Modern Daughters

and the Outlaw West

Modern Daughters
and the Outlaw West

A NOVEL BY MELISSA KWASNY

spinsters book company
SAN FRANCISCO

First Edition
10-9-8-7-6-5-4-3-2-1

Spinsters Book Company
P.O. Box 410687
San Francisco, CA 94141

Cover and Text Design: Pam Wilson Design Studio

Cover Art: Anne Appleby

Cover Color Separations: Henrietta Boberg

Editor: Sherry Thomas

Production: Nancy Fishman, Jennifer Hamilton, Georgia Harris,
Joan Meyers, Camille Pronger and Kathleen Wilkinson.

Typesetting: Joan Meyers

Printed in the U.S.A on acid-free paper

This is a work of fiction. Any resemblance to real persons, places
or situations is not intentional.

Library of Congress Cataloging-in-Publication Data
Kwasny, Melissa, 1954-
    Modern daughters and the outlaw west
    Melissa Kwasny.—1st ed.
        p.   cm.
    ISBN: 0-933216-75-0: $9.95
    I. Title
    PS3561.W447M6 1990
    813'.54—dc20

                                            90-44699
                                                CIP

DEDICATION
_____

for Nancy Daniels

ACKNOWLEDGEMENTS
_____

For their past and continuing support and guidance, grateful acknowledgement is made to the spirits of the land and to all my sisters in Montana, to Susan Griffin and Sherry Thomas, to my family, to the Headlands Center for the Arts and especially, to Anne.

In the small clay pot
...of their melodious names
I will bring back some remnant
...of the hundred fragrances.

Ranier Maria Rilke

1

Frequently, at first, there were flowers: violets, azaleas, wild orchids and poppies, lilac bouquets and single stems of iris, yellow roses, peony, but never seasonal. There were not, for instance, poinsettias in December. Days went by without a sign of them when without warning a perfect vision of tulips, imported and ruffled, filled the sink where her hands were sunk in soap and dishes. Of what she was thinking, she had no recollection. Her thoughts seemed never to determine when or why they would appear. The flowers were a surprise, a comfort and a gift, a sort of mystical Easter Egg Hunt. She hadn't always seen them. They began here, in the town approaching.

Emeryville. At the crest of the Rocky Mountains in Montana. The only paved road rarely brought anyone through and when it did, a cat or dog, and once, the town drunk were knocked down. No one remembered Emery, or what the village was called before that. The history books barely mentioned the state, let alone a former mining town of less than two hundred people, a town whose development peaked sixty years after Lewis and Clark wheeled their boats around the Great Falls of the Missouri. Here, two creeks flowed in opposite directions, one west to the Columbia; one east to the Mississippi. This was a source of awe and confusion to the pioneers when they first arrived and was still a mystery seldom spoken of.

"What am I doing?" she mumbled as the Greyhound Bus skidded on black ice toward the river, skated back into oncoming traffic, then regained control. Ahead, the two lanes of pavement swelled thick at the deep curves, thinned ahead on the long, brown prairies. She pressed her hand against the glass, tracing the red, argillite cliffs, the jawline of a ridge filling the sky. What towns they passed looked poor, burnished and thin as hammered coins. It was barely June, so the fires were stoked and smoking, a bit medieval. But not like ghost-towns. The ghosts were gone and what was left was like the brown grubs she used to find after first frost. Spirit-flown.

Just over the state-line and, as if on cue, every vehicle had a gun-rack. Soon would come the ranches, the rodeo signs, the bad cafes and bumper stickers denouncing gun control, the bars advertising, "Liquor in the Front, Poker in the Rear." The carcasses of a few deer stared up from the side of the road and the mashed remains of a small, furred creature exploded into a spray of magpie and crow. What made her think it existed, another West? Far across these harrowing passes and snow-stilled roads: a different world?

The driver shouted her obscure destination and she watched as the highway took them a mile past town and doubled back, affording her a rear-end view of the dilapidated backyards of cabins, the amateur car lots, the chicken coops and metal dumpsters, the precarious rows of fire escapes backing down the brick behind an old hotel. It was after midnight. Gina, city born, twenty-two, alone, with only a pack on her back, stepped off the bus into air which was chilled, but smelled as if it were going to burst into bloom. She stood in the road long after the bus left, staring up at the mountains scooped from the level town like the walls of a clam shell. The village was sweet with blue light and, to the east, the waning hips of an over-full moon spread her skirts over the railroad tracks as if ready to take a piss.

It was too late for a room, if rooms were to be had. She hadn't thought of calling ahead to find out. "Never lived in a town this small," she said as she walked through what she caught herself calling the residential section. There were, perhaps, a dozen frame houses, a few of stone, a row of cabins. Smoke rising from all but a few of them. A school with a belfry. An abandoned, boarded-up church. She followed the dirt road past the houses. Before she knew where she was heading, she was climbing next to a creek on her way into the mountains. "I suppose it's cleaner up here than any place in town," she said.

What did she know about Emeryville? That it was a gold-rush town, the hills scarred with the hand dug pits of placer miners. Gallus frames still stood on its slopes like sentinels. In the late 1800s, Emeryville was swarming with miners, trappers, whores and bandits from the East, eager, as she was, for a new and less confining way of making a living. Their cabins were built in odd draws far from water. In recent years a motorcycle gang had called it their summer home, and the knife fights were epic tales as far away as the biker bars of Seattle. The first women's weaving union began in Emeryville and a chapter of the Wobblies, gunned down by the National Guard in Butte.

The earth was outlaw, too, Gina had learned from a gray-haired Canadian, sitting next to her on the bus. It was ringed with radon mines. Gina had thought radon synonymous with radioactivity, but the woman, barely concealing her irritation, had said, "Darling, if they were cancerous, why would they call them health mines?" To cure their rheumatoid arthritis, bursitis, lupus and emphysema, senior citizens from Canada traveled to Emeryville each summer to sit in tunnels eighty-five feet below the ground and breathe the therapeutic vapors. The locals called them "frost-backs."

What she had also heard—to be more accurate, what she had been warned against—was that the town was home to an inordinate number of lesbians. At twenty-two, this was all she had needed. A hide-out town of miners, loggers and cowboys, rebels, dykes and buyers of old-fashioned remedies seemed a lot more like the western movie she had thought she was to take part in growing up in Seattle. She looked forward to meeting the town, these women, and wondered if they were all like the woman, walking the tracks, who had given her the idea of Emeryville in the first place, although no one had ever told her that Myrna was a lesbian.

It wasn't because Myrna was Native. Gina was white, but she'd grown up around "skins." In her city neighborhood, she could hardly have believed they had all disappeared a hundred years before on that summer day at the Bighorn. In her neighborhood, the bumper stickers read, "Custer Wore Arrow Shirts." She'd even seen the long-hairs, those who kept their braids and customs who mostly lived away, on the reservations. But, who could have prepared her for the sight, out her window at work, of an Indian man in a trade-blanket coat, tanned leggings, a feather in his black braids, walking so uncommonly slow through the traffic and pawnshops in the freight yard part of town?

She must have watched for hours, infatuated, as the figure moved ceremoniously up and down the tracks. On closer scrutiny, he turned out to be a she, no beaded leggings, no feather. But it was a trade-blanket coat and as much as she tried to get her out of her mind, she would appear and reappear as she did that day, timeless and a child of the times, caught between worlds.

Gina had spent the winter asking around at the Indian bars and only through sheer doggedness did she discover who the woman was and that she was in Seattle visiting relatives. Finding this out had not been easy: "You must know her," Gina would say, after her Chippewa friends introduced her to Myrna's relatives for the fourth time.

"Who?"

"You were just talking about her. I heard you," she would insist, her eyes feeling bluer than usual. She bought another round.

"What did you say your name was again? Tina?"

She had turned to her friends for help, but they just shrugged. "I'm trying to find out about a woman named Myrna."

"Don't know any Myrna, do you, Frank?"

"She's Indian," Gina began.

"Sorry, Miss. No Indians left around here."

That sex was part of all this chasing wasn't at the front of her mind. At this point, Emeryville was a soup, clean and golden with herbs and thin, dried mushrooms. Emeryville was a tea, brewed in a stoneware pot, smelling of pine and mint and served theatrically. A wild, gritty, nourishing scent. So unlike her life in Seattle.

So, here she was in Emeryville, climbing far enough away from the town to make sure no one had followed her. She found a level spot and spread her bag. The creek below was so loud it left no room for her own thoughts. Even the air was immense. She lay on her back, pinned by a sky so much closer than she had anticipated, and it was here, while the stars roared close to her ears, that a quick glimpse of anemone, small, but precise, surprised her.

Numbers, flowers, the paths of birds: there were people trained in the interpretations, those who had a romance with those things. She was not one of them. When she was a girl, her mother dragged her to a church held in someone's home, with folding chairs and a bouquet of plastic roses. She would sit next to her mother, with the same group year after year, Polish and African and Ukrainian women, and wait, as they waited, for the old woman to fall into a trance and call her name. It had always frightened her. "Gina," the woman would scold, "there is a big question mark over your head. You have to listen if the spirits are going to talk to you."

But, what if you didn't want to hear?

Who talked were the dead, most often relatives. After church, Gina's mother would spend days poring over family trees to find out who Aunt Esther was and why she said to watch over the baby. "What baby?" her mother would scream. "Gina, are you pregnant?" Then, there were the spirit guides, who weren't necessarily the wise, the Indian chief every hippie Gina's age claimed to have watching over them. Why an entire nation would be fascinated with a generation of white drug-users was beyond her. The guides, her mother said, could be anyone, dead or alive, animal or vegetable, and they changed throughout a life, some as often as faces passed on a sidewalk.

They weren't on call for just anything, either; for instance, if the keys were missing or the bolt didn't fit back in the oil pan. They operated on a Peter and the Wolf system of exposure. Which was too bad, since when Gina had first been told of this, the possibilities seemed endless. "Fold or bet?" she would whisper.

Did she believe it or not? Not religion, certainly. Not certainly anything. As a woman, the man-up-there was a hard theory to buy, especially since the ones below had demonstrated such remarkable lack of ability. But sometimes a shadow on paper, a susceptibility to music, the sight of someone out her window, would turn her in a direction and she would follow, ending up in a place like Emeryville. And sometimes she would not. This much she knew: she was no prophet. The anemones were not to be looked for, the seeds not planted. They probably didn't grow this far north or this high. As she drifted off to sleep, she decided to invest the sighting with as much authority as she did anything else. Though signs and signals came, they only seemed to confuse her.

It was late when she opened her eyes to daylight, already warm, and still as when she had gone to sleep. She dressed hurriedly. Flanked by columns of pine, Gina back-tracked the dirt road toward Emeryville. Halfway down, she passed what she hadn't seen in the dark of the night before—a ramshackle but oddly beautiful collection of shacks with walls built of a copious assortment of materials: logs, wagon wheels, corrugated metal. A bit of stained glass, a portal from a ship, a two-man scythe—walls grew from these objects of attention out and the rest of the building followed. Blue-framed windows protruded at unexpected angles and an elk antler framed the crescent edge of a door. No electric or telephone lines in sight, cardboard stuffed in many of the windows, but there were definite signs of a poor, but imaginative inhabitation. There was a courtyard of sorts, a pier of barn-planking bordered by the raised beds of crocuses. The metal gates of over fifty different fences kept a herd of brilliant goats from consuming the garden. A hermit, most assuredly. She gazed patiently until a goat stepped menacingly toward her, then she continued down the road.

Every cow town in the West must have a bar called the Mint, and Emeryville was no exception. This one faced the highway, as almost everything in town seemed to, with a brick facade. Gina entered the last in what was once a four tavern town, the back bar varnished walnut and the beveled mirrors, which paraded down the length of one wall, separating it from the short order cafe on the other side. A wood stove was heating the room to a sluggish temperature. She found a seat and waited for the bartender, who was steadily consuming a glass of milk to which he was adding squirts of the house vodka. Ulcers. She'd recognize it anywhere.

"What can I get you?" His face was the mushroom white of day bartenders, his voice weary, although he was only slightly older than she was.

"Coffee, please." Gina watched him move toward the cafe, his narrow hips with more swing than she had ever managed. When her eyes adjusted to the lack of light, she began to notice the other three patrons: a young woman plugging quarters into a poker machine; one very old one, drinking beer with shots of whiskey and crocheting doilies in the neon-blue glare; a bald man who faded in and out at the end of the bar.

"New in town?" The bartender set the coffee in front of her.

"Gina. How do you do?"

"Eddie," he said, extending his hand.

"Eddie, I'm looking for a place to stay."

"Stick around, sweetheart," Eddie winked, started for the cooler, then turned his head and shoulders in a calendar-girl pose. "I always find something by morning."

"That's not what I meant."

Eddie returned to cross both arms over the counter. "That's Hatty over there with her knitting, and over there," he pointed to the fading cowboy on the barstool, who by what looked like an extreme act of will came sharply into focus, "is Glenn."

"Boomboom."

Gina waited for him to say more, but when he threatened to fade again, his lips twisting grotesquely, she asked Eddie, "What did he say?"

"Boomboom."

"I heard. What does it mean?"

"Beats me," Eddie shrugged, emptying his glass in one motion.

By the time Gina left the bar, squinting into what was left of the day, Glenn was gone. But the town was in full swing. Half-ton pickups, manufactured the year of her birth, the inescapable drone of chain saws, power saws and lawn mowers sounding off the canyon walls. Four-wheel drives and dust. Everyone in flannel shirts and blue jeans. There was a general store where a postmistress in a housedress and slippers was sorting through the mail, a gas pump, padlocked, and the locals smoking, waiting in line for it.

Across the road was a peeling, two story building sporting the only block of sidewalk in Emeryville, the concrete cracked and sprouting chamomile. The word, "HOTEL," was fading over the door. Gina crossed to where a woman sat cross-legged on a ragged car seat propped against the wall in the most luxurious pose of sunning Gina had ever seen. Her face directed overhead, smiling to herself, she was smearing oil from a jar onto her lips, over and over as it glistened off her fingertips. She stretched a shoulder against an ear, unfolded her legs and extended her bare feet in front of her, wiggling them like a child in a too large chair, although she seemed at least fifty years old. At the height of Gina's marveling, the woman opened her eyes and giggled. "What are you staring at, little goose?"

"Sorry, I didn't mean to wake you," Gina stammered, embarrassed. "I mean, you were enjoying the sun so."

Her unbound hair was a nest of gray strands, thick as good string. What remained of the dark gold she had inherited from her mother now huddled in the shade of her neck. She sighed. "Yes, it seems further away and lasts less each year." Her voice had the cloying mannerisms of a girl, but where in someone young, Gina would have suspected it, here, in a middle-aged woman, she found it unnervingly charming. "Where are you going?" the woman asked, motioning to Gina's pack.

Gina slipped it off her shoulder onto the ground. She was gazing into the bluest eyes, a blue so bright it seemed impossible, as if the sky could be like that before dawn. Impossible. Doll eyes set in a wrinkled face with hair that was coarse as wheat.

"Gina," she said, holding out her hand. "I'm looking for a place to rent for the summer. I've always wanted to live in the mountains."

"I knew it, I knew it," the woman squealed, hopping off the carseat. "I must have set the tipi up for you." She took Gina's outstretched hand. "My name is June. Come on, I'll show you."

Gina followed June through a lawn to the back yard. Snow was melting in the garden plot, along with a season of compost: egg shells, orange rinds, a pile of banana peels. There was an outhouse next to the garden, a few rusted wheels and truck parts, a pile of crocks and crates of empty canning jars, picked over logs, too gnarled to split, and next to the creek, which had grown loud in the sun, was the tipi, small and smoke-stained, but in one piece.

Gina ducked inside. Yards of canvas were draped over a rope, strung from pole to pole and weighted with rocks to the ground. No one would be able to see through the two layers when the tipi was lit from within, she heard June saying. So much the better, since June's yard was in the center of town. But, how would she cook? Where would she get water? Gina'd pictured herself in an efficiency apartment, not dragging branches from the edges of town, a dreary entanglement of bones and dead limbs, bent against a cruel north wind. She didn't own a saw, a vehicle or even a pan. She suddenly felt unsure of her ability to build a fire. She stood, uncertain, breathing in the windy scent of canvas, stiff in the dryness of Montana. From inside the mottled walls, between the poles skinned of their bark, she could make out the outlines of leaves, still small. She dropped her pack by the fire pit.

"I want to pay you, of course."

"OK," June agreed. She didn't seem to care one way or the other. "If you wait for me, I'll show you around."

When they took off north, over the hills, June led the way in a brightly patterned babushka, her large breasts sagging, braless, under a violet sweatshirt, lightly skipping over boulders in her running shoes, rocks Gina was struggling over. Gina knelt to a white feather in the path.

A good sign. Osprey. Eagle, maybe. She tucked it in the bandanna she'd wrapped around her head. "What were you doing up there?" she called to June. For while June had gone up into her rooms to change into what looked curiously like what she had on before, Gina had waited over an hour.

"I'm never in a hurry for anything, you'll find. The information I am receiving has waited eons to find me ready."

Gina rolled her eyes.

June smiled. "I'm just in love with my own timing."

Gina couldn't have pointed to the route they took. They ran into deep snow, waded marshes until her shoes turned black, strode across the high, empty steppes between peaks, June leading, her peasant colors above entire ranges of dark mountains until Gina finally called for her to stop. June waited on a ridge above the sun with the village below them, soaked in a basin of golden light. Tucked between the steep slopes of the continental divide, Emeryville looked as if someone had dropped the houses of a Monopoly game, letting them tumble into draws and along the rambling dirt roads which ended here in a slope of sagebrush, there in a wooden door bridging the creek. The wooden houses were long ago in need of paint and most were trimmed in the inevitable Forest Service mud brown.

"This is where we live," June said fondly. She seemed exhilarated, as if she could walk all night. Seeing that Gina sensed this, she added quickly, "I'm getting hungry. Won't you join me for dinner?" and tucked her arm under Gina's for the walk home.

Gina congratulated herself. She had only just arrived in Emeryville and already she was sitting in the rooms of its queen. Well, if not the queen, certainly a central and royal presence. June was busy with dinner, sticking her fingers into the many little pots of honey, butter, tahini and who knew what creamy and oily confections, licking them off with obvious relish. The silence was so comfortable that she could hear the creek through June's heavy drapes. It had slowed, now that the sun had set and was no longer melting snow, slowed to an old-fashioned waltz, played by a violin and a quirky, bass clarinet. The drapes were of purple velvet, with a fine mold of dust, and on an antique desk was a victrola. Stacks of vintage forty-fives with cardboard covers of palm trees and bongo players, pink ceramic statues of movie stars, rocks and seashells arranged on a brocade-covered altar with candles and a bouquet of the blue sage which grew thick and ornamental on the prairies: It was a voluptuous room with pillows everywhere. It smelled of drying lavender, roots boiling and the salve farmers used on the udders of their cows.

Gina tried to imagine this flabby yet light-stepping figure in a dress and heels. She couldn't. And yet, June was not at all like a man. Rings were at home on her fingers and she spoke, giddy with the world. Still, more than dress made her sense June had no boyfriends lurking in the bedrooms of the old hotel. June wasn't afraid of her. As women seemed to be with women when men left the room. June liked women and, what was more unusual, showed it. Gina was used to women who couldn't hold a conversation without the masculine pronoun. Here, the rules were obviously different.

They ate, sitting on the floor, at a low table laden with boiled potatoes, cabbage and the watercress June had picked from the creek on the way home. "What do people do around here at night?" Gina asked when they were done. "Sleep?"

"Or go to the Mint." June licked her bowl, holding it to her face.

"You read my mind."

Gina had laced her boots and was almost down the stairs when June called after her. "You know," she said, "that feather in your cap is from a goose."

The Mint was crowded, as Eddie said it would be, full with the rounded shoulders of ranchers, loggers and truckers. The trick to walking into a bar like this, alone, a woman, depended on what you wore and where you sat. Gina chose a stool on the opposite end from the television. Expecting Eddie, she was startled to find the woman she was looking for, not only in the bar, but behind it. Noticing Gina, she padded down the aisle without a click, though she wore cowboy boots. One braid hung behind her, below her belt, and her round belly, the belly of a steady beer drinker, grew like a melon over her buckle. She was smoking a non-filter cigarette and drinking beer from a bottle.

She leaned over the counter and shadows broke across her already black eyes like a storm. "What," she demanded, "do you want from me?"

She was red-lipped, intent, with a dark, no bullshit beauty. Gina was still wondering if she had heard her right when Myrna laughed, a husky laugh that could turn the tables, quiet the worst drunk and have a room of customers waiting for a drink wait a little longer. The kind of laugh that made you realize, in direct proportion to how much you would refute it, that you were taking your life much too seriously.

"Do you want a drink or not?" Myrna repeated.

"Bud, I guess," Gina managed.

Myrna returned with the beer and a shot of peppermint schnapps. "Next time, if you don't ask for the bottle, you get the can."

"Heard ya."

Myrna shoved the shot glass toward Gina. "Had dinner with June?" When Gina nodded, confused, Myrna added, "I'm no mystic. It's the garlic."

Gina laughed. Every dinner item had been crowned with an entire bulb of it. June's skin, although she called herself a vegetarian, smelled like a stew. "She said it works for everything, colds, infections, to repel insects even."

"And rednecks. Horny old men. Nosy bartenders."

"My name's Gina. I'm from Seattle."

"I got family in Seattle."

"So I've heard."

"Chippewa. You know them?"

Gina's friends in Seattle were Chippewa, unregistered, which meant no benefits, no status, no reservation, although the gene which darkened their skin and straightened their hair still caused clerks to follow them suspiciously in stores and employers to question their applications, even with names like Knudson. "In Seattle, they called themselves landless. I always thought that sounded funny. A landless Indian."

"And all due to a series of badly matched marriages with Norwegians."

They talked long into the night, until Myrna closed the bar at two and followed Gina to her new home. On her knees, placing rain-soaked twigs in the flames, her feet crossed behind her, Myrna showed Gina how to build a fire. Later, she demonstrated how the smoke flaps opened and how, above, when they were sitting inside, the stars landed on the tips of the poles like night birds.

"What brought you to Emeryville?" Gina asked. "You weren't born here?"

"Nah, but close. I followed some woman. Story of my life. What about you?"

Gina ignored the question. "Is she still here?"

"Hell, no!" Myrna said, laughing.

Gina woke the next morning to a heap of crushed beer cans, but the air was filled with the scent of honey. She raised herself onto one elbow gingerly and looked out the tipi door. A dry, light snow was piling up into the corners of June's backyard, catching in the folded leaves of the new chard, slowly turning a black cat, curled and sleeping on the outhouse roof, into a winter ermine. But it was warm and the sun shone so fresh that the silhouette of leaves through the skin of the tipi seemed almost green. She stumbled through the door. The entire town was covered with it, coating the windshield of June's 1959 Chevy, drifting into doorways.

As Gina walked to the cafe, people were smiling, less busy, as the cottonwood seeds covered their eyelashes and roofs. It was a sure sign of summer. "People make things so simple and visible, invisible," June had said during dinner. "They think the creek sounds like a water spirit. As if it wasn't. When the sky is grand with thunder, you'll always hear someone say they don't know why they feel restless." Gina passed two aging men on the steps of the general store, telling each other how they had woken in such good moods. "Must have gotten up on the right side of the bed," they said.

Gina would have attempted the cafe, but it was lunch hour and the walls were painted apricot, it was cheerful and smelled of hamburgers. She took her coffee to the bar where Hatty was crocheting. There was no sign of the fading man.

"Where's Glenn?" Gina pulled a stool next to the old woman. Hatty's hands were bony and moved in jerks, furtively as insects.

"Dead."

"Oh, no. I'm sorry."

"Ain't your fault."

"Last night?"

"Last year's more like it."

"It couldn't be. I just met him yesterday."

"Honey, I ought to know. I'm the one picked him up." Hatty's fingers skittered across the strands, needles clacking. "Fell right off that barstool."

Hatty seemed too thin to lie, her body a wrung-out, end-of-the-line kind of thin. Gina tried again. "Does he ever say anything besides 'Boomboom?'"

"Sometimes he sings 'I Left My Heart in San Francisco,' but I gotta prompt him."

A large, square-headed man had lumbered up behind them. He stood there without speaking until Gina nudged Hatty and glanced his way. "Oh, Sam, I want you to meet a friend of mine," Hatty said. "Sam, this is…Shit, sweetie, whad'ya say your name was again?"

"Gina."

He lifted his gaze from a button on his shirt and began a smile which threatened to take the afternoon to complete. "It may not be grand, but at least you've met Sam," he said, astonishing Gina by dropping to the floor in a split that would make a cheerleader proud. No one in the bar even glanced their way.

"Sam used to live in the Home," Hatty continued. "He swamps the bar now." The Home, down the pass from Emeryville, rose from the dust of the prairie, far from towns or water. Caged inside a twelve-foot barbed wire fence, since the beginning of the century it had served as the state's only repository for undesirables: the retarded, the insane, the deaf, blind or just plain ornery. The asylum was also a slave block, supplying busboys, bar swamps, maids and ranch hands to anyone willing to take them. "Eddie's dad found him there twenty years ago in shackles. He's been working here ever since," Hatty whispered, "And when he cain't work, he'll probably get sent back."

"That was quite a split, Sam," Gina said.

It was impossible to avoid June on her way back to the tipi because June was sitting in her outhouse, cracking open the pits of prunes. "You should try brewer's yeast for your hangover," she called to Gina.

"How did you know?" Gina said, wandering over to the stall, which was decorated inside with drying yarrow and an excerpt of the Navaho Night Chant: "With beauty before me, may I walk. With beauty behind me, may I walk." On the floor, a stack of outdated newspapers and a basket for them once they were used. June disdained toilet paper. She burned them later for kindling.

"There's a note pinned to your door, an invitation. There's a potluck in your honor tonight." June cracked a prune pit and dug out the marrow with the point of her knife. She had a toilet inside and running water, but she liked her double-seater. From it, she could see anyone coming down the road and frequently surprised them by waving a greeting from her booth. June was fond of toilets and food, and noisy with both. If she were a cat, she'd be a fat, orange tabby, digging in the litter box for hours.

"Who knows I'm here?" Gina shook her head. "Small town, I guess." She turned toward the tipi. There was still the matter of the aluminum cans.

"There's a bin for recycling under my back porch. River collects them."

"How did you..." Gina began, then changed her mind. "Who?"

"River. That's her name."

"Spell it."

"Like it sounds," June said.

"Oh, God," Gina said, ducking into the tipi for a nap. She woke in late afternoon when Myrna threw a set of keys to the ground next to her head.

"Whose keys?"

"Deeva's. Thought you might like to take a shower. She's out of town."

"You stole her keys?" Gina sat up groggily.

Myrna laughed. "I rent from her. She'll never know."

"I could use a shower. How are you feeling after last night?"

"Tired. Broke. Hung-over. And now, I have to go to work. It's a tough life being a lesbian." Myrna poked Gina with her boot. "Come on, I don't have all day."

"Myrna, who's Maggie? She's having a party for me tonight. For Pete's sake, I've only been in town a day and enough people know about me to plan a party?"

"They can smell fresh blood a mile away."

"Myrna!"

"Ok, it's a small town, remember?" They crossed the road and Myrna pointed to a pot of geraniums on someone's backporch. "When she re-hides the key, she always moves the flowers with it," Myrna winked. "Just remember to put them back."

"I'm a little nervous, Myrna. When's Deeva expected back?"

"Don't worry." Myrna, like June, had her own sense of timing, which she called Indian time, but allowed no one else to. It was devoid of clocks and the calendars with large windowpanes to cross off the days, which she said were for those in prison. She was always late, but rightly so: The meeting she skipped was invariably canceled, the road closed when she called off a trip. "Every four minutes the heavens change," she would say, "How can you expect people to stick to their plans?" Indian time depended not on a clock, but on exact conditions. Myrna picked the huckleberries when they were ripe and she didn't wait to make love until her day off either. She waited until the late afternoon light fell through her high window and the scent of roses in a hot night rose from the woman next to her. It never mattered that she had to be at the Mint in half an hour. A note would be passed under her door, saying the bar was closed that night due to power failure.

Deeva's window was wedged open with a stick, and from it an electric cord ran along the ground a hundred feet and under the front door of a weather-beaten shack. "Wait a minute, is that yours?" Gina followed the cord to the door.

"Welcome," Myrna said, arriving there to open it. Inside was a meager room with planking Myrna had laid over the once-dirt floor. A crosscut saw hung on one wall and a bed was pushed against the window. Through it, clouds were draining to pink in the east. No pillow. A sleeping bag unzipped for a blanket. Of anything Myrna owned, there seemed only one. One oil lamp, one ashtray, one closed trunk. There was a washbasin, a plastic five-gallon jug for water, the rectangular box of a sheepherder's stove. No knickknacks, no pictures, no books, no photographs of family. Gina pointed to the black and white TV plugged into the extension cord.

"Myrna?"

"She'll never miss it. She has three."

Gina sat on the edge of the mattress. "Myrna, why do they think I'm a lesbian?"

"Why else would you move here?"

In the city, she had waited half the night for the skies to clear and a few distant stars, but here, a busy world of planets and meteors moved in directly after sunset. Dusk, and there they were above her as she hiked the dirt road toward a house with candles burning blue from the windows. Gina wasn't surprised to learn that Maggie, who had invited her to this party, lived in that conglomeration of shacks up the creek that had so caught her attention the day before. In a town this small, it seemed nothing would remain strange for long. Even a woman hermit. Still, as she approached, she wished Myrna was not working this night.

Turning up the path, she saw the forms of many people near the fire. When she was closer, she saw that women ringed the fire pit, which blazed as it washed the mountains above in purple shadows. Rolling tobacco, eating with chopsticks and spoons, they joked and talked as if it weren't so odd. Yet, Gina had never been to a party without men. A baby shower once. Slumber parties when she was a kid. And never were women so familiar as these, teasing, kissing each other fully on the mouth. She felt immediately out of place and found a place to stand in the shadows.

"You're late," June said, mid-dip into a bowl of whipped cream. She waved toward the carcass of an unidentifiable animal on the buffet table. "We saved you some."

"Thanks, June, but I'm not hungry."

"In that case," June said, grabbing Gina by the elbow and walking her into the circle. "Everybody, I want you to meet Gina." Obediently, they stood as June began to name them. Barbara Jean, who asked to be called BJ, a bit older than Gina and trim, who dressed carefully, with a sincere belief in accessory, a strand of off-colored beads, certain buttons left undone. "Jake!" shouted the young woman who bolted from BJ's side, her hand outstretched. She was big, over six feet tall, with the practiced stance of an athlete. River was a stout, short woman who wore men's trousers and a vest, had keys hanging from her side pocket. Her hair was blond, a thumb-nail long and stood above her head like mown grass. And Gertrude, handsome, older, who took both of Gina's hands in her own.

When the introductions were over, Gina popped a beer and offered it to her hostess. Maggie was small, bowlegged, tall as Gina's shoulders, her hair cut in the practical crew of Montana ranch wives, atop which she wore a hat, a huge gray stetson. Gina had never seen a woman wear a ten-gallon hat. And what a hat! With its beaded band and what looked like a magpie feather pinned to the felt. "You have something special with magpies?"

Maggie cackled like her namesake. "Everything I own's been scavenged, so I guess so, picked from this and that and whatever I've found in dumps, along the road and from the boundaries of back yards."

Laughter erupted from the group. BJ had uncorked a bottle of wine and was toasting a rock star she'd seen on tv, a woman who played with fluorescent drum sticks. "She's cute, she's rich, she's fast with her hands. What more could you ask for in a woman?"

"Who?" June whined, oblivious of any reference to popular culture.

"I keep her glossy next to my bed," Gertrude said.

"Sure. I just read a survey. It found that, of all kinds of relationships, lesbians have sex the least often." Jake lunged as she spoke, cracking limbs across her knee and assaulting Maggie's carefully laid fire with her boot.

"If women had the right to choose, the rate would probably be lower in straight relationships, too," BJ said.

River spoke above their heads as if to an invisible crowd. "Obviously, it is due to the fact that women without men are almost always working women. Tired, underpaid, worried about money."

"Mothers," BJ added.

Gertrude was watching Gina. "Wait a minute. What kind of impression are we giving?"

BJ checked her watch. "Ah, time for the sitter to go home." Jake and she left, arm and arm, and soon the others began to drift home too. In no time, Maggie and Gina were left staring at the flames.

"Early risers?"

"Country folk," Maggie said. "Getting kind of chilly. Wanna have a drink inside?" As they made their way along the path without a flashlight, maneuvering through the goats and the large population of dogs, Gina asked questions, since Maggie hadn't volunteered a word to anyone all night.

"Did each of those women forget three or four dogs?"

"This used to be the dump. Dogs still come looking for garbage, especially when the moon is out."

"How many people live up here?"

"Women come through. They like to build houses."

"But where are they?" Gina guessed Maggie's shacks were more storage units than dwellings since stacks of grocer's crates, skis, books and pans were visible through their windows.

"They'll be back. They'll take care of the place when I'm ready to have another go at the outside." Maggie hooked her thumbs through her suspenders.

"The outside?"

"By the time I'm forty, I'm gonna have a show in Portland."

"I could have guessed you were an artist," Gina said. Maggie looked like an artist, especially with her goatee, a Van Gogh beard growing quite long from her chin, slicked into a point and which she smoothed automatically.

Maggie's house smelled faintly of goats and nothing was as it should be. Chairs facing a television? A bedroom? A dining room? This was more like a prehistoric French cave. The stairs from one level to another were not stairs, but slabs of granite. A stone fireplace from another century, part of the cabin it was built into tagging along behind, was hung with pots and iron skillets. Easels, canvas, drawing pads and palettes propped against walls and couches, hanging from window ledges; it was evident that eating, sleeping and drawing were on rotating schedules.

A ladder leaned against the floor of a loft and Gina climbed it. Maggie was lighting the lanterns below, saying something about jet fuel, which she purchased at the nearest airport, fifty miles away, burning cleaner than kerosene. Gina had always thought of the indoors as warm and well-lit, but these women's homes flickered, were shadowed as if of secret importance. There was a sliver of a window and next to it, a mattress. Maggie climbed up with a bottle of homemade chokecherry wine and they lay, watching the moon rising above the canyon, crawling into corners, under trees, catching the creek below and turning it silver.

Maggie began to talk long after the coals had died out beyond the garden. Almost through with the wine, she was holding Gina's hand and had taken off her ten-gallon hat. "I grew up here. When I was a kid, I used to think that everywhere I looked were the same, piled-up mountains. I felt trapped by 'em. It was a big task to get over them, believe me. But, I knew that on the other side was the World. When I was old enough, I packed it up, went to New York, Los Angeles. Ten years later, I came back. And you know what? I found myself in the center of a circle of bright blue mountains and I felt like I was in the center of the world.

"Look around you. Generations of lakes, generations of mountains." Maggie waved her arms. "I own this small piece. You see, there was a miner and my great-great grandmother was a whore downtown. Way back then, this was the town dump. He gave it to her, a kind of joke, you see. To prove how much he loved her. The women in my family didn't have too hard a time keeping it to themselves, but little did they imagine, in all their days, that I would build a home here.

"Mom moved out of Emeryville when my dad died. She could hardly wait." Maggie sighed. She didn't see her mother often, nor did her mother encourage frequent visits from Maggie, not since the day she'd shown up with her goatee. Maggie didn't understand the fuss, but then, Maggie had forgotten that it, along with the rest of her lifestyle in Emeryville, was in any way outside the norm.

"I never had a picture of that miner or knew anyone who did. But lately, a fat, red-headed man's been sleeping in my goat barn. He doesn't talk and he doesn't bother anybody. Sleeps almost on top of my goat and she doesn't bat an eye. My blind dog, who barks at me if I walk in front of her, won't even sniff the air though he smells to high heaven and back. Must be no danger, 'cause I figure animals can sense things we can't. But I almost think he's a ghost."

"Maybe he's your spirit guide," Gina said.

"What?"

"Haven't you heard of them? My mother talks of them all the time."

"Well, sure, but I thought they were Indian warriors. Or at least," and Maggie winked lecherously, "tantric specialists."

"Or dead relatives."

"Don't remind me I have ancestors like that," Maggie grumbled. She patted the mattress and rolled to one side. "I gotta hit the hay. You're welcome to sleep here. Don't imagine you could find your way down in the dark."

It seemed like a good idea, although the path back through Maggie's yard seemed more treacherous than the dirt road down to Emeryville. Gina undressed and, pulling the blankets around her, watched until the stars had thickened into sleep. A rustling like wings woke her and she was shocked to feel Maggie's wiry frame descending on her. Maggie, smelling of goat's milk and wine, naked on top of her and heavier than she looked.

"Maggie, what the hell are you doing?" Gina gasped.

Maggie buried her lips in Gina's hair, her pelvis flapping wildly up and down in the motion of men and coming nowhere near an erogenous zone. She struggled to get free, but before she could, Maggie was off her and snoring, her heart beating visible and quick as a bird's.

"Some introduction," Gina scowled, pushing Maggie away with her knee.

The next morning, Gina found Maggie in an antique bathtub outside, a fire smoking under a pile of rocks the tub was lodged on. Maggie waved, reaching for her clothes which were draped over a juniper. Her beard dripped and hung like the tail of a cat caught in the rain. Quick as a flash, she bounded into the cabin barefoot and reappeared with a steaming cup of coffee. "Mornin'," Maggie smiled, kissing her.

"This tastes just like your goats smell," Gina complained, but Maggie just laughed. Goat milk and its companion odor were a staple of Maggie's kitchen: goat milk, goat yogurt, goat cheese, goat meat.

Maggie seemed not the least uncomfortable with what had happened the night before. "How 'bout a tour in daylight?"

They wandered through the patchwork of shelters, one-room sheds, a lean-to built of lumber and limbs of pine. June had already told Gina of the work party Maggie had invited them to the year before. When the women arrived to insulate her home, Maggie pointed to a pile of styrofoam egg cartons for them to staple to the walls.

"I collect what most people throw out," Maggie said, pointing to the large piles of glass, aluminum, metal and styrofoam separated and arranged across her land. Her yard was no different from when it was the town dump, except for the lack of flies and the addition of the hides of hunted animals, which Maggie was curing on her garden fence.

"Can you believe this place was built without power tools or even a transit?" Maggie asked when they finished the tour.

Gina frowned. "Maggie, what do you think about what happened last night?"

Maggie threw her arm around Gina's shoulder. "I'm thinking it could only get better."

Gina smelled cow flesh burning and woke in the tipi to find Myrna outside, cracking a dozen eggs into a skillet already spitting with the grease of a pound of hamburger. Myrna threw a handful of twigs into the blaze she'd built in June's barbecue grill. "I hate cooking over an open fire," she said, handing Gina a cup. Cowboy coffee, boiled and thick.

They both smiled as June came sniffing onto the lawn. "Here," Myrna said, handing June a plate of her one-pan breakfast.

"Oh, I couldn't, I never eat meat." June arranged herself on the grass, her faded, flannel robe bunched up around her thighs, her recently shampooed hair the color of ashes. Regardless, Myrna dished up two more plates and balanced one between two logs on the woodpile. June strolled close on her way to check the sprinkler, snagged a bit on her way back, returned for a pinch of egg. It was not long before the plate was in her lap, her resolution forgotten. "I really shouldn't. I'm breaking a week-long fast today."

"June, where was the brothel in Emeryville?" Gina asked.

"Here. This was the whorehouse." June reached to a patch of sorrel growing beside her and pulled a few leaves. She chewed them while she talked. "Couldn't you tell?"

June had given her a tour before through the dozens of junked-out rooms, back rooms, attic and cellar rooms, each with a door, a bed and a dressing table. They were cluttered with racks of moth-eaten cloth, funny uniforms, extravagant dresses in good repair. The walls were plastered with yellowing magazine pages, newspapers for insulation, and real paintings between post-cards and pin-ups from the various wars. June used the main parlor and a few bedrooms for her own, decorating them not in the style of one period, but in the spirit of them all, just as she chose her garments, opulently if not expensively, from the working class of at least six decades.

June pulled on the lapels of her robe to expose her breasts to the sun, sneaking around the corner of the yard. They were freckled, pink, old-fashioned breasts and lay on her ribs like infants, as if she had placed them there. "I dreamt of that smelly miner who gave Maggie the dump she lives in," June said, then giggled, covering her mouth. "I mean, on."

"I saw someone like that in her goat barn the other day," Myrna said, stopping to listen to an explosion of birds in the cottonwood branches. The birds, not tropical, but small and light, sang as if they slept in pine.

"In those days," June sighed, "women must have seemed like these birds, colorful and bright and from another world."

"Maggie's been feeding him. Says he's out of work. Drifted in from Wyoming," Gina said.

"So, what do you want to know about the brothel?"

"Who owned it?"

"You haven't heard about Rosetta yet? She was quite a gal!"

"What are you talking about, June? That must have been a hundred years ago. How would you know what she was like?"

June stole a glance to Myrna. "Oh, I dream about them all, you'll see. Everyone climbs into bed with me sooner or later." She motioned for Gina to sit down next to her. Gina had seen the small waiting room next to June's, a room with a separate entrance off the hall, designed for the customers of the bordello. But June did not run a bordello. For the community of souls who came to her winter flannel or summer silk sheets came while they were sleeping. They spoke with her awhile, if all they needed was her clothed legs like electric blankets around theirs. Some would dream they were forcing her fingers to loosen their belts if will was what they lacked. Some crawled in, completely naked and cold, spreading her thighs which gave way like the moss-covered banks in the spring. But most of Emeryville, all of whom had visited June's at least once during their nightly travels, came for her to direct their dreams.

Leaving bodies entangled with their spouses, or holed up in their dreary cabins alone, they followed June until they came to the passage, the sentence, the monster, the maze that until then, had wakened them to forgetfulness. With an exertion which made her grunt, squatting and taunting them with catcalls, June would push them into exactly what they feared. A gentle push and a holding back of the drapes if that was all that was required. A shameless trick or trap, if more. "I share their dreams and they fear me for it, but they always return," June told Gina.

Gina narrowed her eyes. "Tell me about Rosetta."

"Rosetta. She was one of those big women who wear lots of make-up and look like a man in drag. Well over two hundred pounds, solid and dangerous. No one looked cross-eyed at Rosetta. The story goes she got herself pregnant. Nothing she tried would end it. Finally, on her knees in labor, barking like a dog, and at a time when women stuck rags in their mouths so they wouldn't cry out, Rosetta screamed. Louder than anyone in this town has screamed before or since." June threw her head back and imitated. "No man's ever gonna stick it to me again!"

"It's sort of a legend," Myrna said.

June's scream had stopped a young couple walking down the creek road. Four blond children tugged at the woman's skirts and her hands rested a moment on her obviously pregnant stomach. "So much for population control," Myrna said. The man wore a buckskin jacket, his long hair in two braids.

"He calls himself Blue Cloud," June said. "Says he's half Indian."

"With blond hair?" Gina said. The recent bombardment of books on Mexican mystics, Indian gurus and southwestern shamans had left the West rife with men dressed in beads and the skins of animals.

"He told Myrna it's going to be a boy. He's already bought him a pistol."

"Alternative lifestyle," Myrna nodded.

June rose to go indoors. "By the way, Gina, have you seen Maggie? She's been looking all over for you."

Myrna's eyebrows raised. June left, the clouds moved in like cows ready to be milked, but still Myrna sat, saying nothing. Gina felt the silence gain weight and bowed her head. Finally, in a low voice, Myrna asked, "Did you sleep with her?"

"Who?" Gina said. She had decided not to tell Myrna about Maggie, though it should hardly have mattered to her. But Myrna was watching her with that look that left Gina little space to hide in. "Yeah," she said.

"Figures. Maggie likes to take in strays."

"What do you mean? I didn't expect to."

Myrna silently packed up her groceries.

"It's not like I seduced her. She seduced me. Is that an appropriate word with women?" Gina realized she was chasing Myrna from barbecue to back steps.

Myrna lit a cigarette.

"I'd been there a week and yesterday she tells me her girlfriend is coming back today. After a week, I was beginning to think *I* was her girlfriend." Gina stopped, as it suddenly occurred to her. "Why does it bother you?"

"Because she did the same thing to me."

"She dumped you, then?"
"No, she didn't." Myrna glared.
"Oh."
Myrna stood to leave.
"What is she thinking?"
"Who knows what Maggie thinks?"

2

"I hate potlucks," Myrna grumbled. "Look at this. Fourteen salads. As if any of these hamburger freaks tossed anything but a softball at home." Deeva's home was crowded with Emeryville women in wool and bandannas, and the invited women from nearby towns dressed in earrings, printed scarves and heels. "Everyone's hoping someone will bring lasagne," Myrna continued.

"Who's that?" Gina whispered, nodding toward an older couple leaning self-consciously against a closet door. The larger woman, in a suit jacket and tie, smiled and waved to Myrna. The other, although crowned with an identical crew-cut, had on what looked like a prom dress.

"She wore it to their first high school dance," Myrna replied.

"No, Myrna."

"I'm telling the truth. She wears it the first Saturday of every month when they go out to dinner at the cafe."

"This cafe?" Gina looked again at the muscled arms spreading over pink taffeta. "What do they think about it in there?"

"They think it's more normal than us going in with logging boots on."

Gina studied the two women, who had probably become lovers before she was born. "I wonder if they vote Republican."

"Boat what?" Deeva had crossed the room and was now smiling with the beatific smile of those who meditate or pretend to. She was lovely, her blond hair swept up in a swirl of purple silk and batiked Indonesian cotton, her Navaho turquoise and crystals, her embroidered Chinese slippers. "Deeva," she said, still smiling. Her friends had given her the nickname, by which she was flattered. She had always fancied herself a singer.

"You remember Gina, don't you?" Myrna said, although Deeva had been out of town since Gina arrived.

"Of course. How are you?" Deeva wrapped Gina in an embrace of sandalwood oil, then began digging into her bag for the photograph she had been waiting to show Myrna. "I have a friend who's been living with the Indians at one of the pueblos in the southwest. The real ones, who are still in touch with their culture," she said, finding the picture and handing it to Myrna. "You know, Myrna, you might like to try it sometime."

"Deeva, I'm Chippewa."

"My friend was studying with a medicine woman. She taught her how to call eagles. She didn't tell me what the technique was. I'm sure it's a secret. But she tried it and forty of them came. She sent me this to prove it."

"She took a photo of it?" Gina said, but before her eyes, Deeva thrust a snapshot of a city of the knee-high, white-hooded birds, who were not exactly smiling into the camera.

"I wonder how she got rid of them," Myrna said.

"It was an inspiration to me," Deeva proclaimed. "We live in this country and we don't take part in any of its ancient customs. Tomorrow is my birthday and that is why I thought it would be perfect to build a sweatlodge on my parcel of land." Myrna was already moving toward the door, but Deeva caught her arm. "Myrna, please, I've already invited most of the women here. I'm counting on you."

"I don't get it," Gina said when Deeva left. "Is she paying you or something?"

Myrna shrugged. "She's my landlady."

It seemed that many of the residents of Emeryville rented from Deeva. She had the distinction of being the town's only investor. "If she's got so much money, what's she doing here?" Gina asked.

"Postponing a difficult career decision," Myrna said, grinning. "I was going to tell her it was traditional to fast before a sweat, but look at these tables, like a pack of coyotes ran through."

By noon the next day, Myrna had dug a deep firepit and Gertrude was helping her cut what looked like enough wood to stoke a barrel stove for a week. Gina arrived in the small clearing next to the creek just as a wind lifted from behind Myrna's left shoulder, nudging the infant smoke from the match she held under the tinder, igniting it at once.

"Lava rock is the best kind to use," Myrna began, although Gina had approached behind her. She pointed to the round rocks that were nestled in the square she had built of logs and pine-needles. "River stones burst when they get too hot."

Gina stretched out on the ground near the fire, exhausted. After Deeva's potluck the night before, she'd wandered over to the Mint, where she had stayed just long enough for Maggie to stagger in, nod absently to her and instigate an argument with an equally drunk construction worker. He was one of the first to arrive of a crew who were rumored to be surveying for a new four lane highway through the canyon. Maggie began by talking about safety, was soon expounding on the ethic of wilderness and by the time she was deep in a heated monologue of how deer couldn't drink when fences blocked the river, the man's face was red and the pitch of his answers dangerously lower.

"Come to the bathroom with me," Gina interrupted and was surprised the old girl's trick had worked. Maggie followed doggedly, slipping off her stool and weaving down the aisle. "How about a cup of coffee?"

Gina sat Maggie at the other end of the bar and ordered, while Maggie glared, silent and sullen, her arms crossed. There was a country to ride through with Maggie, between when she was sober, and therefore too stubborn to talk, and when she was too drunk to. Sometimes this place was a gallop over the surprising-because-so-secret foothills of her mind, sometimes it lasted as long as a couple sides of a cassette, spinning in a tape deck while Maggie chatted in the dark. Sometimes, it felt as if you had pulled onto the freeway and, before you reached your speed, had missed your exit and had to turn around.

Maggie went on the wagon a couple months out of every year, when the rest of her friends had withdrawn their invitations and River had nagged her enough about her responsibility to the community. For Maggie was worse than any miner when drunk, expounding on waste and greed for nights in a row, delirious with prophecies of doom. No one could know she was talking about resources when she muttered, "McDonald's is the worst offender." Christmas trees, littering the curbs of the cities after the holiday, could start her sobbing months later. Myrna had told Gina of more than one occasion when she had watched while some logger, tired of Maggie's accusations, would throw her over his shoulder, her cowgirl boots kicking, and deposit her in a snowbank outside.

Magggie always allowed herself to be soothed to Myrna's bed where, when Myrna arrived after her shift, Maggie would turn steamy and loose. But Myrna was not the only one. More than a few women had wakened with Maggie's hat spread over their pillows. "Don't worry, I love you," she would tuck behind their ears the next morning, fumbling for her boots. And she did. Each and every one of them and as honestly as she could. Gina had tried talking with her about it, making her distinguish between the love she shared with a friend, cutting wood for the winter, and the love she felt next to a woman whose breasts her lips were tracing. Or the next woman the next day after that. It did no good. Maggie saved all the passions of her life, just as she collected glass peanut butter jars and scraps of aluminum. She kept them in some compost heap of her soul that only opened with the chemical key of wine and spirits. Then the words came tumbling out, hard from waiting, scrappy and windblown.

But, this time, Maggie wasn't talking. She was silent so long that when the hat landed on the counter in front of Gina, spilling the coffee Maggie hadn't touched, there was no time for Gina to think. Maggie, her head down like a linebacker, was heading full speed down the length of the bar. The construction worker had just buttoned his coat and was reaching for the door when Maggie butted into his back and, from the yelp he made, she must have hit the kidneys. With a scowl, he swatted her flat.

"Kick her for the town. Kick her while she's down," Sam cheered, pumping his arms frantically, forgetting, in his excitement, that he really liked Maggie.

"Boomboom," Glenn said.

"Stop that!" Myrna grabbed the bundle of loose twigs Gina had been absently breaking and tossing into the fire, thinking of the night before with Maggie.

"What's with you?" Gina said, startled.

"This fire is for the sweatlodge. Don't throw your garbage into it."

"Don't be so self-righteous. I'm hungry, that's all. And tired."

"We're all hungry, but we're fasting for each other. It brings strength to the lodge."

"We're doing this so they can see us," Gertrude said, stepping from behind Myrna and lifting her hands to the violet-shaded clearing and the wild rosebushes lining the creek. "Do you know that saying, Gina? When wild roses bloom, the river stops rising?"

With reluctance, Gina smiled. Gertrude wasn't her real name. When she realized she had a choice, she had told Gina, she thought a writer with a partner named Alice suited her better than any saint or soldier her parents had thought of. Gina had gone to visit Gertrude often since first meeting her at the campfire at Maggie's. Gertrude's apartment above Deeva's was lined with paintings and photographs of women: planting trees, in uniform, fleshy and erotic poses of naked young women, old women, skin, teeth, scars, idols and statues of Sumarian women in the rice fields, Central American women with guns. Her shelves held more poetry than seemed possible to have been written by women, in different languages, from different countries, in different times. Gertrude owned the jacket Billie Jean King wore to her first Virginia Slims Open. It was framed and hanging above her bed.

One afternoon when Gina arrived for a visit, she found Gertrude dressed as the writer would have been, in baggy khaki shorts below her knees, her dark, wet hair over her dark eyes, shower-clean and dancing calypso to Sonny Rollins on the stereo. It was Gertrude who told her that homosexuals were the most self-congratulatory in-group other than heroin addicts.

By the time the other women arrived, the stones, covered with ash, were white-hot and singing. The lodge was built of willow branches bent in arcs to form a small dome and then covered with blankets and rugs. Myrna waited until all the women undressed and crawled through the small flap. She passed in the hot rocks with a pitchfork, sliding them off into a depression she had dug inside. At last, she entered with a bucket of water, closing the flap behind her. They sat, six women, their knees touching in the dark. Their eyes stung from the stones, which smoked as they burned off soil and chips from the coals.

Myrna sat, one knee up, one tucked under her, her breasts visible as stones are visible in the night. With the first sprinkle of water came the steam. "Grandmother Earth, Grandfather Sky," she began, doling out the water steadily as she prayed, dribbling it off her fingers as the heat rose, layer upon layer. The heat swelled like the summer swells up from the earth and a grit of ash coated Gina's teeth. "Not a cowboy sweat," she remembered Myrna saying. She could hardly catch her breath.

Myrna passed the bucket to Gina. She had told them each would get her turn. Gina, embarrassed and awkward as she usually was in prayer, full of the please and thank you of her mother, muttered on and on, splashing from the pail well past the time the heat had run out. With a signal from Myrna, they crawled into the air like ruffled, blinded animals and hurled themselves into the cold snowmelt of the creek. It was deep enough only once a year to drench an entire body.

The next round, the sweat came easier, their bare skin touching, the sweat dripping onto each other's thighs from their brows. "The spirits," Gertrude said and the steam rose about her like mists with the sun, many and personal. Her thin hands rose with it, not clasped together like Gina's, but letting go and touching, tossing invisible rings. When Gertrude spoke to them, sometimes her hands would move like that, as if she were rearranging something.

When River undressed, she had shown them her tattoos, Amazons with wings, double-headed axes, moons and stars, astrological symbols rippling down the rolls of flesh on her back and the muscles on her legs. "Isis, Hecate," she said as she prayed. Someone had to counter Myrna's assumption of "Grandfather Sky." River sighed and continued, "Yemoja, Kwan Yin." It was a thankless job guarding a belief system that was a return to matrilineal thinking, a way of life before the Nordic tribes came down to the agrarian cultures and wiped out the women and those who worshiped women. Especially hard since it was so long ago, filtered down to her and floating with dead bodies and the empty beer cans of Christianity and male history.

Gina listened, amazed. River could recognize the slightest scent of semen in any approach. She took pride in her ability to do this, in her stubborn watchfulness. River read only women authors, supported only women artists, musicians and those in the trades. This was an enormous commitment in Montana. River drove a pick-up truck with a license plate which read, "Wymin." Gina had asked her if she was related to the Wymins in Tacoma.

June prayed bodily, from her intestines. She groaned, shuddered, shaking the limbs of the sweatlodge with her rocking. June didn't plead with her god, she made love with one, her breasts rising, her legs spread.

Deeva began with the Lord's Prayer, sang the soprano part of a Bach cantata and ended with a salute to the four directions. Her god seemed male, and from her apologetic beseechment, Gina could only surmise, was part Jesus, part Buddha and part private detective.

The sky was the petals of white roses at twilight when they returned to town, walking the back trails through pockets where the earth sent a warm last breath to their chilled bodies. The air seemed softer, the grass smell rose and haloed their heads and the pine duff cushioned each step. "The friendliness of the earth here," Gertrude was telling Gina.

Deeva was busy telling Myrna how she had known someone in graduate school who had looked exactly like her.

"Did she have high cheekbones?"

"Yes, I think she did."

"Dark skin? Black eyes?"

"As a matter of fact, that's why I thought of you, Myrna."

"I bet she wore her hair long and in braids."

"Sandy. Sandy was her name. Do you know anyone in Boston?"

"Probably," Myrna said, rolling her eyes at Gina. "Probably a sister."

"Funny, I feel great," Gina said. "When I was a kid, I felt so spaced out after church."

Myrna stopped. "This isn't church. The ceremony is based on the holiness of the earth and the earth is not spacy."

Nevertheless, Deeva forgot her watch at the site and, as they waited for her, brushed by waist-high bunch grass and stalks of lavender daisies, they heard her faintly singing, some medley of "When the Saints Go Marching In" and "Where Have All the Flowers Gone."

"All my relations," Myrna said, laughing.

3

There was a joke among the women that if you were good in your last lifetime, you came back as a dog in Emeryville. Dog heaven, they called it. The dogs ran free and in packs and some nights in the summer when the days last until midnight and the ranchers have driven their cattle up from the brown and into the still-green meadows of the mountains, the town resounds with bovine moaning and the paired howlings of dogs with coyotes, watching above for stray calves or the dead.

Gina left the tipi alone before dawn in a direction to distance the cacophony. She thought with amusement how, during her first months in Emeryville, she would force herself outside to close the smoke-flaps to a sudden rain, to walk through the dim and evocative shadows in June's backyard toward the outhouse or the one streetlight that marked the Mint. She had taken her flashlight everywhere. But, little by little, she had grown fond of the night and her sight, like her fear, had grown accustomed to it.

"What are you afraid of?" Myrna had asked her. "The earth?"

"The stones I hold in my hand when I walk are not for animals," Gina had replied.

Myrna trained her. All summer, when she left the bar at two, she would find Gina. They would choose a direction and climb near or far to where, like deer finding the best view, they would throw their bags down in a bed of medicine sage. There, they would lie, a woman's width apart, Myrna on her stomach with her arms pinned underneath her. They slept with no fire. "Astronomers must live in places like this," she'd told Myrna, the stars migrating above them as they slept. Three months in Emeryville and the winds no longer sounded like a concrete overpass, like two shoes stepping out from behind a bush, like anything, more or less than winds.

It was she who frightened others now, jumping elk sleeping in juniper, deer in bluebells, animals feeding or leading their young to water. It worried her, but she craved to see them, find the nest, search it, for what? A souvenir, a tuft of fur, she wasn't sure what, something she could finger in her pockets. She learned from Myrna to hone a silence from her steps, an erraticness to her pace, to be attentive to dried twigs and overhanging branches. For Myrna could second-guess a trail ahead like musicians anticipate a score.

She had nothing to do but learn this. No job. No appointments. She haunted open meadows, creek beds at dusk, mapped the progress of certain edibles as they bloomed higher, in stages, on the ridge. Only to watch them bolt and run away, their eyes full of terror, to wait for the moment they stopped, which they invariably did, with the curiosity hunters banked on. But, she was not a hunter. No, with her it was different. Those who used both arm rests at the movies, the sprawlers and the tall ones in front, those with loud radios at the beach, those whose first acts of ownership were fences; she was not one of these. But even so, a strange stance of self-righteousness, a sensitivity to trespassing had begun to appear. "This is common,"

June said, catching Gina clicking her teeth at every jeep going up the creek. "It happens to some of us."

Gina phoned the Fish and Game regularly, if a beaver hadn't moved for five hours or a dead porcupine might have been shot. The more she walked, the more she grew to know the mountains of Emeryville, the more she saw trouble in need of her solving. "This is common," June said. It wasn't the distrust of nature gleaned from the locals at the Mint. "Too dry, too early," they were always fretting. "Not enough snowpack," or "The trees will be ruined by the early snow." As if the land was unequipped for decision-making. No, it wasn't nature she distrusted. If Gina heard a gunshot, found a wounded moose, a truck parked near the gates of private property, she was convinced someone was poaching. She had a clear idea of the brute. A blond, heavy stranger. Quartered elk swung from the rafters of his barn. He was proud of what tags he had drawn for moose or mountain sheep or bear and how much his rifles cost. He needed the meat.

June fueled this fear, warning Gina that in a month, Montana would become a war-zone. June said that in hunting season, the carnage lined the roads and trails: bones, sacks of rolled skins, entire families of hooves and heads dumped like litter. Soon, June said, every other car would pass through Emeryville with a body strapped to its roof. The bars would be full at twilight with men dressed like soldiers, the bars Myrna said opened before dawn. Already, the local newspapers had published photographs of neatly severed heads, a rack of antlers scalped from a moose, the men smiling and holding their trophies to the camera. "Montana," the bumper stickers said, "where men are men and sheep are nervous."

"Poor sheep," Gina had said, "and it's the same with hunting. No one thinks animals have consciousness."

"Gina, be reasonable. You're new here," Myrna had argued. "You can't oppose hunting. People have always hunted here. And all the feeding grounds are gone."

"Thank goodness for the highways. If it weren't for road kills, we'd have starving deer begging at our doors, wouldn't we?"

"Gina," Myrna sighed, "you have to live with what has happened before you. Like it or not. You can't pretend it doesn't exist."

It was barely morning and Gina had been thinking and walking all night. A high-pitched scream spewed into the air and a red-tailed hawk landed with its umbrella dip into a nearby fir. The music of the lower birds erupted and Gina whistled back, trying to match pitch to pitch. As she came over the crest of a ridge, the sage below pale, still flowering, the grasses sparkling with first frost, she saw that the mountains she lived under were gone and in their place was a wind, running fast ahead of winter like a scout. As the clouds made way for the sun, she found herself standing in front of an enormous outcropping of rock which had disentangled itself from a thicket of huckleberry leaves. The sun hit and the rocks exploded into light.

"Borite," Gina whispered. Myrna would have found that hysterical. All summer, Gina had carried a book, "Wildflowers of the Rocky Mountains," memorizing each species. She had thought Myrna interested, too, until the day her cataloging was interrupted by Myrna's laughter. "Eggs and Butter? You've got to be kidding? Fairy Slipper? Naked Lady? Virgin's Bower?" Myrna had touched the petals of a delicate pink flower. "And who would call this Common Knapweed? Probably some common fellow named Knap." Myrna never picked wildflowers, but then, Gina had never seen Myrna collect or even strive to include the earth in her life the way Gina felt this new-found need to. Myrna would sit for hours on a rock in the creek, her shoulders draped forward like a bear, naked and dunking herself in cool pools. But she wouldn't be thinking or naming or calling anything in. When Gina asked her what she was thinking, she'd say, "I'm not. I'm concentrating."

Gina had to admit that borite was a ridiculously banal word for the alchemy of time which had turned this stone into gold, clattering from the mouth of the cliff like teeth. She wondered why she had never heard of this crystal rock before. Suddenly, a doe came crashing through the downed timber and into the open prairie toward her. It slowed, flicked its ears as if something troublesome were buzzing there, but continued, its head cocked, eyes wide, waiting for some movement to betray someone. Gina held her breath. It was so near she could hear its breath, rowdy and coarse through its nose, not more than five feet away. She could have taken three steps and touched it.

She was determined to not break her gaze, although it scared her, so close and so trusting. Why did it trust her? The fur on its chest was almost like a bird's, feathery and flecked with white, the flanks imperfect with scars, the dewclaws caked with mud. She couldn't believe it. It was almost too much, the way it was still mincing toward her. What if it moved into her completely? What if she became deer, like those stories Myrna told her, with this strange cliff of crystals signaling at her back? Something was the matter with it for it not to be afraid. And what if it jumped on her? Where had she heard of deer rearing up, their hooves attacking a camper? She shuffled her boot through the kinnikinnick, breaking the spell, and the deer froze, then bounded down the slopes of sage. With every landing, the ground exploded with small rocks.

Gina watched the deer grow small between the patches of aspen and cottonwood, turning a quick yellow before the frosted limbs of winter. The fog lifted and smoke began to rise from the houses below. A snow on the further peaks had turned them formidable. Tucked along the seam of the creek, swinging toward town and marked by red willow, was another seam, barely visible, which occasionally shot a signal up to where Gina stood. It was the highway she had come in on.

Her eyes followed the road. There was the town, almost hidden by foliage. There was June's hotel, where she would be digging red and brown potatoes, bouncing them into the dirt. Snow was beginning to circle the valley again, the large garden catching the flurries, but June, inside the four poles of the fences, would still bend to her potatoes in the gray, electric light. Later, her kitchen would smell of chokecherries boiling for syrup. Gina turned to the crystal rock. The sky had absorbed the sun again and the borite withdrew like a miser with its gifts, turning into simple and dull, lichen-covered stone. If she was going to leave Emeryville before winter, it was time.

"Myrna stayed in a tipi all winter once. Talk to her." Maggie was stirring a soup of the vegetables she had found

in the garbage bin of a supermarket. It was the last catch
of the season, before snow would prohibit an easy perusal
and ice would blacken the overripe fruit. Maggie, with
June, hit the supermarket dumpsters whenever they were
in the cities and was proud of their finds: cases of avocados,
soft for spreading, brown bananas for bread, one broken
jar of peanut butter which spoiled the whole case. They
worked as a team, Maggie scaling the sides and landing
knee-deep in iceberg lettuce, tossing nectarines and
peppers to June, who packed them carefully as eggs. Sometimes, there would be others, Indians and the wives of
unemployed miners. Then, Maggie would call out the day's
contents like an auctioneer. "Peaches! Who wants a couple
peaches?"

Maggie turned from her soup. "She said it was quite
cozy once the fire got going."

Gina was studying the plastic bags tacked and taped
to Maggie's windows, the wool blankets nailed to the walls.
Maggie's home smelled of the sacks of potatoes moved in
for the winter, but a sourer, more pungent aroma pervaded
the close quarters. Rolling over with a belch, the redheaded
miner pulled a pile of quilts tighter around him on the floor.

"Maggie, where's your girl friend?"

"Which girl friend?"

"Your girl friend, Maggie. Remember? The one you
kicked me out for. I've never seen her."

The odor of stale beer had soaked into anything
porous in the room. Gina stared contemptuously at the
miner. Maggie wasn't disgusted by much, she could tell. So
little, in fact, that the people of Emeryville called on her to
remove pack rats from traps and children called her to bury
their dead animals. Only a week before, June told everyone
how she had walked in, held her nose and pointed behind
the wood stove to Maggie's missing cat, dead for days.

Maggie was pulling a threadbare sweater over her
shoulders and kicking the door open on her way outside.
Gina followed her to the woodpile, where Maggie began
cracking limbs across her knee. Her chain saw hadn't
worked in months. Instead, Maggie gathered sticks and
the trunks of uprooted trees which were light enough to
hoist into the bed of her truck, aspen left by beaver or the
rotten and many-branched logs discarded on the roadside

by others. Her 1958 pick-up was unlicensed, but ignored by the authorities as it made its way laboriously up the country roads in autumn.

"Your girl friend, Maggie," Gina said again.

Maggie shrugged. "I said she was coming. Not that you had to leave."

"What?" Gina asked, incredulous. "What?" She stood, openmouthed, speechless. After months of confusion, of Maggie's late-night visits to the tipi after the bar, Gina had been determined to confront her at her own house, only to find Maggie cooking soup with no trace of another woman for miles.

Did Maggie love her? No, that wasn't what Gina had come up to find out. Only Maggie would stop chopping onions like she did when Gina knocked on the door, put down her knife and listen to Gina's story of the crystal rock and the deer. "We were planning on showing you that outcropping," Maggie had said, obviously impressed, "but I see you found it yourself." Only Maggie would rifle through her things to find the doeskin bag she had slipped into Gina's pocket. "And next time," Maggie had winked, "don't be so unsure of what you call to you."

Were they lovers? That was not the question either. Maggie's fingers, tasting musty as clay and smoke, tasted of the parts of Gina's body where they had lingered. Did Maggie want to see her any more? That was a question for soap operas and popular songs, not this life with women. Emeryville was small and Maggie would see them all, every day if they wished and, to answer another question, love each with an innocence and exuberance which Gina was growing to hate. And she surely didn't want to move in with Maggie. What was it then? Single. Married. Adultery. Affair. "Damn it, Maggie. I'm confused," Gina said. "What is going on with you?"

Maggie had the look of a woman who spent the summer alone in the mountains. Fields of wild iris, the relaxed stance of a deer off-season, the solitude of the nights had moved into her. She set down the broken chain saw she had been tinkering with and crossed to where Gina was standing. She leaned her trim, rancher's hips into Gina's thighs. Carefully, she began to undo Gina's crossed arms and recross them around her. "I've missed you," she said. Already, the air had cooled and carried on it the sun-warmed needles of pine, curing logs and the fire still burning in the shack. When Maggie unbuttoned Gina's jacket, the snow was sifting through the tops of fir.

"Your soup," Gina reminded, as Maggie's fingers, slick with motor oil from her saw, slid across Gina's breasts.

That fall, Gina made a career out of getting to know the women; potlucks and poker games, non-stop work parties and wood gatherings where twelve hours spent together forged an intimacy only siblings could rival. Evenings were at Gertrude's or with Myrna at the bar. Breakfasts at June's were long, drawn-out affairs where out-of-town visitors were either guests of honor or subjects of conversation. At June's they would drink tea and make lists of ways to earn money without getting a job. June was veteran at this and ingenious. When times were tough, she hung a sign, "Antique Store," in front of the hotel, opening her labyrinth of rooms to tourists and dickering furiously over some treasure she had forgotten was there. Selling firewood, saving aluminum cans, these humble projects turned to extravagant schemes in June's kitchen. They would have Emeryville declared a historical landmark and restore their old homes to their former opulence. Gina tried to imagine Gertrude's rooms, roped off and labeled with signs indicating "Signed Copy of Gyn-Ecology" or "Jill Johnston's Bowler Hat." The country inns were Maggie's idea. Bed and breakfast clubs in a charming mountain town of artists. Myrna offered her own advertising: "Wake up with eccentric women." Gina wondered who would get up in time to make breakfast.

Gina and Myrna settled into the late afternoon autumn light at Gertrude's, warmed by the fire and waiting for Gertrude to serve the chamomile they could smell brewing. Gina tried to imagine what Gertrude was looking for out her window, for it was her habit and it was uninterruptable. No matter who met her after work, who was tugging at her arm like a child, Gertrude would motion for silence, sit in her chair and look and look over the wood houses, the playground, the runoff as it came splashing through the back yards and down from the mountains. She sat there longest in the winter when, without the foliage, through the bony lace of the cottonwood, willow and aspen she could see farther, see deer sleeping, see tracks and ridges previously hidden. Soon she was thinking, the snowy earth would come over that farthest hill.

June had a similar habit of window watching, but her interests were different. June drew back the curtains just enough to hide behind. She never missed her village waking and she checked on it periodically through the day. Her gaze, however, never reached above the chimneys, its range never past the radon mines. She noted each fire started later or earlier than usual, which lights were shut off at night, each Canadian stepping off the bus and moving stiffly to the one open motel. "Are they relatives?" she would ask a neighbor with an out-of-town car in their driveway. It was June who first saw the old man from Edmonton carried off the bus and wheeled down the street toward the health mines.

He had a broken hip, she discovered, wouldn't let a doctor near him. Every day, June watched as he let himself be wheeled painfully along, holding to the sides of the chair, his face contorting over the ruts. She watched diligently for a crease of pain to unfold, a cane to appear, for him to march out of the mines, hands held above his head like a prize-fighter. Finally, an ambulance came to carry him to the nearest hospital where, she later read, he had died.

Finally. It was a phrase synonymous with inevitability and used as frequently in Emeryville as "C'est la vie," is used elsewhere. They waited knowingly for the next thing to fall over, die, rot, meet its timely end. It reassured them. They were right not to expect too much. When the town's first cabin, built in 1827, began to weather, the logs softening, sliding toward earth, someone suggested historical renovation. The roof caved and someone mentioned restoration. Finally, it crumbled. "Dust to dust," someone said. Finally, a grocery store opened, but more importantly, closed. Leaving a trail of shot dogs in front yards, bullied teenagers threatened with knives, and harassed women, the motorcycle gang finally became bored. Gunning their engines, pulling wheelies one last time through the gardens, the gang disappeared with flames behind them in the Old Jail they had been using as their clubhouse.

"By the time we arrived," Myrna was saying, "the inside of that stone jail looked like a barbecue grill."

"Didn't the gang bother the lesbians?" Gina asked.

"Not since the night River whipped them at pool."

"River?"

"Fresh from the gay bars in San Francisco. She even had her own cue."

Gertrude joined them, serving the tea in stoneware cups. "Did you hear that the route has been approved for the new highway? Straight through these mountains."

"As usual, by the time they announced that, they'd been working on it for weeks," Myrna answered. "The call for public input was sandwiched in between the livestock report and 'Neighborhood Blurbs from Betty.'"

"June said it will cost twice as much as the other route, that they'll have to level mountains, divert the stream and disturb those uranium tailings close to the river. But the business men in Milltown have lobbied for it."

Myrna scowled. "The construction workers are already crowding the bar. Last night, I gave a guy his beer and he grabbed my hand. Now, you know nobody grabs my hand if I don't offer it. Said he liked squaws. Said he'd had his eye on me all night."

Gertrude glanced at Gina. "Well?"

"I said, 'Oh yeah? Well, I've had my eye on you motherfuckers all my life.'"

Gina looked up from the netted veins of leaves she was staring at in the bottom of her cup. She was thinking of the hundreds of orange surveyor's stakes she had watched June pluck from the lines. Organic sabotage, June called it. She was thinking of the four-lane through Washington's high passes which had brought her here. "You should see how the dynamite slices clean the granite. Not even balsam root will take hold. But I suppose there's no way to stop it."

"They already have the funding," Myrna nodded.

"June wants us to dress up in feathers and skins, paint our faces and parade down the old highway, lamenting and passing out leaflets."

"That sounds like her," Myrna said impatiently.

"River thinks we should blow up the trucks."

"That sounds like her." Myrna rolled a cigarette on a saucer in her lap. "That would slow it down, but we're never going to stop it."

"Jake thinks we should just forget about it. Keep the low profile we have."

"Deeva wants to hold a ritual of some sort. She says that with all the power we have collectively, we could stop the destruction of the canyon," Gertrude added.

"Fat chance," Myrna grumbled, opening the window to blow out the smoke.

"What kind of ritual?" Gina asked.

"She says she knows how to lead seances."

"Oh," Gina groaned. "Who does she want to call back?"

"Rosetta," Gertrude said.

Myrna grunted.

"Wait, Myrna, it does seem appropriate. After all, she was the town's first famous woman. A property owner, self-employed, in control of her body. She's a legend. Maybe she'd have a suggestion."

"What would a whore know about the highway commission?"

"Myrna," Gina suggested, "Maybe you could think of someone. A medicine person or something?"

Myrna glared.

"Calm down. It's a harmless thing. Although, I have to admit, it makes me uneasy that Deeva insists on holding it in June's backyard."

"That's nuts. June's backyard is in the center of town," Gina said.

Gertrude smiled. "Yes, center. I think she stressed that word."

A couple of weeks later, on the date Deeva had set, late autumn rain was arriving from up the creek like marathon runners, unsteady, but determined. Gina was in the Mint, trying unsuccessfully to convince her friend.

"Be careful when you mess with the dead," Myrna said.

The bar had changed. Glenn was only making rare appearances and the miner friend of Maggie's was hanging out there every night, slapping backs with the construction crew, punching polkas on the jukebox and telling bad jokes. The crew was horny and belligerent and few women ventured in. Hatty sat, surrounded by men she had resolved to think of as the enemy ever since she heard they were going to blow up the streambed where she had gone fishing every evening since Frank died.

No one remembered that Hatty had ever been married and few knew of the place, next to a juniper, above the curve in the river, where there was a deep pool full of cutthroat trout. Hatty barely remembered Frank herself, at least not with fondness, but she loved that green pool, the walk there alone in her windbreaker, pole on her shoulder, night crawlers in her pocket. It was a thin living, taking tickets all summer in the health mine she didn't own, selling doilies to bank against the off-season and the frozen-over pond. Hatty lived on Early Times, draft beer and trout. The curse she leveled against these men was for the cutthroat trout and the quiet Frank had finally left her in.

"You girls shouldn't be afraid to come in here," Hatty yelled across the bar to Gina.

On a busy night in the bar, there were those Myrna could count on, those who would cause her trouble, but there was always a wild card. Myrna kept her eye on Hatty. Hatty had a temper with roots in the Mint. As a young woman, she'd packed a shotgun and was not averse to blasting the mirrors out when she caught Frank with anything female, just to get his attention. Lately, she'd been bringing bags of bananas in, throwing them at the feet of the workers and yelling, "Monkeys! Apes!" Myrna watched her raise her fists.

"When Dora and me were your age, they made us get our beer in buckets at the backdoor. You're lucky. So, don't let these clowns stop you," Hatty continued.

"Hey, that's right," one of the men yelled. "Come, sit next to me. I won't hurt ya."

"We should have scalped all of them a long time ago," Myrna whispered.

"Whatsa matter? You gals ain't queer, are ya?"

"Unless you got an outstanding proposition, which it don't look like you do, it ain't none of your business," Hatty yelled back.

"Shhh, Hatty, calm down," Myrna said, setting down a shot glass of rye. "This one's on me."

"Sure you don't want to get Eddie to work your shift?" Gina asked, pulling on her coat. "Deeva would love to have you join us."

"Whatever you do over there is your problem."

The rain was slowing when Gina crossed the two-lane toward June's back yard. Before she turned the corner, she heard drums, and soon she had joined a handful of arthritic visitors to the health mines, who were clapping and taking snapshots of the band as they stood under a makeshift awning. There were at least ten women perched on June's steps, oblivious to the weather, costumed in wool jackets and cowgirl boots and playing a wild six/eight Bembe. In front of them all was Deeva, directing the orchestra of tin cups, Brazilian rattles, guiros, pots, frying pans, snare drums, tamboras, bongos and spoons, shouting and wiping the last of the rain from her conga drum with a bath towel. Near the creek, Maggie was fanning the smoke of a dampened fire.

"How did you learn to play African music in Montana?" Gina asked Gertrude, who had a counter rhythm revolving on her samba bells.

"We haven't."

Deeva handed Gina a cup and a stick to beat it with. "I thought it would be nice to play music before we begin. And isn't it wonderful? The townspeople have turned out to see what we're doing."

"They already know what we're doing," Gertrude said to Gina.

The sunset had the blood of November in it and a moon was rising. Deeva blew a whistle and the music lurched to a stop. "I want us all to form a circle near the banks of the creek, where Maggie has built us a splendid fire." The tourists started to follow, but a few words from Deeva and they turned back, disappointed.

When Gina reached the circle, Deeva was strewing dried petals and seeds from a basket. They held each other's hands while she chanted words out of a book she kept referring to. "A ritual cookbook?" Gina whispered to Gertrude. The women wore the look of amateurs at a square dance, ready to be embarrassed, but eager.

"Now, with our eyes closed, I want us to visualize a hearty matron with black hair," Deeva said. June had loaned Deeva Rosetta's velvet and rhinestone belt and together, they stretched it to its full circumference, illustrating, for those lacking imagination, Rosetta's exact girth. "You've all seen the photographs," Deeva continued.

Gina had never known anyone to will the dead into manifestation. She thought if they didn't show, they didn't show. Deeva, however, seemed sure her credibility would be ruined forever if there was no sign. Gina tried hard to picture Rosetta. She was sure no one expected her to arrive bent double and wrinkled. People always conjured the dead at an age which was never the age they had died. Which age would this be? At her most beautiful? Wisest? At nineteen, thirty, forty-five? Gina tried to imagine Rosetta as a young woman of her trade, but her only comparison was the thin girl on the street in Seattle, in short boots, fishnet stockings and leotard.

The heavy silence of concentration fell over the group, and out of the corner of her eye Gina watched a bear-shaped shadow approach the edges of the lawn. "Give us a sign, Rosetta," Deeva was imploring. The other women, necks bent back, were scanning the sky, apparently waiting for Rosetta to fall into the belt like a fish into a net. "Let us know you are here," Deeva said again when, outside the circle, the shadowed figure collapsed softly into a mound in the new mud.

Gina was the first to break the circle, rushing toward Ellen, a large woman of about her age who worked with Gertrude at the Home. Ellen had been in Emeryville before anyone—was born there as far as Gina knew—but none of the women spoke to her and no one thought to ask each other of her history or to visit her home. Ellen shuffled through town, eyes to the ground, ignored. And now, with her body lying in a heap at their feet, Gina wondered why she had never thought that odd.

"She's got hypothermia!" someone yelled and before Gina could stop them, Deeva arrived with Gina's sleeping bag and stuffed Ellen into it. In an instant, Deeva had stripped off her clothes and was crawling into the bag with Ellen.

"It's sixty degrees," Gina protested. Hypothermia was the state disease, a condition the Park Service, tourist brochures and school assemblies warned against. One moment, you were feeling fine, a bit wet perhaps, and the next, your temperature was plummeting, your limbs weakening and you eased into a sleep like drowning. Gina bent to Ellen's slumbering breath. It smelled like marijuana.

Deeva was rubbing her body briskly against Ellen's. "Someone call a nurse."

"She is a nurse," Gertrude said. "So am I and I doubt she has hypothermia. Deeva, stop. I think she's coming to."

Ellen was stirring. She opened her eyes to find herself nose to nose with Deeva. Soon, she realized she was in even more intimate contact, and with a total stranger. "What's going on here?" she screamed, trying to squirm out of the sleeping bag. "Who are you?" Ellen stared in horror at the ring of women above her, staring back as if from a great height, their blue and red faces flickering in the firelight demonically.

Gertrude turned to go. "Shit," she said to Gina. "Shit."

Dreamers like a severe winter.
-Gaston Bachelard

4

A barely perceptible shift in the density of stars, a veil
blown about, nothing she would swear to. "Are you sure?"
Gina said, shielding her eyes to the night sky. "I thought
they were colored. This looks more like sand in the heavens
or dust." June and Gina were snowshoeing across the
crunching hills to a knoll where they could see Orion and
watch the faint beginnings of the northern lights.

June squinted. "So, this is how those born in winter
must feel, dry and crystalline." June was born when most
animals in the north were born, in the late spring when
they have two seasons to become strong. She kept her body
a nice animal temperature, too, slightly above normal. Her
feet were powdered liberally with cayenne and buried
under two layers of cotton and thick rag wool. The red
pepper, she swore, improved her circulation, while it
turned her soles ocher. She wore long underwear to bed

through May, and in winter wore so many yards of down, wool and flannel that she waddled like an infant in a snowsuit.

June did, in fact, own a snowsuit, but she saved it for only the most bitter weather, when going outdoors was unavoidable—the fecundity of dumpster oranges, the over-full compost pail and her plastic-sealed windows too much even for her. She had found an extra-large mechanic's overall in one of her back bedrooms and had quilted it with down feathers. Jake had tried to suggest the use of poly-ester batting, which would be thinner and lighter, but June would have no plastic next to her skin. She embroidered sequins on the pockets and added her collection of appli-qued flags of the allied nations. It took only one washing for the flags to run into pale streams of dye. To the children of Emeryville, the apparition of June, moving like a winter sunset, streaked pink and yellow and red with feathers escaping from the seams like snow, the light catching the sequins as it did on the frozen ice, throwing it back and forth, shimmering like an orchestra of flutes and cymbals, was a solstice ritual.

Sound traveled the thick air slowly. A front had moved in and swallowed the town. Twenty-five below for ten nights in a row. Few of the old cars started, even though their engine heaters were plugged in, the cords trailing under their owner's front doors like leashes. In the homes below, faucets were dripping to keep the pipes from freezing. It was a cliff-edged time, when the back tires of pickups slid on upward grades and teetered, creek-side. When hands lost feeling, could be sliced to the bone without pain.

Myrna, so the story went, wintered in a tipi in a year far worse than this one, the year the trees popped and split in December, Milltown Lake froze solid; the eleven-cord winter the locals speak of in hushed tones as if not to awaken it. Some of the women had visited her there and liked to tell of it, how they left the cabins and fires of town, crossed with trepidation the tree that had fallen twelve feet above the creek. Most remembered how good it smelled, of kerosene and canvas frozen stiff as rawhide, the wood-smoke clinging to it. They spoke of pockets of balmy air near the dogwood, of a darkness near the spring, foreboding, as if a bear slept there. They tried to describe the enormity of the quiet, only the sound of water murmuring under ice, as if all things near the tipi were the tipi, too. As if the tipi was only part of the endless winter they were visiting.

"Are you crazy?" Myrna had asked, astonished, when Gina offered to share her tipi during the coming winter. "When I have this warm shack and a stove?"

"But it sounded beautiful. I thought you enjoyed it."

"Gina, I enjoyed what I had."

Once Myrna realized there was no talking Gina out of it, she helped her prepare. They built a floor with two-by-fours, stuffed it underneath with straw. A tin airtight stove was moved in with a pipe inserted through the smokeflaps. Myrna lashed a triangle of pine to the three strongest poles and strung limbs between to make a loft. "It's pleasant to sleep up there, warmer, and when the wind blows, you rock a little."

June donated a mattress and they piled it with any available blankets. When the first snows came, Myrna showed her how to bank snow against the outside walls for insulation. It was warm when the fire was going. Once the fire went out, as it invariably did, the warm air evaporated like a drop of water in a desert. Myrna had forgotten one thing. One night, Gina woke to what she thought was the returning motorcycle gang, gunshots, fireworks and flying debris, but which turned out to be glass bottles of beer and jars of fruit exploding as they froze. That was the night June first dreamt of Gina crawling between her flannel sheets. By January, Gina's real limbs were warm around June's waist, her dry fingers tucked under the skin of June's breasts, her hair, like this night they were braving, sterile and windswept next to the heavy scent of the favorite forage of deer June rinsed into her hair.

They slept close as cats and naked as two children, although Gina's mother would never have approved of such closeness or nakedness between sisters. Neither seemed surprised to find the other there, close or naked. It was a comfort. June's ample breasts floated from one side of the bed to the other, like the sea, in tidal fashion, sometimes landing across Gina's arm, then slowly draining off from it. One night, Gina caught the nipple, just the tip of it, and

June lolled back toward her. June's skin began to curl into any cavity of air between them. Neither knew when to call the turn of sex. Maybe it was the night June backed her body closer, over Gina's thigh and rode there, pausing, settling closer.

Some nights, they would just touch, Gina losing her fingers in the folds like bath water, clean and warm, running her hands through them, soapiness trailing her sleepy fingers. Some nights, June nibbled and sucked on Gina's ears, her shoulders, lapping like a kitten, her dry tongue in tiny, eager strokes until Gina would push her away. Neither knew when to call the turn of sex, one night or the other, but sometimes, impatient with comfort, Gina would find herself above June, her fingers reaching, like the time they found the narrow caves the sun made in ice near the creek and flushed, how they'd laughed as the water melted down their hot fingers.

"Gina, look," June whispered. The sky was rocketing, the northern lights majestic and pastel. When Gina lay in her bed as a child, the traffic lights travelling the ceiling of her room came close to this. June lifted her finger to her ear and they listened as the coyotes howled low and close. The birds had migrated, all but the small gray ones and even they had stopped calling.

Their gloved hands caught like the bare limbs of aspen below as their eyes followed the white groves down, down to the shallow pan of a town, nestled under a cloud of smoke. Down to the very tiny earth-movers, road-graders, the encampment of diesel trucks, the long line of laboring vehicles invading the canyon like mercenaries. June squeezed her hand. She saw, too, what cliffs, what curves of the river would be removed. There, near the river, where Myrna had just last month picked grocery sacks of chokecherries. Downstream, where the birds had beat her to it. That trail, which led Gina once to nighthawks dive-bombing at dusk for their prey, the cliff where she'd heard the wounded, half-human cry of a bobcat. Alone. Walking. Curious. In so short a time, Gina had a personal mythology of these cliffs and canyons. It was too soon to point to a spot, as though to a house burned down, and say, there, there was once a cliff. I remember.

From the ridge, the machines looked ridiculous as toys, despicable and small as the red bugs June picked from the leaves of her cabbage plants in July and ate while Gina watched, horrified. Could they destroy so much? The day after the seance, the engines of three bulldozers refused to turn over and a boom broke, swinging into the pelvis of a young man from Wyoming. No one mentioned the drumming or the protests and Sam swore he had seen a van with New York license plates pull up next to the trucks late one night after the bar closed. Construction had stopped, due not to the accidents, but to the half-foot of snow atop the roofs and a cold sky so near it was pushing snow off the trees in avalanches.

"We'll show you what power is!" June yelled suddenly. Her voice, solid and weighted as a ball, bounced down the blue and black slopes, down the hills of fragile sage.

Gina stared in awe as, in seconds, June's sudden breath coated her hair and face with a silvery web of frost.

Myrna stood with her foot wedged in June's back door, blowing smoke-rings through the crack. "If I was rich, I'd buy Hatty plastic for her windows."

"Close the door," June whined. She was busy preparing tea from the many green jars in her apothecary of herbs, selecting pinches and sprigs from the dark, unlabeled glass—twigs, barks, the purple flowers of borage. She pulled a rabbit ear from a stalk of mullein, which was hanging from the rafters to dry. Then, muttering, she shucked a stem of comfrey into the pot. Gina worried when June started her teas, averting her eyes from the shriveling brown and green seeds which were drying on a window screen, suspended above the stove. She wondered if June had dried the small, red cabbage bugs.

"If I were rich," June said, "I'd buy up all the undeveloped land and leave it just the way it is."

"Your private Bohemian Grove?" River asked.

"For the animals. They're going to need to go somewhere." June handed out the cups, steaming from the muted green all her teas turned to. Despite the cold weather, the women arrived every morning at June's, kicking the snow off their boots, warming their hands over her oil-barrel stove, the holes in it glowing like eclipses.

"But Jake doesn't want to move to Europe," Gertrude was saying, as Deeva continued to list the friends she would install with lifetime pensions or send to tropical paradises, and Jake, the janitor, whom she would send to art school.

"Well, she should."

"You all disappoint me. You sound like such capitalists," River interjected. "After all, there are things we can do to improve this community without money."

"Oh, River, what more do you want? We already man the volunteer fire department."

"Watch your language."

"I think River's right," Deeva said. "For instance, she's been going door to door, giving demonstrations of herbal medicine."

"I bet that goes over big," Myrna grumbled.

"It's not just education, it's a necessity. In case you haven't noticed, the town is rife with influenza."

"Yeah, you know Hatty's very sick when she can't make it to the bar."

"She seems determined to die in there," River sighed. All her free time was spent in Hatty's room above the Mint, brewing soup until the air grew sweet with garlic and the pillows smelled of honey, ginger and kelp. Despite River's best efforts, Hatty would touch nothing but puffed rice, pouring it into the empty margarine tub she used for a bowl.

"Hatty's brought more chicken soup and pint bottles to more old folks, sick folks and new mothers than you and I can say we've known, and she's swabbed a great deal of black eyes. Hatty's been present at every funeral, cooking for the widows and driving the family to the service in Eddie's sedan. Emeryville's got more than its share of deaths and wife beatings and Hatty is conveniently located in the place most of them happen, in the Mint." Myrna lit a cigarette. "So, you can understand why she isn't bending backwards in gratefulness."

"She told me to leave her alone," River pouted.

"Then, leave her alone."

"She don't take kindly to nursin'," June said, mimicking Hatty.

"She doesn't mean it. Alcohol has got us all under the thumb of the oppressor."

"River?" Myrna narrowed her eyes.

"OK, so I've grown fond of the old gal."

"Haven't we all," Gertrude said. "She's cranky, but she always defended us."

"Even when we walk in the bar holding our new girl friend's hand."

"Myrna, I have a right to public affection," River said.

"It was Bill Lewis's bachelor party."

"That doesn't excuse their behavior, shouting 'Dyke!' like it was a football chant. Nothing Hatty said could be heard over the din."

"I think those construction workers are getting the local men riled up," Gina said. No one mentioned the highway much, though the first swath they cut of lodgepole pine and fir was visible from the lowest hill and in each of Emeryville's yards was a stack of green wood for which they had risked the differentials of their pick-ups. "Ever since that worker died, the crew have been suspicious."

"They don't think that was our fault, do they?"

"I don't know. Do you?"

"Hatty doesn't use their green wood," River said proudly.

"Hatty doesn't ease the animosity either. You laugh at those bananas she throws, but those men don't think it's funny." Myrna frowned. "I tell you, the bar's getting to be a three-ring circus."

"Sam was in rare form last night," Gina said. "Dancing and punching A-6 over and over. You know the tune:

> I was talkin' with yr mother
> just the other night,
> said I thought you were an asshole.
> She said, I think yr right,"

Gina sang in her best western twang. "They thought he was funny until he winked at Myrna and me and said, 'Those of our class should stick together 'til the last.'"

"How about when he told Bill Lewis, 'The day I turn odd is the day I walk with God?'"

"That's terrible," Deeva said, shocked. "Sam must not realize the implications."

"Deeva," Myrna said, "When Eddie's father found Sam at the Home, he was in four-point shackles."

"Well, I do feel sorry for him. I know he's your friend."

"He has one friend. A social worker brings him to the bar at Christmas and he rocks back and forth from one foot to the other near the poker machine like this." Myrna rocked forward, "Back, you idiot," then, back onto the other foot, "Against the wall."

"What are you saying?"

"I'm saying Sam is more than aware of the implications."

Gina peeked around June's curtains at the white earth, white sky. "I dreamt last night of snowbanks pocked with rain. The tubes of ice around the willow had disappeared." Since moving in with June, Gina dreamt of weather moving in from the top of her head, storming through her body, passing out her feet. At first, she was off. Terribly. Willow smelling of rain, but when she woke, it would be below zero.

Living with June was easy, easy as sleeping, easy as falling in a hole, a big dream, the cave of a Montana winter. Each night, crawling under June's woolen quilts, it was as if she were crawling into the season itself, the earth and waters sealed, as she was sealed, under blankets so heavy that once she was under, she was pinned. There, Gina slept ten, twelve, fourteen hours at a time and when she woke, there was June, asking about her dreams.

"June, I put no stock in dreams," she had said.

"You have them?"

"Of course. Everyone has them."

"You like to ignore things that happen to you?"

"They don't happen. They're fantasy, a bombardment of haphazard images. People appear, disappear, phrases of songs, blades of steel, foreign names, petals, pots, planters of foliage. I dream of a friend dying and I call her and she's never felt better. I get tired of being wrong."

"You're not wrong. You're just slow."

"Now, what is that supposed to mean?"

"Don't you bump into the dream in your life sooner or later?"

"Sometimes. Hell, I don't know. What are we talking about?"

"We'll work on precision. We'll start with the weather. I never met an animal that wasn't prepared for a storm."

Gina was doubtful, but after a month of her body rocking with wide swings of temperature, June calculated that Gina's predictions were, at worst, off three days.

"Let's see," June said, relinquishing the honey jar to her guests and following Gina to the window. "Yes, yes," she said, looking over Gina's shoulder, delicately drumming it from behind. "It sure feels like something new is about to be blown in."

When the chinook came two days later, no one could sleep. The sky broke through, the wind blew pure and warm and the creek, no longer muffled with ice, ran sexual, lapping and licking with such a thirsty sound that it was as if crowds were drinking from its sides. The sun sent children onto the porches, the steps of the general store, the school playground. They sank into the greasy mud, swinging their arms and gesturing with a width that a week before would have seemed to their brittle bones too reckless.

Only the old men stayed indoors next to their stoves in the high country, drinking canned milk in their boiled coffee and grumbling about how they didn't get good, hard winters like they used to. Only the old men, worried about an early spring, a dry summer, a high fire danger, about their grandchildren growing up "weak as Californians," only they missed the arrival of the double-wide trailer and the station wagon bearing the sign, "Wide Load." It rumbled into town, flashing with orange lights, and the children trailed behind it like a carnival. When it took the only right-hand turn up Emeryville Creek, coming to a halt in the vacant lot where Hatty dug worms, at the end of a row of houses, at the bottom of the very best sled hill around, the Reverend Jimmy Raymond Boyd climbed out of his car and faced his audience.

He was of medium height, thin, with hands which hid in the pockets of his suitcoat, jingling coins. When he walked, he stooped, one arm circling his waist as if he were clutching something valuable or painful. His wife, Loretta, stood by his side, waving like a campaign wife.

In silent appraisal, the locals noted the make of car, the quality of fabric, the brand and number of appliances they unpacked. It was nothing they could name, but they were as adept at recognizing tribal features as the Natives, who could tell Cheyenne from Sioux. Maybe the ears, which stuck out from under his hat, the fleshy nose, maybe her sandy hair the color of the midsummer dust on dirt roads that blurred the distant views. Whatever it was, they reached consensus without any consultation. The preacher and his wife were of them, poor, and thus, inconsequential. They turned, disappointed, toward their homes.

In a week, a banner went up over the double doors of the only chapel in town, the one-room church which had been empty for decades. "Revival Meetings," the sign said. Soon, the power company had arrived to restore electricity, and three young men were hired to shovel out the bat shit, remove the beer bottles and take down the boards from the windows. Before the new glazing had dried, the riverlets in the road had turned back into lightning bolts of ice, and winter returned, much to the relief of the old miners.

"What do you think he does for a living?" Gina warmed her hands over the wood stove on an early-darkening afternoon in the Mint. It was only four-thirty, but the snows on the hills were already deep blue. "He must do something on the side."

"Side of what?" Myrna had just exchanged a week's tips for a roll of quarters and was futilely plugging them into the poker machine. "Only five families have joined the church since he opened it a month ago. What do you think he has, a membership fee?"

Gina watched the screen from across the empty room, "Too bad you got the six. That would have been a full house."

"Stay out of my game, Gina."

Eddie stole a glance in the mirror and smoothed his hair. "Maggie's friend, the miner, joined the church."

"Boomboom," Glenn said. During the war—no one was sure which—Glenn had suffered a stroke while the artillery thundered above him. He had regained all his faculties except one, the use of language. Although he spent years in VA hospitals, no amount of speech therapy

could coax a sound out of him. It was a miracle he could
speak at all, let alone sing. Hatty interpreted, repeating
each garbled, sea lion roar, waiting until he paused when
she would nod to his audience and say, "High on a hill and
windy sea."

Hatty rehearsed Glenn just as she rehearsed the bar
kids: the sons of the short-order cook and the offspring of
Emeryville's alcoholic mothers. "Now, show me how you tie
your shoes," she'd say and they would groan. "Show me,
you brat," she'd repeat, grabbing hold of an ear. "You want
to end up like me and your mama?" Just as she rehearsed
the preteen pool hustlers: "Throw the first few games, win
one, then let them win another."

"Reverend's been preaching you girls is witches,"
Hatty said and fell into a fit of coughing.

"Which girls?" Gina moved closer to Hatty.

"He's claiming that lesbians are witches and says
there's evidence you've been having rites on the hillsides."
Now that Eddie had her attention, he began filing his nails
and concentrating on a plastic diaper commercial.

"What kind of rites?" Gina shrieked.

Myrna, who had exhausted her luck, returned to her
stool. "Control yourself," she whispered.

"Mutilating animals, cursing innocent people,
obscure sexual practices," Eddie winked, answering Gina,
"that sort of thing."

"He can't be serious. Who's going to believe that?"

"He says he's going to run you out of town."

"What do you mean, 'you?'"

"Well, I'm certainly not a lesbian," Eddie said,
shoving a beer toward each of them. "Cheer up."

"Bad sign when somebody moves to town in winter,"
Hatty nodded.

"How does he know we're lesbians?"

"Honey, it doesn't take a private detective to figure
that one out," Eddie said.

Gina thought of River on the street with her tank top
and tattoos, her new girl friend from the city with her
shaved head. River banking the eight ball six games in a
row, telling the heavy equipment operator whom she had
just beaten that the nuclear family was an anachronism.

"River," Gina whispered to Myrna, "probably ruined it for us all."

"Come on, Gina," Eddie said. "Where are your shopping bags, purses, high heels, *Family Circle?* What about your trips to the beauty shop, your pregnancies, weddings, showers, divorces? Instead, you have chain saws, pickup trucks, flannel shirts. Women's legs sticking out from under the open hoods of vehicles. I swear, Gina, you're getting as blind as that Deeva who parks her second car down the block so we won't think she's rich."

"Like who else would have a Mercedes?" Myrna laughed. "Don't worry. This town has tolerated leather-jacketed dropouts backing them against the wall at knife point, not to mention loggers so drunk they once shot out Eddie's prize possession." Myrna pointed to the row of Lewis and Clark vodka bottles displayed on the bar's mantle, bottles cast in the likenesses of the original explorers; Sacajawea, her alcoholic husband, York, the scouts. It had taken years for Eddie to replace them.

"And they call you queer," Hatty said, nodding to the drunken man who had awakened and was now slouched at a corner table, his hand in his opened fly.

"Eddie!" Gina screamed, "Kick him out of here."

Eddie strolled over to the man, whispered in his ear, and the drunk swayed toward the men's room. "Chanting and drumming in the middle of town probably wasn't such a good idea either," Eddie said. "This is cowboy country, not Tahiti."

"Did the Reverend tell you about that?" Gina said, suddenly feeling a need to whisper. The cafe was filling for dinner and, out the window, the brilliant snow falling after dark.

"Of course not. He only came in here once. I said I didn't drink in his church. He shouldn't preach in my bar. But the word is out."

"The miner joined the church," Hatty explained again.

Gina and Myrna exchanged glances and stood to go. Outside, the village noise was hushed by snow, layers and piles which deafened the spin and skid of tires arriving from over the pass. Snow that began in the evening like this would fall until dawn, would send elk to the lower meadows and terrified drivers searching for the orange reflectors which marked the sides of the road.

The door to Deeva's shed was locked, but the bolt was hanging by two screws. Myrna removed them expertly, slipped in and reappeared with two sets of snowshoes. It was obvious she had done this before. When she had replaced the lock, she fastened Gina's shoes and trudged ahead, the wool mackinaw she wore all season dark against the bright snow. Gina struggled behind, angry at her continual lack of skill with these bearpaw shoes which felt more like flippers. They plodded between houses lit with the blue light of the only television channel from Elklodge, the announcer mispronouncing all foreign names and places. Soon, even these lines would heave with the weight of the storm, the spinning tires would cease and slip backward, all animal travel would halt. When they reached the Reverend's trailer they turned to see that Emeryville had been snuffed out by the blizzard.

But the creek was hard to lose. It twisted under and over the ice with the shimmery sound and roll of tympani. The smell of water was everywhere, tinny and fresh as blood, the thick flakes melting on their faces. It was hard work moving up the dirt road, which was quickly becoming only a path. Myrna stomped ahead, breaking trail, her head tilting up to the sky which billowed like a shaken blanket, and down to the tracks being covered. The dark pinnacles of fir narrowed in front of them as if they were lining a tunnel. It felt as if they were entering a different world, this path like those which lead through the jungles to the ruins of an invaded land: Palenque, Chichén Itzá. Gina had seen the photographs. But here, there were no temples, no pyramids of stone. And yet every stone, every tree, the earth she pressed her feet into gave evidence of an ancient, human presence, the air itself crystallized as if with past ritual. Salish. Kootenai. Shoshone. Ten thousand years before that, Clovis, those who made the tools the archaeologists still found on hills nearby. Only fifty thousand Indians left in Montana, but the land spoke strong of their passage.

Gina stopped, squinting into the blizzard. Something had shifted. The sound of something restlessly stomping the ground. The night trunks were flickering with the blaze of snow. The snow and night swooped speckled and close, big-bodied as an owl, confusing her. Myrna had turned to face her. Her braids with the flurries seemed otter and ermine, black and white, and in one hand, something she leaned against like a staff. A musket? Gina stared. Myrna's feet, only a second ago strapped in snowshoes, were bound in hides. But torn ones, oiled and dark with blood or mud, and her clothing hung in tatters. Still, the sound of something stomping, feathers, dark and white, the entire night lit and colorless. Myrna stood, unmoving, her face thinner and shadowed, pocked with disease. In a swirl of snow, near the edges of the forest, her black eyes flashed accusations of a time neither of them remembered, but which seemed to be repeating. Myrna stood, angry, calling the woman in Gina out.

"What makes you think you're the first to feel the loss of this land?"

Frightened, Gina backed down the road, crossing her shoes behind her and landing in a racket of bones and rawhide thongs. When she looked up, Myrna was back to herself, her hands in the pockets of her wool jacket, her hair feathered with snow. Myrna pointed to the lamplight above, fighting its way through the blizzard. "Hey, kid, think you can make it that far?"

Maggie hadn't heard a human voice for over two weeks. Not a radio, not television, not a neighbor. She opened no newspapers, magazines or books and she talked to the goats in their own language, a sweet, storybook baahing. She talked to herself not at all. Through the hours of splitting wood, feeding dogs, goats, cats, through drawing and sleeping, her thoughts appeared in notes, the pitch of chickadee or junco, the rumble of the creek below. They appeared in lines and squalls and in desperate washes of color. Every deer wandering into view, every break in the weather, every dream seemed providential. A knock on the door would be the angel or devil she had been waiting for.

"The miner joined the church," Myrna said when Maggie opened the door. She had been sketching by lamplight the many candles in corners, tables and windows. The room was aglow like a wake. Slowly, Maggie rolled her pencils in a cloth.

"I know," Maggie said.

"Do you also know that he's told the whole town about the seance and the dykes and God knows what else?" Gina shouted.

Myrna shot her a look and Gina withdrew to the floor, her arms wrapped around her knees. Myrna was right. She should have known better than to try to shake a response out of Maggie. Maggie's life was unfit for quick response, especially in winter. To Maggie in winter, shapes, ideas and time slowed to great movements; the crustal plates squeezing the continental shelf, islands sinking, extinctions, mutation. They would be lucky if Maggie said anything at all. Gina waited while Myrna and Maggie sat, heads bowed, but not praying.

She looked around. Maggie's cabin was untouched by the collapse of electric or telephone wires. The wood and glass loomed elemental by firelight, the dirt hidden by the dark, the frayed blankets folded in a colorful pile. The shelves held jars filled with pink beans, brown rice and flour. The jars the town recyled to her still bore the factory labels of the peanut butter and pickles. Gina looked to the sink where water ran into a slop bucket underneath. When she had stayed here, she had emptied the soapy contents each day as she finished the dishes. But Maggie could eat off the same plate for a week, wiping it off with newspapers which she then burned for kindling. To Maggie, cleanliness as a virtue was nothing compared to the sin of mothers who used disposable diapers. Her god tallied the cans recycled, noted the pious use of toilet paper. To Maggie, it was a universe of limits and limited resources. But her love, Gina thought, yes, Maggie had said it was limitless.

Maggie piled a few pieces of lath, some with nails still embedded in them, into the cookstove. "It was my fault. I sent him down there."

"To the church?" Gina asked. "Have you lost your mind?"

"To the trailer. I thought he could spy a bit. I always get suspicious when somebody moves to town in winter." Maggie reached for her pipe. "He came back converted. Must have been that chicken dinner Loretta fed him. He got tired of bean soup, though he never was too picky to stuff himself."

"I never understood why you let him stay here in the first place," Gina said peevishly. "Unless there was something I didn't know."

"You said he was my spirit guide," Maggie said, laughing, and punctuated it with a loud crow caw.

"Just 'cause they're dead doesn't make them wise," Myrna said, contributing a wolf howl.

"Just 'cause you're Indian doesn't make you dead," Maggie countered, demonstrating her elk bugle.

The cabin was beginning to resound with animal calls. "So, where is the miner now?" Gina asked, irritated with their levity.

"Far as I know, he moved to the Reverend's wood shed. Said I'm a sinner 'cause I sleep with women." Maggie continued their game by snorting like a pig. "I said that must make the Reverend one, too."

Myrna answered with her hawk imitation, Maggie switched to a bobcat's howl and soon, the goats were on top of the roof and the coyotes returned their calls.

The printed flyers littered the empty streets of Emeryville like tumbleweeds, crisscrossing the road, torn from telephone poles and windshields by the wind. It was the void-of-course, edge-of-the-weather pause between seasons before the hawks returned and what buttercups had appeared were buried again and again under snow. Ellen caught one of the flying papers with her boot and bent to pick it up.

"Concerned About Your Community?" it said. "Come To An Emergency Meeting At The Chapel Tonight. 7 P.M." In smaller print: "Catholics welcome. Bring your wives."

Ellen slipped a joint out of her pocket and smoked it as she headed toward the chapel. She had never attended anything but her job and her mother's funeral. "Religion is a gamble with worse odds than the state lottery," her mother had frequently said. Ellen had once considered it, sending out prayers like chain letters, but she never got an answer. "Knock, knock," she would say, but all that answered were the dead who flocked around her like gulls to a trash can at the beach, never the divine. And did they tell her anything new? "What's up there?" she would say. "Just tell Hilda it's lovely and I'm waiting for her," they

would reply. However, the arrival of Rosetta, an entire
month and a half after Deeva had first called her at the
seance, who came back from the dead, in the dead of winter,
introducing herself to a near-sighted and nonplussed Ellen
at suppertime, was different.

"Hypothermia?" Rosetta had laughed brashly, the
rouge out-of-date and waxy on her cheeks. "Well, I have
been called an ice queen."

Ellen jumped back. "You surprised me. I didn't hear
you knock." Remembering her manners, she set another
bowl on the table.

"Thanks, honey, but do you have anything stronger?"

Ellen passed the cooking sherry. She was trying to
place her. Perhaps an aunt? "Refresh my memory."

"Rosetta. You called me, right? I used to live here."
Ellen's cabin had low ceilings and too many corners.
Shadows, lace-edged, banged against the walls like moths.
Cobwebs grew thick on any flat surface, and on the mantle
was an unexpected display of the personal objects of
another generation's ladies; wire-rim glasses, veiled hats,
lace gloves pinned in hand positions to the walls. The
windows were painted shut and the scent was of incense
burned regularly. "This place gives me the creeps," Rosetta
said.

"You lived here?" Ellen asked. She was watching
Rosetta from behind the fleshy circles of her cheeks as if
from a great distance.

She lives an entire life back there, Rosetta was thinking. Rosetta could spot a virgin when she saw one. "Not
here. In Emeryville. I owned the brothel."

Ellen was relieved to learn that Rosetta was not a
previous tenant or one of her mother's relatives come to
reprove her for not getting married or going on a diet.
Rosetta looked convincingly alive except for the slight
funereal cast to her bobbed hair and she smelled of
lavender. She was getting better at her experiments, or
this was not your average dead person. "Do I have one of
your gloves?" she asked.

Ellen was a dabbler in the occult, which to her was a
self-taught potpourri of witchcraft manuals, tarot decks
and European herb catalogs. She mixed herbs, bringing
them to a boil over her electric stove, chanting formulas in

the Latin she had learned in nursing school. This was not a hobby. Ellen was convinced she had been burned at the stake as one of the nine million witches in a previous lifetime. Since childhood, she had been afraid of matches and she could rarely leaf through a book on Renaissance art without her hands shaking. She practiced good-luck charms on the friends she never made and turned men who called her fat into swine. Following the directions in books, she had purchased intimate articles of apparel from secondhand stores—a lace slip, a pair of glasses. It was with these that she first discovered her particular knack for calling the dead. Soon, she was flooded with messages to loved ones left behind. She never passed them on. The dead never left phone numbers or forwarding addresses.

"Forgive me," Rosetta was saying, "but your place looks like the home of a hatchet murderess in the nineteenth century."

"What's your message?" Ellen said.

"My message? Listen," Rosetta frowned, her hands on her large hips. "I got word a while back that there was trouble. What's going on in the old town? Somebody gonna dig up my grave?"

"No one tells me anything," Ellen replied matter-of-factly. Blue Cloud, the young man from whom she had been purchasing marijuana for years, couldn't remember her name. And Ellen wasn't a virgin at thirty-five because of her weight. In the homes of Emeryville, where what salads were served were macaroni and where flour and sugar filled the craving for fruit, heavier women than she fed children. After ten years of employment at the Home, Ellen still took her breaks alone. There was something about Ellen. Even Gertrude, who could be counted on to befriend the shy or the unpopular, would have nothing to do with her.

Ellen was, by all appearances, ordinary as most. She didn't remember when she hadn't worked for a living, having spent her youth taking care of a mother who spent her nights in the Mint and her days on the couch. "Takin' care of mama bring you luck," Hatty always told her.

"Please, Miss. I'm running out of time," Rosetta said. "Isn't there anything new that you can remember?"

Ellen paused. She had forgotten about Rosetta. "There's going to be a new highway. Not through the graveyard though."

"Hurry."

"Oh, there's a church open now."

"Church? What kind of church?" Rosetta walked toward the door. "So, that's what trouble is," she said, slamming it behind her.

"The church is the trouble," Ellen said to herself as she approached the church and heard the Reverend Boyd shouting before she reached its heavy doors.

"Immorality attracts immorality," the Reverend stormed, pacing before the rows of pews some misguided zealot had sewn calico cushions for. His voice boomed as the doors closed behind Ellen. She quickly found a seat. She was startled to see how crowded the church was, more people than lined up for the monthly government cheese giveaways, more people than went to the July rodeo in Milltown. Ellen sat, fighting the fog which entered her brain whenever she was stoned and someone was lecturing. She concentrated on the zigzag stitching on the parka of the woman in front of her.

"There are people who will tell you to live and let live. There are those who will say that homosexuals aren't hurting anyone but themselves. Well, I say those people are stupid! I say those people are dead wrong! When you are a homosexual, you are committing a crime against your parents. When you are a homosexual, you are committing a crime against your community. When you are a homosexual, you are committing a crime against your partner. Against yourself! But, worst of all, when you are a homosexual, you are committing a crime against the nature of God!!!"

Loretta was listening like she listened at home, focusing her gaze like an actor on a nail hole in the wall above his head. "But, dear," she had said, "I don't really know what a lesbian is."

"It's our ticket out of these small towns in the middle of nowhere."

The Reverend Jimmy Raymond Boyd hated the West. He hated cattle, their languid, stupid pace. He hated the prairie dogs, who ate their own dead when killed on the road. He hated the roads, slippery; and the hungry, waiting. The big sky overhead made him feel like a rabbit dyed red with hawks circling above him. The cold made him cough and the winds made him panic. But, most of all, he hated growing up poor in Cody, Wyoming, the end of the line for Buffalo Bill, although that famous man had never deigned to live there.

Jimmy's father was a preacher and his father before him. Consequently, Jimmy hadn't thought twice about becoming one himself. As a child, he had lived all over the state, following the boom towns which sprouted in the wake of the oil drillers. Across the empty prairies, they staked their survival on the biological facts of death and marriage. It was there that the Reverend developed his love for television. He spent every night in front of it and the free hours he found during the day. Television gave him hope, the possibility of another life. On television, he saw other preachers. In Georgia, Florida, in Texas and South Carolina. They were tanned, well-fed missionaries. They didn't eat canned soup and saltines for supper. When they gave sermons, an orchestra of strings ascended behind them like a flock of doves.

As a young man, he had thought a lot about the money the oil drillers made, the retirement benefits, the insurance, the vacations. Those men never read the Bible. They never read anything. And they were doing far better than he or any of his family had done. They came to his services the way they went to the fast-food stands, without thought, for convenience. And now, Emeryville. Before he moved to Emeryville, this church roof was leaking and the kids used the building for a party house. The town hadn't seen or missed the presence of a preacher in fourteen years and from the looks of it, could go another fourteen more. After three months, his paltry congregation consisted of four ragged families, a drunk in the back, his wife, the miner who lived in his woodshed and two sisters who sat with bowed heads and matching flowered dresses, peering into their hymnbooks hopefully. They were to be disappointed. There was no singing in his churches.

Another mistake in a long line of mistakes which seemed to be leading him in a downward spiral toward dilapidated parishes and progressively unconcerned brethren. When his father died, he had left him this: title to a church in a small town by a creek in Montana, five acres near it, hundreds more lying undeveloped on the outskirts, an island of private land surrounded by railroad and federal property. "If I was you, I'd sell it," he'd advised. "It'll take a stronger man than you to wash that area of its sins." Jimmy, however, was not going to look a gift horse in the mouth. Land of his own? A place to start? Acreage to sell, to develop, timber rights, mineral rights, grazing rights. And all in the name of the church. No taxes. He could sell it to tourists in the spring, before they knew the winter. There could be copper, gold, and, he had heard, perhaps uranium.

He was sorely disappointed when, after selling everything they had saved and worked hard for, Loretta and he rolled into this town of dark mountains with their new house trailer. The property was useless. Treeless with sage-strangled hills and more rocks than soil. "What can you do with this?" he had shouted after the villagers left that first day, dismissing the slopes, the ridges like bony dogs scaled by wind. He couldn't sell it if he tried. But, at the low point in his despair over the impossibility of living forty miles from anywhere with a prospect of making a decent living, where nine months of winter closed the routes connecting the ghetto of Emeryville to the rest of the world, where the people were in far worse and more resigned states of poverty than he, were half Catholic, for God's sake, an angel came to him in the form of a dirty ex-miner and whispered in his ear, "There are lesbians in this town." It was then that the Reverend Jimmy Raymond Boyd had a hunch his luck was going to change.

The years of studying the preachers on television were not in vain. "There are lesbians in this town," he shouted, clutching the lectern as if it were a life raft, pacing the pulpit as if it were a stage. Exclamation was important. Exclamation and accusation. "Once they start buying property, their kind will stream in from the heathen cities. They will come in droves, with shaven heads and beards, axes and tattoos, so the Bible tells us. They will take over your streets. They will be teaching your children." He

stopped abruptly and shook his pointed finger at them.
"Think about it, good people. Your daughters stolen, your
wives leaving for other beds, your pets the objects of
satanic rites. You, if you are concerned, have the power to
right this wrong.

"We can force our government leaders to take a stand
on this issue. So far, it seems a little too delicate for them.
A little too personal, perhaps?" The Reverend's audience
was, by now, either asleep or plotting revenge against the
women who went home from the Mint with the best-looking
women in town. "You need people in the capital with
courage. People willing to go to the Governor, if need be, to
embarrass those in law enforcement. Someone to bring the
extent of our problem to the public." He held out his hands
as if in benediction. "That is why I am forming this
organization. Christians Against Homosexuality.
Together, we can win. Please sign up on your way out the
door."

"There are witches here," Ellen said to herself as the
congregation filed out under a gray sky rising between the
shoulders of the pass. Women who could cause booms to
break and slide mysteriously into the bones of workers.
Who could throw monkey wrenches into highway plans
and nuclear power plants. Who could look at men they
considered bad for the gene pool and render them im-
potent. Here, there were women like her, who could learn
from her, who could teach her. That they were also lesbians
only made them easier to pick out.

5

Every evening, the river grew, slicing the canyon with untamable force, scooping up earth and undermining trees until the water was dangerous with speeding limbs and spitting a chocolate brown. It was the time of only the bravest rafters, of weekly reports of casualties, when the snow of a long winter swelled the waterways in a few short weeks. Under cover of the creek, roaring truck-heavy down the granite banks, June's wood was stolen, *Lesbian Cunts* was spray-painted on the side of BJ's home, River's cat disappeared and Gertrude received the first of a series of obscene phone calls promising her an introduction into the joys of heterosexual sex.

Despite reminders to plug in the heat-tape, to keep the taps dripping, to crawl underneath the building at the least sign of slush armed with a blowdryer, Deeva let her pipes freeze every winter. When this happened, she was off for a few months to the more temperate zones. If the pipes cracked, she had them replaced. If the apartment flooded, she hired Myrna to clean it. That her pipes were located en route to Gertrude's apartment above were an oversight she repeatedly apologized for. But this year, alerted by rumors reaching her in Baja of the Reverend Boyd's campaign, Deeva cut her trip short, returned to Emeryville and immediately called a meeting.

Her drapes were drawn, her usually open door bolted from the inside and Gina had to knock three times before Deeva hissed from the other side, "How do I know it's you?"

"Mercedes," Myrna said.

"Very funny." Deeva opened the door.

"We should have stayed at the Mint," Myrna said as she made her way to the back of the room. She was never ready for the hash of parliamentary procedure, consensus and therapy session which seemed to attend these meetings of what she called too serious and cold-irritable women.

Maggie, boots propped on Deeva's coffee table, her black dog curled, one eye open, at her feet, was smoking a pipe which filled the air with the scent of kinnikinnick and wild cherry. With her pipes and the fat cigarettes she rolled like party favors, Maggie could transform any room, even Deeva's fluorescent one, into a hut on the edge of the forest. Maggie was the only woman who dared to violate Deeva's no-smoking rules, although she was asked repeatedly to take it outside. Maggie would nod and roll another one on her knee.

June's body was spread over two rugs and engaged in a yoga posture which resembled a cat licking its behind. Gina gave her thick-stockinged foot a squeeze as she walked past and June rubbed her head against Gina's leg, purring. Jake was on the floor next to June, stretching her long limbs over BJ's white wool lap and ignoring the threatening glances this earned her. BJ hadn't sat on the floor since grade school and she was not happy about it. Gertrude waved as Gina and Myrna made their way toward the floor pillows she'd saved for them. She passed a thermos, filled with hot chocolate and schnapps and elbowed Gina, her eyes scanning the crowd. "A person with a talent for blackmail could clean up."

Gina knew only half the women present, sitting cross-legged on the floor, leaning into walls, straddling ledges. Many of them dated men publicly, were known to show up at volunteer fire department meetings on the arms of boyfriends. They went to such extremes that even Gina had wondered: those who wore pumps on their way to get wood, those who jogged up the steep creek and back each morning in pink running shoes and pastel sweats. These were the women who wore dresses in the bitterest weather. The school board president, who had turned down every application for janitor or teacher by a woman since she had been in office and only relented when Jake's name fooled her on the resume. Next to her, ready to take charge at a moment's notice, was Pruet, chief of voter registration in the county, who had shamed its entire thinking population by bemoaning in a newspaper interview the fact that she had to let the Indians vote. "Half of them can't read," she was quoted as saying, "and next, they'll want the ballot typed in Sioux."

These women were visibly uncomfortable in Deeva's home, in such proximity to women they had tried to ignore and with whom, until now, their only affiliation was their common place of residence. They stared at the floor, tapped their fingernails against their purses and did not betray, by even a glance, that they might know each other.

"I've always wanted to start a girl scout troop," Gertrude said, breaking the silence. "We could advertise. Skilled instructors."

"Overnights," June added, while a few of the women searched the room as if for guards. Several stood to leave. Several flung insults and soon women were shouting at each other until Deeva pounded the floor with a hammer. "Order! Order! Gertrude was just kidding!"

It could have been the tie or the authority commanded by the tailored men's suit, but when River stood before them, clearing her throat, she had their undivided attention. "Although we may not have much in common, we are all women and in times of crisis we should stick together."

Myrna rolled her eyes. When River first moved to Emeryville, she had said the same thing. Rural life had functioned without feminist theory before that. Neighbors helped each other once on principle, twice in an emergency. Anything after that was a strict and intricate balance of trade agreements. Needless to say, the promise of a day's work outdoors with women, strutting their tools and skills, was not the draw it was to River's friends in the city. "If she offered a keg of beer or something," Myrna had told Gina later. Nevertheless, River had convinced enough women to donate their trucks, saws and labor to rechink an abandoned cabin and stockpile enough firewood to heat it for two winters.

June had embraced it as a brilliant ploy and promptly sent out invitations to lesbian groups throughout the Northwest: *"SUPPORT RURAL WOMEN,"* they read, *"SEND A WOMAN OF THE COUNTRY TO DO IMPORTANT POLITICAL WORK IN HAWAII."* June received twenty-two dollars, enough to cover postage and encourage her to plan a bigger campaign the following year.

Pruet noticed, in a panic, that she had left her unclasped purse next to Myrna. She was attempting to retrieve it, spearing the bag's handle with the pointed toe of her pump, when Myrna pulled a roll of dollar bills from her back pocket, smiled at Pruet and began counting them one by one onto the floor.

"What's the big deal? So the Reverend knows about us? No one goes to church," someone began. "Most of the people here are offspring of Irish Catholics."

"He is talking about calling in the police," River said.

"What do the police have to do with us?"

Pruet set her purse on her seat and stood nodding, despite herself, to River. "It is illegal to be a homosexual in the state of Montana. The law reads: Sexual conduct with a person of the same sex can be punished by ten years in prison and/or a fine of fifty thousand dollars."

Deeva was pounding the hammer again. "Whatever happens, you must promise me my relatives will never know."

"Ah, nobody believes you're a lesbian anyway," someone shouted from the back.

"What do you mean?" Deeva smiled, unsure whether this was a compliment or not. "I am, too."

"Prove it," someone shouted.

"You should talk," someone else said.

Robert's Rules of Order dissolved into a concert of insults and accusations based on each other's perceived steps in and out of the closet. "Stop!" River finally screamed. The last car through the red light was Deeva, freed at last from proper etiquette by the din, shouting at no one in particular, "Shut up, you old crackpot!"

"They can't arrest us for suspicion," Gertrude said. "What can the police do? Peek in our windows?"

"The law reads, 'in the act of,' however," Pruet admonished, "they will be watching those of you who insist on calling attention to yourselves." Pruet scowled at Maggie, but Maggie was snoring, her bandanna pulled low over her forehead. Even awake, she wouldn't have understood the uproar—she hadn't slept with anyone for months.

BJ had donned reading glasses and pushed Jake's legs off her good wool pants. "I'm worried about my children," she said.

There was the typical silence. BJ's motherhood, through some mysterious, mutual agreement, was invisible to these women. She often wondered if it was because they didn't like children in general or hers in particular. She felt as though she was asking for charitable contributions by mentioning the word. The last time she had mused about her youngest girl's conception, even Jake had objected. She was invariably asked not to bring them, not even for holiday dinners or Halloween. When anyone invited her to go camping or to town, they first asked if she had gotten a babysitter. A support system, an extended family of women; these ideas had bitten the dust long ago. Here, as when she was married, her children were watched by poor teenagers.

"Your children know?" Pruet asked, horrified.

"I didn't raise stupid children."

BJ had moved to Emeryville with no skills and no car after her divorce. She had never enjoyed the outdoors. Her pale skin and red hair remained the same shade, even in summer. The dark winter afternoons when her children were in school, she sat with an electric blanket wrapped around her and played Chopin on the piano. But the country was safe. And cheap. And far from a husband and a family who could not understand how, after ten years of marriage, she could leave a man defined by what he was not: a drinker, a gambler, a philanderer. Within those borders, she had been taught, he had unlimited freedom to slop around.

Moving her piano was the one thing he had ever helped her with, and she paid for it with the endless weekends he missed with the girls. When he delivered the instrument, Jake had volunteered from off the street. His three buddies and Jake were friendlier, carrying that piano, than she had ever felt with him. Two years later, she cropped her permed hair, changed her name from Barbara Jean to BJ and took her ankle-length skirts to the Salvation Army.

"What we need to investigate is what this preacher has in his closet," BJ said to the group. "He could cause a lot of damage."

"I think we can all agree that no one is to speak to the press," Deeva said, changing the subject. Reporters had begun appearing from under every rock, from the far corners of the state and beyond, lured by the letters to the editor the Reverend had been writing to every weekly or monthly rag. "How to Curb the Homosexual Menace in Your Community," he titled them, listing the suggestions from the Christian Citizens group he had organized: Refrain from speaking to, purchasing merchandise from or selling and renting property to any known homosexual. The reporters had been hounding the women for weeks. They were kind and concerned. They wanted to interview the other side, to approach it from a standpoint of civil rights. Vigilantes in modern times. Threats. Vandalism. Nothing sensational. The rights of children. "How are the lesbians taking the provocations from the minister?" they asked, in countless phone calls. "What lesbians?" the women would answer.

"I've shipped my love letters in a locked chest to a friend's," one of the women said. "I'd advise you all to do the same."

"I have a line on a new lipstick," Gertrude offered sarcastically.

"Girls, I think that is good advice. Tone it down. No holding hands or otherwise in public. Keep your shades drawn and tell your friends to send their postcards in envelopes. Why invite trouble?" Pruet glanced reprovingly around the room. "And I hope we never have to hear another rumor like the one the Reverend's been spreading around town."

"Who would tell Pruet gossip?" Myrna whispered.

"Last Sunday, the teenager who waits tables in the cafe announced to the entire congregation that one of you pinched her. In the rear."

"Who? Who?" the women shouted and the meeting erupted in laughter.

This was not the response Pruet intended. "You know who you are," she accused, but her stern tone only provoked more hilarity. It was minutes before order was restored.

"My neighbor cornered me in the cafe last week," June said, wiping her eyes. "She told me about a German doctor she'd seen on a talk show. He said that homosexuality was a chemical imbalance which happened when the pregnant woman was under stress."

"There's always a theory about what went wrong, not right," Jake said.

"I told her that if that were true, half the mothers must have been under stress while pregnant."

"Half?" Pruet gasped.

"So, I fudged?"

"This must be the preacher's work," Gertrude said. "Yesterday, one of the nurses I work with leaned over the table and whispered, 'I just want you to know that me and the gals talked about it and we don't mind if you're a lesbian.'"

"What did you say?"

"I said, 'We don't mind if you suck your husband's penis either, although it is none of our business.'"

"Oh, my Lord, you didn't?" Pruet said.

"Everyone's gone crazy," BJ said. "Jake's burned all her magazines. She calls them illegal paraphernalia. She saved one valentine from her teacher in high school, but crossed out the signature. She's thinking of changing her name back to Mary."

Jake squirmed. "Look, some of us have lived here all our lives."

"Some of us pay taxes," Pruet added.

The woman Gina had first seen in a prom dress now had a comb tucked into her back pocket. She nodded toward the newer residents. "We never had trouble before."

"It's not the town. Hell, we're half the fire department and the whole volunteer staff of paramedics. We pick up their beer cans in the spring and organize the flea markets in the summer."

"Hey, Maggie, remember that year your booth was the back of your pick-up?" A few of the women winced at the memory of Maggie's old truck, with its one flat tire, coats and hats, pots and pans strung along the wood rack, even a nest of give-away kittens in the cab. Maggie had left to get beer and three days later, her gypsy van was still there, only covered with a foot of snow. The truck stayed there all winter, all but the kittens.

"I don't get any complaints from the locals." Carolyn ran a miniature junkyard in her back yard and fixed most of the locals' cars. When she couldn't, she sold them. Twenty-five year old cars and trucks were one of the state's biggest exports.

"Well, who doesn't like us, then?"

"Bill Lewis says he's gonna tar and feather the lot of us," Maggie said. "Pulled over on the bridge just to let me know."

"I don't imagine the guy who breathes heavy on my phone likes me too much, though he swears he does," Gertrude said.

Gina patted Gertrude's knee. Gertrude had begun practicing techniques of creative visualization after the tenth call she received from a man who told her his dick was in his hands. She pictured a penis withering like the dried apple cores her art teacher had taught her to costume and call witches when she was a child. She bought a handgun and dug out her tapes of martial arts. Gina rarely caught Gertrude dancing to jazz anymore, though it reassured her somewhat that each afternoon Gertrude was barefoot on her hardwood floors, her brown belt pressed and hanging from her practiced body. Gertrude no longer dreamt at her window, but before retiring at night, she scanned the streets and alleyways with an increasingly acute night vision.

"And I don't imagine whoever painted my house was concerned about the education of my children," BJ said. Jake had bought a gallon of white paint and erased the message on BJ's house, planning with each slap of the brush what she would do when she caught the culprit. She had been so angry, BJ had had to paint the stone pathway beneath it.

"We could picket the church," River suggested.

"Sure. What a great police lineup that would make."

"I'm already boycotting the bar." June had vowed never to set foot in the Mint again after a burly local sidled up behind her and whispered in her ear, "The reason you're with women is 'cause you never had a real man."

"A woman'd have to be a fool to go in there now," Deeva agreed.

Myrna stood to leave. "That reminds me," she said, tipping her hat, "I gotta get to work. Collect my fool's wages."

"Myrna, you know what we meant," Deeva called out as Myrna threaded her way through the room of seated and now silent women. As she passed, Maggie and Gina joined her. All three were out the door before Myrna said, "Yeah, I know what you meant."

Following Myrna into the bar, Gina eyed the row of men so bored that anything coming through the door besides the splash of rain filling the footings they had been ready for weeks to pour would be entertainment. They looked like soldiers, synonymous, dressed in their work clothes, drinking the same brand of beer from the bottle, facing the mirror as if they were blank-faced passengers on a bus. Since their clandestine entrance, ducking in the backdoor, Gina could almost hear each of the men's exhalations as they turned to stare at the two women.

"Hey, Myrna, how come you always get the pretty ones," a man yelled, breaking the spell.

Gina stood stock-still. "'Cause you're so god-damned ugly," Myrna yelled back and the men at the bar burst into laughter. Myrna waved Eddie home and took her place behind the bar. She set everyone up with a free drink. "The truth is," she told Gina, who was still amazed, "it's a luxury to have enemies in a town this small. You think Harold wants to walk the mile and a half through spring snow to check on his horses when Maggie lives next to their pasture and has fed them through every winter for ten years? Or Helen Riley's gonna leave her job early if a call to June would put wood on her fire before the pipes freeze? Anybody at all drive to town for honey when River, sure as hell, has stockpiled jars of it?"

"The locals kept the Reverend's commandments pretty much for a week," Maggie nodded, "then they left 'em to those who don't live in Emeryville and to the young men they have no control of. And they don't sell us any property 'cause they don't own any."

"Speaking of which, did Maggie ever tell you about her run-in with the reporter?" Myrna asked Gina, leaving to wait on three ruddy youths who had returned home after an afternoon spent hopping the bars which dotted that stretch of highway with more frequency than towns. They straddled the stools, scraping mud off their lug-soled boots onto the railing.

"If the ladies at that meeting only knew," Maggie grinned. It was true, they had agreed in private session and behind drawn curtains. They repeated the phrase to each other as if in a trance: More public attention will only cause more trouble. Even if the hills at night were closed to them. Even if no one was to walk the hills alone during the day. From the list of names supplied by the Christian Citizens, the reporters could not find one woman who would talk. Only one remained uncontacted, owing not to her lack of cooperation, but to her lack of a telephone or street address. In a last-ditch effort, the major daily from Great Falls sent a rookie to track her down.

Speeding into Emeryville, the reporter must have wondered if her car had rent a veil into another century. Chickens in the road, men whittling on the wooden sidewalk and a crazy, gray-haired woman who appeared at the side of the car, waving and screaming, *"Slow Down!"* with the vacant look of prairie women too long in sod houses. Why would lesbians be here? In a ghetto too poor to be quaint, garbage strewn everywhere and protruding through the receding snow, cigarette butts and beer cans, canned food labels and missing gloves. Why would they be here with no indoor plumbing, no movie houses, not even a restaurant? A pack of dogs dodged her front tires as she turned up the lane and by the time she reached the cattle guard which marked the climb to Maggie's, she wondered if she was on the right track.

Thick ocher smoke rose from the knoll and the trail was deep with mud which had dried up a month before in Great Falls. Either the occupant always stepped in the same holes or she had only left and returned once. The reporter leapt from one footprint to the next as she knew cats did in the snow. A repugnant smell was wafting down the trail. There were no "No Trespassing" signs, but when she saw a human standing next to the flames of a fire, she approached cautiously. "Don't shoot," she called ahead.

Suddenly, she was face to face with a cabin-smelling woman who stared at her quizzically, her short hair tucked under a ten-gallon hat. From her chin, the fabled shred of a beard hung straight as a Chinese emperor's. The reporter looked to the fire where, in horror, she recognized the skinned form of a body, skewered on an enormous spit. She counted five fingers and five toes. Torn between the impulse to run and the need for documentation, she thrashed in her handbag while the fat crackled into the flames. She pulled out her camera and, backing away, shot a frantic series of stills.

"It's my bear," Maggie had said, pointing to the missing head which glared at them, still furred, from a nearby stump.

The reporter was not entirely convinced. Maggie's fishing waders were spattered with blood and she gripped a carving knife in one hand. "Did you shoot it or stab it?" the reporter stuttered.

"Nah. I have a deal with the warden."

"The game warden hunts for you?"

"When they confiscate game from anybody they don't like—out-of-staters, government employees, longhairs— they bring it to Maggie. When the hunters skin out their meat, they drop the tails and feet off on their way down the hill. The rangers even bring me dead porcupines for the quills. There's a special way you pick 'em up." Maggie's house was a gallery of mutilations: raven-headed quirts, rattlesnake canes, baskets sewn from the dewclaws of deer. A pit she had dug in the slope was a mass grave of feathers, antlers, wings. If Maggie ever installed electricity, it would be so she could put all of this in a freezer.

The reporter was staring at the bear. She felt ashamed to be so disappointed. "The bear?"

"This one's a road kill."

The reporter remembered why she had come. "Maggie, are you a lesbian?"

"Who's asking?"

"I'm a reporter from the *Great Falls Gazette*."

"That stuff about the warden is off the record."

"Well, are you?"

"No, Ma'am. I'm a Christian."

Maggie laughed and laughed, slapping Gina on the thigh. "I should have planted a fat kiss on her lips and told her that could be the first line of her story: 'Maggie greeted me with a kiss.'"

"I guess the story never got printed because no one would believe it," Gina said as Myrna rejoined them at the end of the bar.

"Maggie invited her to stay for dinner," Myrna said, "but she declined."

While they were talking, Hatty dragged herself in, a stick figure grown even thinner. She fumbled for a stool next to the three young men. "Things are livening up," Myrna said, going to set a beer in front of the old woman. "Honey, what are you doing out of bed? That flu isn't getting any better."

Hatty ignored her, turning her attention instead to the three sons of Irishmen, whom she had known since their birth. "Whose money you drinkin' on, Kid?"

"That ain't none of your business, Hatty."

"You still waiting for that highway job to come through? I told ya they'd never hire any of you boys. They brings their own with 'em. No matter what the politicians promise."

"Then how'd that woman get hired on?"

"That's what I'd like to know," the youngest joined in. "She ain't even experienced."

"Reverend says you girls take hormones to grow them beards," Kid called out to Maggie.

"You got hair on your chests as well?" another began, his boots kicking excitedly against the bar.

"Seems as if we could find out."

Myrna, her hand on the pistol below the counter, said very coolly, "Do you want to get served in this bar or not?"

"Sure they do, Myrna," an old man from the back insisted. "They're just fooling around."

"No, sir, you don't understand. We're sick of them flaunting it in our faces. Coming out of nowhere and taking our jobs. Coming in with all their ideas 'bout changing the town. Clean up this. Improve that. Teach us this. And actin' too good to even talk to us."

"Reverend says you girls put a curse on that Wyoming guy. Says the crew don't like the locals much now."

"Hold it right there," Hatty croaked, "I killt that man. Didn't nobody else help me."

In minutes, the bar lost its romantic light. The cooking grease and nicotine, usually ignored, were a mold on the ceilings and lamp fixtures. Gina stared at the peanut shells underfoot, the mangy dog scratching next to the jukebox. The customers already had their own opinions about the death of the highway worker. Hatty only confirmed their suspicions. Only it was not she that they suspected.

"Was mine. My curse. Hatty Norris sab'taged that machine."

Suddenly, Kid grabbed Gina around her waist and pulled her close. "Quit coverin' for 'em, Hatty." He headed toward the door, dragging Gina along with him. "You girls so smart, you can show us how you do it." The other two men leapt, guarding the door. The bar was so still that Gina heard the night drop like a rock from her hand. No one moved.

"Oh, yeah?" Myrna shouted, blasting a round of the pistol past their ears. In seconds, everyone was on the floor, Eddie's prize Lewis and Clark bottle collection was in shards and Myrna, holding the telephone like a flag in one hand and in the other, her gun, said, "You'd better leave. I just called the cops."

"Boomboom," Glenn said.

"You know, you'll probably get fired for this," Gina said, the shots still ringing in her head. She helped Myrna sweep the cathedral of glass off the floor. The mantle was empty, except for Sacajawea and York.

"You cain't even shoot," Hatty mumbled, hobbling out the door.

"I got goats to milk," Maggie nodded and left. One by one, the rest of the customers eased themselves out the door. "Close up early, Myrna. If ya want, come on up," Maggie said on her way out.

Gina was still trembling. "Myrna, I got to tell you something."

"You really wanted to go with those boys."

"Don't joke. I've been thinking. Maybe Montana's not such a good idea right now."

"What are you talking about? Those hoodlums just gave you a little scare."

"A little scare? They were going to rape me," Gina snapped. "I want you to come with me. Out of here. Maybe back to Seattle. Somewhere they don't care who sleeps with whom."

"We might have to go further than Seattle." Myrna lit a cigarette. "I can't believe you're serious about leaving."

"Just until things cool down. It doesn't have to be forever."

"Nah."

Gina was close to tears. "What could possibly make you want to stay here? It feels like we're in jail."

"Gina, this is my home." Myrna paused. "My people are from here."

"Come on, Myrna. The Chippewa didn't arrive until the 1870's. This was Shoshone land. Your people were a long way from home."

Myrna slapped her cigarette pack on the bar. "And who are you to tell me what I can and cannot call home?"

"The ruins of somebody else's home."

"Besides, why me? Why don't you ask Maggie?" Myrna blew smoke in Gina's face. "Or June. Since you're such a hot number."

Gina blushed. "You don't understand. It's not what you think. Besides, I'm moving out. I'm moving back into the tipi. And I'm going to move it up the road to Deeva's land next week. I've already asked her."

"Why?"

Gina took a deep breath and covered one of Myrna's hands with her own. She felt the pulse move through it the way Myrna's eyes moved under her lids those long summer nights while she slept. This was the woman who had opened the mountains for her, who slept unprotected under stars with a past blowing her dark hair which blessed her and was fragile. This was the woman she was fast moving toward a meeting with and whom she felt utterly unprepared for.

"Myrna, I've fallen in love with you."

Myrna's raucous laughter stung. "You?" she gasped. "You? You have to stop yourself from signing love on your letters to congressmen. If you had a checking account, you'd sign your checks, 'Love, Gina.' You love everything, the sky, the earth, women..." Myrna noticed Gina's fallen face. She stopped, but her voice was not kind. "Listen, Gina, that word is different for me. It binds us."

"But I do love you."

Myrna smiled, removing her hand. "Then, stick it out."

Gertrude didn't remember the hypothermia incident until the third sharp curve she almost missed, going eighty in her fifteen-year-old Chevy, B.B. King wailing from the Cook County Jail, drowning out all but her pictures of Ellen, stalking behind her at work. She let her foot off the gas. "Shit," she said aloud.

Gertrude relished her drive through the canyons on her way home from work. Though it took over an hour, she met few cars, would only pass hay wagons. She always plugged in a tape, took off her shoes and stepped on it, for going a hundred only brought a five-dollar fine. Driving fast and owning a gun were more important in Montana than free speech and the right to vote, and were more frequently exercised. But now, not only did she have to trade her samba for self-defense, her satisfied survey of the seasons and the neighborhood she loved for a nightly military vigilance, her drive home from work had been ruined.

As it was, work was not easy. A succession of laws and civil rights cases had reduced the residents of the Home to those too severely retarded to cope on the outside, the insane and a few political prisoners. When this happened, the emptied asylum became the new, federally-funded low-income clinic. Amid women who would have been dead years before had she not stopped them from slamming their heads into walls, biting their fingers to the bone or cutting their wrists with any sharp, available object, surrounded by boys on Thorazine and men in diapers, she now had to nurse the endlessly poor with their botched abortions and their drunken accidents. When Ellen, after years of eating lunch alone, set her tray next to Gertrude in the cafeteria, Gertrude had choked on her tuna salad and prepared to bolt.

They had eaten in uncomfortable silence. Gertrude had spent too much time learning to rely on her intuition to throw it away for the sake of courtesy. She, who was always so courteous. Especially with women. For Gertrude loved women, their feats and gestures, the register of their voices, their marshy red-green smell of vegetation. She loved flirting with them, pampering them, trading their hiding places with each other. So why avoid Ellen? June's body approached Ellen's size, was older, paler, hung in large folds like the draperies of the masters and was infinitely sexy. Yet, yes, Ellen's flesh appalled her. And Ellen's silence, black-masked and lying in wait with the neediness of a highway robber. One would drown there. Although that had never stopped her before. The pain of women challenged her: to tease out their dogged strength, to convince them. She would never relegate women, as River did—"Yes, yes, I know you tried your best," River would say,—to the status of damaged souls.

Halfway through her jello salad, Ellen had elbowed Gertrude and whispered, "Rosetta sent me."

Startled, Gertrude had glanced self-consciously around the cafeteria. "Rosetta? I don't know what you're talking about."

Ellen had winked. "I share your religion."

"It's not what you're thinking," Gertrude had stammered. "Those are my friends."

Ellen had bent close to Gertrude's ear. "I think I'm ready to join you."

Obviously misunderstanding, Gertrude had blushed heavily and, picking up her half-finished tray, rushed to deposit it in the trash on her way to the rest room.

"Shit," Gertrude repeated. "The seance." They should have never messed with that seance. That Deeva, always some bright idea. But Ellen had only been on the edge of their circle. And Gertrude had known that night that Ellen wasn't cold, but stoned. She was sure of it. She'd smelled marijuana on Ellen's breath. Maybe Ellen was stoned when she mentioned Rosetta. But how would she have known who they were calling? She was outside the circle. And what would Ellen want from them if she knew?

In the weeks that followed, Gertrude spent her drive home running over the conversations Ellen insisted on having with her, aiming her front tires at the words as if they were the prairie dogs the cowboys liked to aim for. Ellen was no spy for the church or the papers, that much Gertrude had decided. There was nothing Ellen wouldn't divulge. How she knew she was a witch. How she wanted to be a better one. The only thing that kept Gertrude from eating her lunches out was a stubborn self-defense that was taking an odd form and incredible endurance. For the conversations were never easy and the answers were not simple for her.

Could she cast spells?

"No, of course not," Gertrude would answer. But what would she call it, when cross-legged in the sun her eyes began to widen like a cat's, taking the world in, and she could feel something round and shining grow into her? At those moments, she could do anything, visit distant friends, cure sick animals, spin webs of protection over entire watersheds. Everything Ellen claimed she wanted to do. But to call that beautiful assurance witchcraft? It made it seem criminal and small.

Did she put curses on her enemies?

"No, of course not," Gertrude always answered. Yet, the seance? The photograph tacked next to her phone?

Gertrude had intended to tell the other women. To warn them that Rosetta had come, but only with questions, no answers. That they had bungled it, that Rosetta was as Myrna had insisted she would be, an arrogant, if independent whore. Or worse yet, to tell them that someone, not part of their group, attracted to the dim light of the fire Maggie had tried in vain to bring to light that night, could compromise them. She still intended to find the right moment. But, through the many questions, the assumptions Gertrude took offense at, pacing back and forth in the cage of Ellen's definitions, biting her fingers like the women where she worked, Gertrude was unsure whom she was angry with.

And did she believe that to lie with women was part of this witchcraft?

"Ellen, sexuality is a personal choice, not a religion!"

"It has nothing to do with power then?"

Gertrude was increasingly exasperated. But paradoxically, day by day and over time, she began to find herself waiting at the corner table for Ellen at lunch and, when she noticed several raised eyebrows from her co-workers, she began to visit Ellen at night and in her home. It was Gertrude who noticed the co-workers with apprehension. Ellen's years of banishment had led her to interpret any attention as welcome.

Would Gertrude call herself a Christian?

"No."

Well, what would she call herself?

Gertrude wore a small tattoo behind her left shoulder bone, shaped like a crescent moon. Ellen had seen it once. What did it mean?

In Ellen's home, Gertrude would glance nervously at the gloves and jewelry tacked to the walls. She still imagined bats flying off the shelves or worse, even after coming for months.

"Why do you let the church bully you?" Ellen asked.

Gertrude accepted a glass of sherry and recited, "More public attention will only cause more trouble."

"Aren't you proud of who you are?"

"Stop, Ellen. You don't know what it's like."

"They can't burn you at the stake anymore."

Gertrude hated these turns of the conversation. "The law states: ten years and/or fifty thousand dollars."

"Why doesn't someone challenge the law?"

Not that they hadn't thought of this, but in the end, they couldn't decide who it was going to be: someone educated and confident in public speaking or someone working-class so the people of Emeryville wouldn't be alienated. Should she be a mother, a student, a woman in a traditional or non-traditional job? Should she be someone

they liked or someone they were sure the public would like?
With parents or without? And if they could find someone
willing to martyr herself, is that the kind of person they
would want?

One evening, sitting in Ellen's kitchen, Ellen, picking
her teeth with a sliver of kindling, asked, "Can someone be
a lesbian if they are still a virgin?"

Gertrude was touched. For the first time in the inter-
rogations, she answered, "Yes."

"Do you think I'm a lesbian?"

Gertrude had her own question. "Ellen, why do you
keep that horror of a back yard?"

Ellen appeared as if struck. It had all started out
innocently enough, with a stuffed squirrel she bought at a
rummage sale and placed in the limbs of her weeping birch.
When she found a hawk, unclaimed in the garbage bin
outside the taxidermist's office in Milltown, its wings un-
furled as if in attack, she hung it on a string from the higher
branches. It was a creative thing really, a hobby. The
collection grew, and with it, the bizarreness of the wildlife
scenarios as Ellen began receiving stuffed and embalmed
deer, moose heads, snakes and small birds as gifts for
Christmas and her birthday.

Ellen never asked for them, but they showed up like
the dead for which she had become a lightning rod. Well-
meaning relatives, stuck for a present to give someone with
no discernible likes or dislikes, who ate everything with an
amazing insouciance, were only too glad to find a collector's
streak in Ellen. Children and eventually any form of
animal or bird refused to come near the place. Peering over
her fence became the initiation rite of the youth clubs and
it was a favorite place to push people into for Halloween.
Ellen had concocted not only every predator and prey scene
she could think of, but, egged on by her growing reputation,
devised pictographs of torture, a snake under the ampu-
tated foot of an elk, an otter swinging from a rope by its
tail.

"People collect all types of things. What about the
cups with mushrooms? The trivets with ducks?"

"But, Ellen, your animals were once alive."

"What about fur coats, leather furniture, the stuff
Maggie makes?"

"How do you know what Maggie makes?" Gertrude did not intend to discuss any of her friends. "I'm sorry. I shouldn't have said anything."

Ellen stood at the back door, her hand already on the knob. "Let me show you. It's really not so bad."

Gertrude tried. She tried so hard, as hard as she remembered her mother trying when she had asked her to enter the sauna with her naked daughter and her naked lesbian friends. She understood her now, limited by her own prudishness. She hung her head, as her mother had, and avoided Ellen's eyes. "No, I'm sorry. I can't."

Ellen was near tears. "People drown kittens every day in rain barrels. They take the heads from geese and slaughter cows. They kill elk and deer, saying if they don't, they'll die. It's because mine are stuffed, right? Is that what doesn't appeal to you? Well, I'm not even the person who stuffed them."

"I can't believe you don't know the taboo you're stumbling over. How weird that you've put them all out there together."

"What about the Mint with those moose heads? What about the glass eyes of the grizzly staring at you over your salami sandwich?"

"But kittens, Ellen? You have kittens out there. Where'd you get them?"

Ellen peered through her window at the only back yard off limits to Emeryville's children. The night obscured the wildlife refuse, but not enough to blanket the polished eyes of deer and the dozens of small creatures hanging surreally from the tree. "Gertrude, what are the rules? Who gets to make them? Do you?"

Gertrude stood, mute and afraid.

"Don't you think a body filled those shells you arrange on your windowsill?" Ellen asked.

No answer.

"That spinach you ate for lunch wasn't once alive?"

Ellen stamped her foot. "Gertrude, you eat chicken, don't you?"

"You didn't eat them?" Gertrude gasped.

"No, of course not," Ellen said.

BJ was sweeping the kitchen when she heard Ellen's name, the words "Emeryville" and "lesbian," but before she could turn up the volume, the radio signal was buried in the layers of an approaching storm.

Deeva was watching the evening news with her aunt in the city after having had dinner at her favorite, but poorly-lit restaurant. Her elderly aunt was still squinting and fiddling with the brightness adjustment when Deeva saw the Emeryville church, then a snapshot of Ellen and finally, a brief but too revealing scan of the homes. "Look," she cried, pointing out the window and quickly changing the channel. "Horses!"

"What happened to the news?" her aunt complained, switching the set to another channel. "Lesbians in Emeryville..." it announced before Deeva slammed in the knob and the screen went blank.

"I hate the news," Deeva said. "It's always so depressing. Will you read to me instead?"

"Emeryville? That's where you live," said her aunt, removing the reading glasses from their case.

Deeva handed her a book. "Lots of towns are called Emeryville. That one was in Mexico."

A week after Ellen had walked into the county jail, held out her wrists, fists clenched as if anticipating nails rather than handcuffs and declared, "I am a lesbian. Arrest me if you must," the women gathered at Gertrude's under cover of the night.

Emeryville had become a town under siege. Patrol cars, which June had vainly requested after the threats of rape, were now parked across from their homes. To the former need to close curtains and bolt doors was added the restraint on any unconscious displays of tenderness. For a week, their bodies grew so narrow without touch that it felt oddly unnatural to hold hands in private. Their gaits stiffened and looseness of hip seemed a fact of their youth. As if overnight, the petting, ruffling, wrestling ceased. Their bright colors were replaced with a military neutrality.

Gertrude's apartment was, to the women weary of the drudgery of fear, a refuge, with candles, lace tablecloths and gypsy dances playing from her stereo. June was rubbing BJ's feet with oil warmed on the wood-stove. Maggie was sketching their portraits, wandering the room with one pants-leg pushed to the top of her boot, like a wino staggering from a doorway. Lovers who hadn't touched for days felt amorous. Their hands found each other's under tables.

"They can't arrest someone for murder if there's not a body," June said, as Gertrude set up the black and white television she had dug out of the attic.

"That's right. How can Ellen be a dyke if..." Jake stared at Gertrude pointedly. She, like everyone else in town, knew of Gertrude's evening visits. "Or, is she?"

"Give me a break," Gertrude snapped.

"She's your friend, isn't she? You must have known what she was up to. Why didn't you let us know?"

"How was I to know she was going to do this? I haven't seen her for a month. She was mad at me."

"This was exactly what the Reverend was waiting for," River said.

"Now, wait a minute. I know we didn't ask her to be our spokesperson, but we'd never gotten around to deciding who would be. We would never challenge the law." Gertrude was surprised to find herself defending Ellen.

"Frankly, I'm glad the cards are on the table," Maggie said. "It'll be a relief to quit pretending we never heard of the word 'lesbian.'"

"The civil rights organizations are already interested. And it is an archaic law. Maybe we have a chance," Gertrude continued. "We have to remember who our enemy is."

"Speak for yourself. I've got two kids to protect," BJ said.

"First, she goes to the police. Then, she agrees to this press conference. Now, the entire state will watch someone who isn't even a lesbian represent us tonight. Or is she?" Jake said again.

"And what is your criterion?" Gertrude demanded, her eyes flashing with anger. She had no idea how it had happened, but somewhere in the last few months, she had stopped defending herself against the person she was in Ellen's eyes. But that would be even harder to explain now.

Deeva interrupted by lightly tapping on the second story window and amazed them all by climbing in off a rope tied to the roof. She looked equally absurd in the police uniform she was wearing.

"Deeva, policemen don't wear red lipstick," Myrna said.

"I know, but if I was stopped on the way here, at least they wouldn't think I was queer."

"Not that my children aren't delighted by grown women dressing up as cops and soldiers, but what's with the fatigues?" BJ said, pointing to River.

River had arrived in army khaki, camouflage paint wiped across her face. "We need to think of new ways to protect ourselves. The situation has gotten worse."

"What kind of ways?"

"Ammunition. Arms. At least, some of the younger women are interested."

Gina groaned. "I don't think I'm prepared for this," she whispered to Myrna.

"You're a spirit, sister," Myrna said. "You're prepared."

"Another thing. If we're going to fight, we've got to be strong and healthy." River swiped the cigarette from out of Myrna's hand. "We've got to stop being so dependent on capitalistic drugs."

Myrna retrieved her tobacco and re-lit it. "Sitting Bull smoked."

"She's on the air," Jake called and they carried their wine and chamomile, their coffee and tobacco to the set.

Maureen Pool was Montana's only talk show host and she appeared now on the screen in her signature cowgirl hat, her hips spreading under a flounced, calico skirt. As was her trademark, she turned her back to the viewing audience to display the slogan, "If you can rope me, you can ride me," embroidered in lasso-lettering on the leather of her fringed jacket.

"Welcome, rodeo fans," she said, facing the camera.

"She sure is showing her age, isn't she?"

"Shut up, Deeva," Jake said.

"I'd like to begin today's program by introducing my special guest. *Good Evening, Montana* is proud to present the Reverend Jimmy Raymond Boyd." In the glare of the television lights, his face took on the phosphorescent and fluted shape of a flashbulb, giving authenticity to his calling as nearer to God. Next to him sat the woman who had set the alarm clock in a roomful of sleepers and was now lying awake, waiting for it to go off.

"Here we go," Gertrude said when she saw her friend.

"Ellen Manchester," Maureen began, crossing her legs to reveal the tri-tone cowgirl boots. "She is challenging the law against homosexuality in our state. We'll start with you, Ellen. Or would you rather I said Ms. Manchester?"

"Ellen's fine," she mumbled.

"Ellen, why are you doing this?"

Ellen stared stoically ahead. "Someone has to do it."

"Right on!" Gertrude shouted.

"Now, Ellen, why would you want to identify yourself with this cause?"

While Ellen remained silent, the camera panned from Maureen to Ellen, then back to the Reverend, who shook his head tragically in Ellen's direction. Maureen looked impatient. "Ellen, are you a lesbian?"

"I think so," Ellen said softly, as if suddenly unsure why she was there.

"Some lover you are," Myrna said, jabbing Gertrude in the ribs.

Maureen rearranged her hemline. "Reverend, as some of our viewers have already heard, although this young woman is determined to remain in jail, she might be released soon. Can you tell us why that is?"

"The present law uses the term, 'engaged in the act of.' In this case, there is no positive proof. That is why I am working with the lawmakers in this state to change it."

"This is a travesty. She says she's guilty. The public thinks she's guilty. And yet she won't be prosecuted." Maureen had an idea. "Reverend Boyd, would you like to ask a few questions of our guest?"

The Reverend smiled. When the sheriff's department had called, he had acted quickly. It didn't matter whether Ellen was arrested or not. He knew the absurdity of enforcing the present laws. But here was the chance of a lifetime. This would be only the first of his television appearances. He looked at the calm woman to his left. Some show of defiance, some anguished confession, even an outright but visible lie would be more convincing that the assurance and ease with which these women accepted their mutated lives.

"Ellen, would you consider yourself representative of most of the lesbians in your community?" He turned to his audience, "Whose number is well above the 10 percent considered to be our national average and which is increasing by leaps and bounds."

"There are many like myself."

"And would you agree that the form of lesbianism practiced in Emeryville is especially, shall we say, heretical, to the extent there is promiscuity and even witchcraft?"

"You can't snuff us out."

"Exhibit A," the Reverend said, and the television screen filled with a photograph of Ellen's backyard, complicated by arrows and labels diagraming the various species and their diabolical relationship to each other. Ellen's hands flew to her face.

"She didn't think they'd find out about her yard?" Jake said.

"Ellen, is this your back yard?"

"Yes."

"Is it true, as the police have told me, that there are little kittens hanging from their necks there? Black kittens?"

"Only one black one, sir."

"Kittens hanging from their necks?" the Reverend shouted.

"They were dead when I got them."

"Ellen," the Reverend sighed, while the screen returned to Maureen's set, "do you believe in Jesus Christ?"

"Jesus is a product of the patriarchy."

"I shouldn't have loaned her my books," Gertrude said, her head in her hands.

"This, my friends," the Reverend managed to say, "is what I have been fighting. What I pledge to fight. For those of you who dare to call yourselves public servants, this is the issue of the next election."

"State legislature elections are this year," BJ said. "Which means he's probably got a few candidates in mind."

Good Evening, Montana took a commercial break and when Maureen returned, she was perched on a barstool

which markedly resembled a saddle. "Stuck for something
to do on your next family outing?" she was saying, as the
camera followed her from the bar to the facade of a re-
constructed fort. "Pioneer Town," it proclaimed in letters
burnt into the logs it was built from. Jake turned the
television off and Maureen smiled and waved as she faded
from the screen.

"With this, he's declared war," River said.

Myrna returned from the kitchen, where she was
helping Gertrude pour tequila straight into large tumblers.
"Holy war," she said.

Deeva was pointing the fire poker at the wall as if she
were at a blackboard. "To the Indians, the vision quest was
like this. A time to confront evil and outwit it. See which
was braver, who had more power on their side."

"I thought the vision quest was about faith, not evil.
I thought you were searching for something to help you be
brave," Gina said, glancing at Myrna for help. Myrna
shrugged.

"I heard a story of someone going into a grizzly den."

"The grizzly wasn't his enemy, Deeva."

"Her enemy," River said, correcting Myrna.

"Does faith always have to be about confrontation?"
Gina asked.

"Religion has always been used to take power from
women." River refused her tequila and sat on the floor,
angrily lacing her boots tighter. "All it teaches us is to let
someone else take control."

"But River, that is what is so wonderful about it. To
know that, ultimately, everything is taken care of." Deeva
smiled convincingly.

"Yeah, like the thawing of her pipes," Myrna
whispered to Gina.

"What about you, June?" Gina said. "What do you
think?"

June was sucking on a lemon. She smacked her lips.
"Religion is like produce. It eventually rots."

"Religion," BJ said, bundling her sleeping children to
go home, "is a set of rules and we haven't been obeying
them."

Easy to pray to something
           you love,
cats like schooners,
the obligato
of northern rivers under ice.

Three deer are three wishes,
grazing under a moon,
puffed like a bird,
its quick, visible heart.

Grandmothers,
I'm whistling for you
in the low, thin call I save
for specific things,
the cat to return
in the morning, my neighbor
to not hunt the deer or me.

6

Gina found the first clump of pink campion growing on the
south slope, surrounded by many junipers and a crust of
the late snow, on the day of Hatty's funeral. The faucets of
melting snow opened from Maggie's eaves and the sun lit
early on her woodpile. The door was open and Gina entered
it. Maggie didn't acknowledge her until she had placed a
shade of indigo into the cumulus center of the cloud she
was painting.

River was right to have sent Gina to fetch Maggie.
For Maggie, standing completely naked in front of her,
brush in hand, looked as if she had no plans to stop. She
opened her arm and Gina felt Maggie's bare breasts, cool
even through

Gina's flannel shirt, Maggie's smell a thicket with
wood smoke caught in it. Maggie held her there, breathing
slowly. There had been a time when Gina wouldn't have
pushed her away.

"Hurry, Maggie. The service starts in an hour."

"I thought Hatty wanted a party, not a service," Maggie complained, but began digging through her trunk. She brandished a long, raven feather which she pinned on the brim of a felt hat.

"The service is in the Mint, so I'm sure she'll get her wish." Gina watched Maggie sort through a secondhand assortment of monochromatic shades of black.

"I thought it was tomorrow," Maggie grumbled. Maggie could seldom name the day of week, but she knew, because of the still-flowering buttercups that there was no need this year to fear the summer fires. She noticed the winter had been easy on the animals because she had seen a set of triplets, the fawns gangly on their thin legs. In harsh years, she knew there would be only one.

"Heard you and June have been kind of cozy," Maggie said as they finally headed down the dirt road. The creek was lapping brown and spilling onto their path. The wild roses had small, pink buds.

Gina stared in astonishment. "Thought you didn't like to talk about those things."

"You're my friends. I'm happy for you."

"It's not what you think. I've moved back into the tipi. And I moved it out of her yard and a mile up the creek." Drenched from rain and the knee-deep water, running colder each day, covering rocks they had only hours before stepped on, Myrna and Gina had moved the tipi to a spot on Deeva's property invisible from the road. Far from June, from town, from the other women. It wasn't long before Gina began to feel like she did during hunting season, only this time, she was now the deer, exposed. Every night she hunkered, listening for their voices, their footsteps; men out to prove something or hunt something or get revenge. Her flashlight was a continual spotlight on the dark spaces between trees.

"So, how do you like suburban life?" Maggie asked.

Gina squared her shoulders. "It's safer than living in the center of town."

"All by yourself up there?"

"Of course I am."

"What about Myrna?"

"What do you know about Myrna?" Gina snapped. The conflicts with Myrna erupted as regularly as the dynamite lighting the slopes of the canyon a television blue. The nights in the tipi, when what was left of the moon crept under the canvas, spreading moon-blue on the grass, through the smoke flaps and onto Myrna's shoulders, Myrna's words rising and falling like a chant, the moon fell, too, into the empty space between them. Wind caught in the branches of the cottonwood, the creek sang differently over each rock. Each bird, each needle, the currents moving in and out of each other: Everything felt different, but it wasn't. Since the night Gina had told Myrna she loved her, nothing had changed.

Myrna always left for work. When Gina met her there, Myrna'd buy her a beer, wink as she did to Hatty, to Eddie, to all those she liked. It was exasperating. Here Gina was, ready to devote her entire life to the one moment when Myrna, kneeling near the fire, would smile at her, slipping open each button of her shirt. But, to Myrna, this kind of devotion was not only unexpected, it was unwanted.

"Myrna, if you want to stay in Emeryville, I won't leave either," Gina would say.

"Do it for yourself, not me," was all Myrna said.

Gina hated it. Since she was young, she had resolved to avoid the role of the waiting one, the wife. But now, with this woman, she found herself waiting more longingly than she would ever wait for a man. She timed the walk from the bar to the tipi and fretted each night when Myrna didn't show after her shift. Whereas before, she had dropped in the Mint whenever she felt like it, now she waited to be asked. If Myrna took a walk alone, she felt deeply hurt for days. A hesitancy entered their friendship. The self--sufficiency demanded by Myrna was leaving her stranded.

"She says I follow her around like she's going to save me," Gina told Maggie as they neared the town.

Maggie chuckled. "What else does Myrna say?"

"That everyone wants what the Indians have. Their land, their labor, their culture, and now, their secrets."

"She doesn't mean you, Gina. She's just testing you."

"That's just it. Why does she have to test me? Why can't she just trust me?"

Maggie stopped walking and raised her eyebrows. Her smoke-stained hands cupped Gina's face and she kissed her.

"I always feel like I have to prove something to her," Gina pouted.

"Yeah," Maggie said, shaking her head and continuing down the trail, "maybe you do."

River was stoic when she greeted Gina and Maggie at the door of the Mint. "I found her, a shot of whiskey on the table in front of her, that windbreaker pulled tight around her waist." River was not the only one with dry eyes. Hatty's life had not been easy.

"Death always comes in threes," an old woman grumbled, slumped on her stool, her mourning garb a black sweatshirt. She was chain-smoking. Gina scanned the crowd. Amid the black-suited men and churchwomen, the Swedish and Irish women stuffed into shirtwaists, the battered wives who had cooked and the teenage boys with hats in their hands, the local men in dark work clothes, ready for a party, June, in wine-colored velvet and a rhinestone tiara, was conspicuous. Gina moved to her side and June squeezed her hand, nodding toward Myrna.

Myrna was bartending, her black eyes unfocused in a way that meant she had begun the celebration early. She snapped a beer open rather too loudly and raised her can. "A toast." Myrna tipped the beer to her mouth. "Hatty defended us all, regardless." All the barstools were occupied and chairs pushed against the walls. The men and women grew silent, watching Myrna, their eyes only shifting to see who entered the bar late. The dark room opened and closed to sunlight like a lens.

"Boomboom," Glenn said.

Gertrude came straight from work, still in her nurse's whites and carrying a dozen mums, their edges brown and curling back as if from the recent winter, a weak-willed stem of daffodil, the lost scent of shopworn narcissus. She stood by the door, alone. The bouquet, careless, aging, so unlike her, hung from her hand like an afterthought.

"Ellen," she said to Gina, who approached, worried. "She had them sent to work so I could bring them."

Gina forced herself to ask, "How is she?"

"What do you mean, how is she? She's still in jail."

"But, the charge..."

"The charge won't stick, but they haven't arraigned her yet and she doesn't have a lawyer. We should be picketing that place. We should be burning it down."

"Have you seen her?" Gina asked sheepishly. Gertrude, so efficient, her short black hair pied with gray, looked harried, inefficient, her uniform too big on her, the work, which Gina had never realized must be hard for her, unsmoothed yet from her face.

"No, I haven't. Have you?" she snapped. She paused and her expression changed, as if the anger, facing out, turned around. "I haven't had time. I'm covering half her shifts. Besides, I don't want to do it alone. It'd be like me telling her we're not all behind her."

"We aren't behind her," River said. "She acted on her own."

Just then, Deeva arrived on the arm of a young man who was definitely not from Emeryville. The ruby in one earlobe was a dead giveaway. River caught her firmly by the arm. "Standing up for gay rights is sure a lot easier if they all know you have a boyfriend waiting in the car."

Deeva wiggled free, shocked. She could hardly have missed how her friends had grown quiet around her. Or how, in a town where no affair was a singular act—those you talked about your new lover with were probably just breaking up with her—Deeva's love was not a subject for discussion. Since the first potluck she had dared to invite him to, the message was clear: her disappointments in love were to be expected, her exhilarations not to be trusted. Her encounters with any of the women took on the self-consciousness of strangers. However, they had had two months to get used to him, and she hadn't expected to be confronted now.

"What's it to you?" Tears formed in Deeva's eyes. "River, we've been friends for a long time. What's the point in condemning me?"

"Lesbians getting boyfriends and straight women claiming they're gay—I'm beginning to wonder what the point is myself."

Deeva's voice was uncharacteristically hostile. "To tell you the truth, it's been a long time since any woman in Emeryville made me feel attractive."

Heads turned as Eddie stepped from behind the bar in a three-piece suit, a white carnation in his lapel. The tension broke and people smiled, at last, at one another. They nodded their heads. A white carnation. With this detail, Eddie had restored to the ragged gathering the missing dignity they had wanted to bestow, but felt incapable of. Before they emptied the cups which were repeatedly being filled, someone had stopped and made an offering. What they had been trying to muster throughout their associations with Hatty, before they began to drink, before they felt too proud to thank her, was suddenly affordable. Hatty would be remembered. And someone would remember them, with a suit of real wool and a white carnation. It was the way it was to be done.

"Every Thanksgiving, she gave a feast for the town," Eddie began. They were so relieved, they forgave him the vinyl chair he was standing on, the receipt pad he was reading from, the Indian woman who served and the transvestite who met them at the door like a funeral home director. "We had only the grill in the cafe. But, did that stop her?"

"No!" they cried in unison.

"No, indeed. Hatty built an oven in the back lot, out of bricks left from when they dismantled the smelter."

"Remember the year Hatty put more sherry in her than in the dressing? She could hardly balance the plates."

Hatty's life passed before them, the doilies she had crocheted, dusty now on their bureaus, the hunter-orange caps she knitted, never worn, almost thrown out. She loaned them cigarette money. She asked about their mothers. But Hatty made sure you never mistook her for your mother. Hatty did not feel responsible for everyone. She helped when she could. Not grandiosely, not unendingly, but as simply as giving a coat left in the mine office to someone without one.

Now, it was River who had made the arrangements, notified the friends. The pot of lentil soup remained untouched on the buffet, along with her whole wheat bread. To the people of Emeryville, this was the fare of war years.

But the donations she had begged of meat pasties and pies were a hit with the offspring of miners. River scurried back and forth between the stools with little sentimentality, little patience but with deep concern, pouring coffee, uncovering dishes, banking the stove. Hatty would have approved.

A blizzard of sunlight from the suddenly opened door blinded them. When their sight returned, the Reverend Jimmy Raymond Boyd stood in his shiny, threadbare suit. A passageway cleared and he stepped quietly into it. Eddie stepped down from his chair. "Excuse me, Reverend, but let me read the will, so that those who want to attend a religious service can choose to do so and follow you out."

"And those of us who want to respect Hatty's wishes can stay and celebrate," the old woman in the sweatshirt snarled.

As executor of the will, Eddie held the tablet of yellow, lined paper solemnly and remounted the chair. "Hatty, as you know, didn't have much. She leaves her cat and her furniture to River, if she will have them, excepting the photograph of her mother, which she leaves to Sarah Corrigan, who has always coveted the frame. Her clothes will fit Viola and her television should go to Sam. If Myrna can use the blankets, she can have them." The room of Hatty's fans applauded. "She wants to give the new preacher in town," Eddie said, hesitating over the handwriting, fine as Hatty's lace, "her most earnest curse that when his time comes, for disturbing the peace of this town, he will die on the street like a dog."

Eddie smiled uncomfortably. "We didn't expect diamonds, did we?"

"The old gal was funny. Too bad there's no money," Sam said.

Those who had not followed the Reverend, slamming furiously out the door, were not laughing yet. They weren't sure how to celebrate the death of someone who had just insulted the only person in Emeryville who could offer hope of a better afterlife. Glenn managed to sing one chorus of his only song before fading out for the last time from his barstool. Eddie left soon after, his job done. Gradually, the women collected their empty dishes, pots and pans.

"Hatty died because the few pleasures she had were going to be taken away from her," River said, pulling on her coat. "Fishing the creek, talking to us in the bar." She pushed the pot of lentil soup into June's hands. "The doctor told her a long time ago to quit drinking."

"Hatty was stuck like the rest of us are going to be when those at-least-I-can-get-a-waitress-jobs don't materialize. Then we'll be fighting each other for the few janitorial jobs left," June said.

"If she didn't like it here, why didn't she leave?" Deeva said.

"To do what?"

"I guess we'll be going," Deeva's boyfriend decided, pulling Deeva, who seemed unaware that Myrna was on edge, toward the door.

"So you drive a beat-up pickup truck," Myrna nodded to Maggie, "or your clothes are from the Salvation Army. So you can't get a job or you don't want to use your college education to get one. If worse came to worse, if your home in the country fell through, if the loan was due, the difference between some of you women and the poor people in this town would wash up like shells at low tide. You have family, friends. You have secrets stashed in drawers."

Deeva and her friend left hurriedly. "Play the juke-box, Sam," Myrna said, tossing a coin across the room. "And none of that country western crap either. I can't take it."

"Hatty gone. Glenn's disappeared. The motorcycle gang burned out," Maggie said, knocking her beer bottle against Myrna's. "Dykes getting boyfriends. Feels like the end of an era, old pal." Maggie removed the raven feather from her hat, smoothed it ceremoniously and held it to an imaginary sun above her. Bouncing back from the mirrors was the sickly yellow reflection from the bulbs of the wagon wheel chandelier. "Give a safe journey to our sister, Hatty," Maggie said.

"Maybe you should save the prayers for when you're sober," Gina said.

Usually, River was the only person who dared reprimand Maggie for drinking. The rest of the women ignored her impudence in exchange for the communication. When Maggie was drunk, she seemed less the lonely figure, hermited in a shack on the former dump, eating out of garbage cans and straining over drawings which ended up under the leaks in her roof. When she wasn't drinking, she was the eccentric artist they believed her to be, austere in her dedication, amusing, if not adorable. They looked the other way when, the next morning, hung over, Maggie would slink back from one of their houses to her own.

"What's with you?" Myrna asked Gina, lighting Maggie's cigarette with her own and handing it to her.

"I just wish we could be a little more solemn around here," Gina said, watching the ease with which Maggie leaned across the counter and brushed a few strands of hair from Myrna's forehead. "It doesn't seem right. It's a funeral." Gina was fuming, despite herself. She knew how rare it was to be in a roomful of women and find one Maggie hadn't slept with. Maggie knew how Myrna's legs folded under her in sleep, how Gertrude's body stiffened and rode the borders of the bed like a sail. She had loved each, intricately, her touch webbed as the tips of branches, or panoramically, with vision.

"Whoa, girl," Maggie said, picking up Gina's hand and kissing it sloppily. "Sorry we've been ignoring you. We love you, too."

"Sure, everyone loves everyone around here, don't they? You women are driving me crazy."

Myrna and Maggie exchanged looks and shrugged, resuming their conversation. Gina had anticipated a certain uncomfortableness between the two, not this steamy uncommitted heat rising as their hands flew to each other and back like a hive of bees. They lit each other's cigarettes. They shared them. The role she was to play in this intrigue was obviously not as significant as she had thought. After all, she had been Maggie's lover. And wanted to be Myrna's.

Gina tried to think of something to say. They were speaking in signs and runes and certain phrases they had come to know over the years as friends, a wealth of images shored up from their daily attentions. Gina listened, but there was no way in. She wanted to shake Maggie, as she watched their excitement grow, leading each other past the known theories, challenging each other to the first true intuitions they were hungering for. She wanted to stop

Myrna, cling to her, plead with her to wait, to explain.
There was no place for her. Even as the jealous one.
Because the currents between Maggie and Myrna,
intimate as sexuality, were not sexual. It was a way of
knowing they were sharing, a way she felt incapable of.

As if they read her mind, Maggie and Myrna simul-
taneously turned to her, exactly like the older sisters they
were, and stopped to let her catch up. "Gina, stop sulking.
This is Hatty's party, remember? If you want to stay and
celebrate with us, fine. We'd love to have you. But you have
got to lighten up," Myrna said.

"I might as well leave, so you can sleep with Maggie
tonight." It was the only thing Gina could think of to say.

Myrna sighed and opened another beer. "Gina, what
do you want from me?"

"Nothing," Gina muttered on her way out of the bar.
"Not a goddamned thing."

"Where's your girl friend?" June asked as Gina
entered. She was squatting in the living room, candles
burning in a circle around her. The walls were paisley with
shadows. June did not lift her eyes from the cards she was
studying.

"She's not my girl friend. But, if you mean Myrna, she
seems to prefer the company of loggers, the highway crew
and Maggie." Gina flicked on a light. "OK, OK, I'm afraid
what I've got here is not the great love I had imagined."

June held a tarot card to her forehead, closed her eyes
and mimicked the accent of a gypsy. "You want for her to
die without you?"

"Of course I don't."

"Then?"

"She doesn't take me seriously," Gina said, realizing
how childish she sounded, but continued. "It's dangerous
to be here now. I can feel it."

June motioned with one finger for Gina to wait and
disappeared into a side room. "What kind of danger?" June
called.

"Remember the doe blinded by your car the other
night? I feel like that when I wake alone in the tipi. Just
like that deer. Pinned. I feel like something violent and

heavy is heading toward me. Something I have to be strong for."

"What does Myrna say?"

"She says since strength can keep me running, I should watch what I pray for. Funny, isn't she?"

"What about your dreams?"

Lately, Gina's dreams had steered clear of the iron springs and featherbed of June's hotel. "I don't need help, June."

"No?" June was silent.

"OK, it's there, too, that heaviness."

"What does Myrna say?"

"Why do you keep asking about Myrna? Besides, I don't talk to her that much anymore. She spends all her free time in the Mint, playing the poker machine and drinking with the guys."

June returned to the parlor. In her hand was a battered, stand-up bass, her feet were bare and she had changed into a velvet, strapless gown. She straddled the instrument, peeled off the gloves and strummed the walking notes of a medium tempo, B flat blues. The creek lapped a high-hat, four/four and June, fleshy and melodramatic as Gina's mood, began to sing:

> "Oh, sometimes you treat me worse
> Than a man would. Oh, sometimes
> You treat me worse than a man would.
> You drink and you gamble
> Like I thought no woman could.
>
> "Oh, bad love's not just from husbands,
> But I expected more from you.
> Bad love's not just from husbands,
> But, honey, I wanted more from you.
> If women ain't no better,
> I'm gonna get me a husband, too.
>
> "On my knees was not the answer,
> No, that's not who I am.
> Begging, scrubbing and a' praying,
> No, that's not who I am.
> So, if I'm crying 'cause of you, honey,
> Your name might as well be Sam."

June stuck her hip out like a ship turning into port and in her best blues wail, performed her coda:

"I couldn't tell him what to do,
And now, I find it's the same with you."

It was a quick, hot summer, the kind that flames with a short wick, poking its head out of drifts of spring snow, calendar pages of snow on which "last storm" was written and crossed out over and over again. The snows continued into June, when for two glorious months the foothills were a dream of wild orchids, paintbrush and lupine.

The only work available coincided cruelly with the most beautiful days. Gina began to plant trees for the Forest Service. River replaced Hatty at the mines. Myrna worked extra shifts. The highway, behind schedule, geared up and the crew worked through the nights under huge lamps, the machines puffing and glaring in the dark like a city broken off from the great metropolises of the East. During the day, the canyon rumbled with continual explosions, audible in even the far clear-cuts Gina was working in. Cliffs sheared into house-size pieces, tumbled into the river and the dry air was a cyclone of dust. When she returned from work, past the leveled mountains, past the ever-changing skyline, the smaller stones rattled down the hills and the nights moaned with the sound of large trees falling.

The women fell asleep next to each other, exhausted, and everywhere there was talk of saving money to get out. The highway contractor had needed to hire a woman to meet the quota and Jake was strong enough for two. Most of the lesbians had stopped talking to her since she took the job. They had thought she understood. That it was more than the improvement of the road, the diverting of the streambed. It was the last blow to a life they felt was slipping away from them just as they had come to treasure it. It was the way the first explosion, which seared the pink-tongued cliffs of granite, bit into them.

"It just goes to show," they said to each other, "all lesbians aren't feminists."

Jake began to frequent the bar, where she got along better with the men on her crew—men more in debt than she was, with homes hundreds of miles away, men working to pay off trailers and color television sets and supporting families. They talked of fishing or bet on the baseball games. When one of the women, who still braved the construction workers and the local young men in the bar for a pack of cigarettes or a coke, walked in and the men began their taunts and solicitations, Jake would stare at the gold coins pressed into the plastic of the counter and say nothing.

These men were like her brothers. Her brothers would beat the shit out of her if they knew she was queer. They were proud she could outrun them, outdrink them and tune a car, just as these men were when she won the bet or worked as hard and as long as they did. They didn't want a woman working with them, but if it had to be, they didn't want her to fail. It was too embarrassing, like watching their wives play catch on the Fourth of July. Jake was on their team. Being a lesbian wasn't. She let them choose between calling her Mary or Jake. They chose Jake.

When the women started arriving in her hometown, Jake had expected some kind of Shangri-la of electricians, carpenters and tradeswomen. She would be surrounded by capable women, women with money of their own and tools, women with libraries and experience in gay bars, sexually strong women, serious, in charge. But instead, she was surrounded by the same rural morality she had grown up with and judgmental, bitter women, used to making tidy sums and now, finding few jobs and no chance of anyone trusting a woman to do them. Women easily shocked and unevenly divided. And now, even BJ, who seemed so eager for a new life, nagged her like a housewife, for money, for sex, how the job took all her time, how she never spent evenings with the children.

June was the only one who enjoyed the wide purple months. "Most beautiful summer we've ever seen," folks still said. The scurry in town did not affect her. Her face stayed pale under an enormous Chinese straw hat, which she wore when she fussed in her garden. June's garden was not a product of work, but of undivided attention. Nor was it confined to the wires of her fence. Daisies, raspberries, the giant blossoms of zucchini, all overflowed into her yard. A spinach plant was an arm's length away for someone sitting in the outhouse. On the path to the back door, one thin row of carrots. Bromeliads, a stalk of blue corn appeared just as one was about to put a foot down. Weeds flourished, self-important as hybrids. One weed, which ranchers and environmentalists alike had vowed to exterminate, grew behind an American Beauty rose, its noxious but dainty flowers hidden from the authorities in the same way the hippies hid their marijuana plants behind tomatoes. June grew eggplant, sweet corn, all the crops impossible in Montana in even the best years, grazed on the weeds she never pulled, invented languages she practiced, gesturing to the blackberries.

"Thought you might like to take a stroll," Gina said to June, who was stepping between the potato hills, waving as if she were dispensing incense at an orthodox church.

"Long time no see," June said. The hikes they had planned during the winter remained only markings on topography maps in June's desk.

"Been busy," Gina said uncomfortably.

June smiled. Gina was standing awkwardly at the gate, disheveled as usual. June chose her wardrobe carefully, to amuse, to provoke, just as Maggie used hers to touch past or hopeful ways of being—the Cheyenne scout, the daughter the mother wished she'd never had. It amazed June that Gina could achieve her effect so unconsciously. Years of hippiedom, friendship with Indians, physical labor and now, her absorption into lesbianism, had left Gina with Guatemalan skirts swirling around her logging boots.

"Where are we heading?" June said.

As they walked east of town, the late afternoon heat released the caught breath of the sages, the withering stalks of balsam root, the tinder of pine. The wild flowers were thick in the meadows and an occasional breeze gossiped brilliantly in the aspen. In summer, the birds would sing straight through midnight, when in the few violet hours of darkness, they continued a faint chanting. "Glad it's cooled down," June said, panting.

They were already a mile up the slope. Gina, who had been hauling saplings on her back for months, hadn't noticed that June wasn't keeping up. "It's not much further. There's a trail I've been wanting to follow for a long time."

"Where does it go?"

"I'm not sure. A peak, maybe."

June watched their shadows climb the hill. "It's a little late to start heading for a peak. Besides, we've followed most of the trails around here." June's eyes narrowed. "Did someone tell you about it?"

"It starts right over there. Up that gulch." Gina turned to go.

"Oh." June reached blindly behind her to where, rough-shorn, a rock grew out of the open field unaccompanied. June had an affinity with rocks. They rose around her, perfectly suited to their tasks, chair-size, stool-size, sunning-one's-body-in-the-creek-size. They fit the cup of her hand, the ridge of her shoulder. Friendly, they warmed her cheeks. They were there for her feet on precarious ledges, for her hands. They were protection, buttress. She filled her home with them, strung her neck with them.

Gina returned to where June slumped on the rock, her bare legs blue-veined and red with nettle burns. June's arms were more toughened than tanned and the dry climate broke over her face in dozens of tiny currents. "What's wrong with you?" Gina frowned.

The sun dipped low and climbed the distant hills, beginning the almost endless hours of twilight. June pointed in the direction of the trail. "You go on," she sighed. "I'm not up to those kinds of hikes anymore."

Gina was skeptical. "What do you mean?"

"I mean, I'm too old, damn it. You think you can just show up out of nowhere and expect me to follow you. You don't even know where you're going."

"Since when did you have to know where you're going?"

"When I don't know, I don't drag other people along."

"Forget it, then. Forget I even asked you," Gina shouted, heading toward the forest. Blue was already lapping between the trunks and she entered it, angrily. She found the trail easily. As she marched along it, she felt June watching behind her like a shadow. The path rose and fell and soon, its familiar rhythm quieted her. What was she afraid of? This was her territory, more than the town could ever be. She had made it hers. She felt silly, trapped in that tipi, scared to go out. Like when she first arrived and the mountains were closed to her.

Gina thought of June, leaning into that stone, tired, but gathering strength. The hills were full of them, people like June clutching pebbles, lacing their fingers through the bitter leaves. They might be sick or kneeling and they came often or once, despite warnings that the water was brackish, the trees diseased, the soil dangerous with fallout. They still came. And, for what? For this salve of beauty? A creek, like this one, running serpentine and bundled dark in willow?

She was making good time, climbing through the higher trees, the ponderosa, lodgepole, alpine fir. Work had strengthened her legs and she was proud of the way she could speed through the large, unthinned trees without a sound. Myrna was slower and her tracks pointed in. Something in the way she pressed made it impossible to tell in which direction she was going. No one tracked Myrna down. Even she, though she had been so sure she could.

Once, Myrna had shown her, by placing her palms together, moving them with undulations like a fish, what it was like to be Indian in the twentieth century. Like water flowing around many rocks. Is that what she thinks of me, Gina thought, as something to get around? "We should talk," she had told Myrna, but Myrna, who used sign language often, drew circles in the air and in dirt mapped ridges, who traced the folds of every feeling, held things, let them go, had only groaned and held her stomach. And what would she say, she who held such faith in the verbal, in getting things out into the open like shaking a rug? That their differences used to fascinate her and now, they were a threat? That what they had here, they could have anywhere?

The trail stopped and above her, a ridge spread into an antler of peaks. She picked her way up shale, between the wind-beleaguered trees she held onto, her breath pounding and sharp-edged stones clattering from her feet. The boulders she had been hopping shone behind her. The wind was sharp and fast. She was exhilarated from the climb. When she gained the shoulder, she was shaking.

The ranges grew green below her and the waves of foothills drained into the deep canyons. Past the sparkling lakes below her, past the lightning of the creeks they drained into, the spreading into river bottom, past the tiers of flowers, the bluebells blooming late near the peaks, lay the pocket of Emeryville, the tin roofs splashing whenever the sun hit. All that life built on top of the lives of others: June and the brothel. Maggie and the miners. Once, Gina had teased Maggie that her home was built on top of garbage. "Everyone lives on top of garbage," Maggie had said, taking offense, "entire cultures." And then, there was Myrna. Which culture was hers, the one which dug up the bones of those it had murdered and called them talismans? Or the culture of the bones? "What if somebody slipped into Arlington Cemetery and took all the soldier's medals and watches and their good leather boots?" Myrna had said. "You wouldn't read about it on page twenty-seven." And which was hers, Gina's? What could she own?

A muted explosion grabbed her attention. Below, smoke groped its way out of one of the draws. It was dynamite. She couldn't escape it even all the miles up here. Was it Hatty's pool or where June had found the first patch of wild iris, close to a spring, shaded by bluffs? Was it the pool where Gina had made love to Maggie, the duff pillowing her head? Was it the pool where she had watched, only a week before, as Myrna cast her fishing pole into the green? Was it now filling with flagstone?

What fools they were! To think they could save anything. They couldn't even save themselves. They thought the place protected. By what? And worse, they thought they protected it, gathered inside the limbs of the sweat-lodge with their vague hopes and their dreams. She turned to follow the sun in its uneven descent and a much less rugged trail opened in front of her. Soon, she was walking on a two-track hunting road, blasted through the rock. Sixty-five hundred feet in the mountains and next to the road, a stack of green wood, cut for fence posts. She crossed a shortcut made by cyclists, the riverlets eroding down the banks like insects from an overturned log. She found a black plastic sack of garbage. A styrofoam cup. She had to get out of Emeryville before everything she had learned meant nothing.

"Damn it," Gina said, picking up a rock and throwing it. For once, Myrna was wrong. Knowing a parade of others felt the same way was no consolation.

A shot rang out, so close it caught part of her breath and ran with it. Gina came to a halt. Ahead, across the clearing, a cliff rose, its crest drifting into the overexposed sky. Was there smoke below it? She was still miles from town and it was nowhere near hunting season. Was she trespassing? The cottonwood swayed in tropical slow motion and the leaves rattled above her, lethargic as palms. Suddenly, she could not be quiet enough. She knew it was all mixed up together: the attack on the canyon, the attack on the women, Hatty's death and Myrna's resistance. The long line of history spread out in front of her, one after another, the wounded, always the wounded figure in landscape, listening to something which in the end could not save it. Why did she think she was different? The faces and dangers of the last few months became alive and she was paralyzed, in a delirium of fear, fear of the land she had come to feel more at home in than her body.

She heard something crashing through the downfall and thistle like a deer, but heavier than deer. A man entered the meadow, raising his gun for a second shot. His back was to her, a stone's throw away. She thought of the deer, at dawn near the borite, a moose, loping hunchbacked past her campfire in winter, the pale winter elk, cloud-colored and calm. She thought of June, her fawn-colored hair, June incorrigible about the suede jacket she wore hiking. What if June had followed? June who could bugle like an elk and did so for amusement?

She knew she should stay. Knew she could stop him with a shout. But what if he turned on her, and she so far from town? Did he already know she was witness in this meadow to him? Or was it she he was trying to frighten, and what if there were more? More men? More guns? She could no longer stop her legs from running. Past the yellow blooms of arnica, trampling the red flags of paintbrush. She was racing when she entered the familiar drainage of

Emeryville Creek. The second shot, and it was as if a body, soft and limp, fell inside her.

Myrna sat in the cool on her stoop, the coal of her cigarette in the last of the light, as Gina rounded the corner toward her, her face flushed and panting.

"Slow down, my girl. What happened?"

"There was a man with a gun," Gina gasped.

Myrna grabbed Gina's shoulders. "Where? Was he after you?"

"I don't think he saw me. But he shot something." Gina burst into tears. "He killed it. I'm sure of it."

Myrna brushed the hair from Gina's face. "Where were you?" she repeated.

"I was hiking. Somewhere above Emeryville Creek, I don't know where."

"What the hell were you hiking alone at night for?"

"We used to do it all the time," Gina glared.

"That was before, Gina," Myrna said, still holding on, "before the trouble."

"I didn't see what he shot. I couldn't stop him." Gina wrestled away. "I'm going to call the game warden."

"Gina, he probably *is* the game warden." Myrna returned to her stoop. "Come on. Sit down. You're upset."

"Of course, I'm upset. I felt like I was going to be killed up there. Or who knows what. You never listen to me!"

Myrna struck a match off her boot. "Don't yell at me, Gina."

"What makes you so goddamn brave all the time?"

"Look, Gina," Myrna sighed, "I've worked a long time for this. You don't get it just 'cause you want it." She smiled then and winked. "Or by getting in my pants."

Gina was still scanning the forest for movement. She turned on Myrna, wild-eyed. "You don't think this means anything? It means it's time for us to leave."

Myrna rose and placed her palm around the back of Gina's neck. "This doesn't mean you're gonna leave without me?"

"Don't," Gina said, brushing away Myrna's hand. "Someone might see us."

"What?"

"Don't you understand? There's a war going on."

Myrna turned toward her house. "Well, then, they've won."

June had been drying gladiolus from her garden and weaving the blossoms into leis. She sold them to summer tourists and mine visitors and gave them to what friends would wear them. In certain light, they resembled wreaths of dying, fragile butterflies. In others, nothing so much as a string of used tissue.

"Seems like everyone is leaving," June said as she slipped a lei around Gina's neck.

"Now, I'm just taking the job so I can save up some money. I'll be back."

"Time for her to start thinking of her future," Myrna said, not without sarcasm.

Gina ignored her, reaching her arms around June's waist. "Hard to pass up such a good offer. They plant trees half the year in Washington. And I'm broke."

"Funny how it came just in time," Myrna said.

"I suppose I'm going to have to resign myself to the fact that I'm never going to have a career," June whined.

"Honey, you've made a career out of having no career," Gina said, kissing her.

"Come on, I'll walk you over," Myrna said. "Time for my shift anyway."

Sam had hung the orange flag, signaling the driver of the one daily bus that there was a passenger. He stood outside the Mint, a blue-billed cap on his head, to which a plastic replica of a cow-pie was attached. "You're a Shit-Head," it said, "if you don't drink at Mary's Bar."

"Thanks, Sam," Gina said on her way into the Mint. It was empty, mid-afternoon, and Myrna bought her a beer.

"I hope you find it, my girl," Myrna said, clinking her bottle against Gina's.

Maggie had given Gina one of her favorite stetsons, as if she didn't feel conspicuous enough with June's lei. The bumper sticker which she couldn't see, pinned on the back of her jacket as a last-minute joke from Jake, was printed with the famous line of Chief Joseph: "I will fight no more forever."

Sam ducked his head in the door, excited to have spotted the metallic flash which meant the bus was passing through the red gates of the canyon. "Guess I have to go," Gina said, standing. Behind the bar, Myrna continued to wash wine glasses.

"See ya," Gina called and let the door slam behind her.

But as she stepped on the bus, the motor roaring, she heard the door of the bar open. She turned expecting to see Myrna running toward her, suitcase in hand, or begging her to stay, but there was Myrna, gorgeous and backlit in the doorway of the Mint. And sure, so goddamned erotically sure, cigarette in hand. "Gina," she was calling, "you look ridiculous."

7

The evening the snow fell, an amnesia of snow that wiped out green and any thought of green, the stranger of snow that stayed so long it became family, the solid fact of snow that came with no messengers and no small flurries, the needles of the fir trees brushed across the surface of the moon like claws.

Entangled in a dream of addressing a crowd of thousands, each word forced through a bout of coughing, River woke, feverish, to the sound of dogs. When she lived in the city, the argument of traffic, the sirens, even the woman who wore high heels upstairs, had not wakened her. They had only reassured her. They were there if she needed them. But in Emeryville, this continuous barking, baying and sniveling of dogs, day in and day out, always woke her to fear. As if they were coming to get her.

She had been ill for weeks. Up early to open the mine, which was getting damper with the end of the season, she had caught Sam's cold while bringing him oranges. River gagged thinking of that room. Sickness for weeks, Sam's cigars and the unidentifiable perfume. When she had asked, Sam told her that two nieces from Oklahoma had come to visit and the fact that he had relatives had so excited him that he wouldn't wash his hands until they sent him a bottle of the fragrance they wore as they had promised. Eddie had put limits on Sam's enthusiasm. "I've already got a barmaid in logging boots. That is enough."

A particularly uproarious jamboree brought River out of bed and onto her feet. She grabbed her gun and, before she knew it, fired three shots above the heads of the pack, grappling in the flurries under the street light.

"Hey," she heard someone yell, "that lady tried to kill my dog." It was not as late as she had thought. A few teenage boys were walking home in the dark. They ran to the spot the dogs had been and pointed to her window.

"What's the matter with you, you old witch?"

"Yeah, what'd those dogs do to you?"

River pulled her head back into the room. The boys were still yelling. A few rocks hit the side of her cabin. She sank into the chair, pulling the cardigan closer, her thumbs circling each other like Hatty's had done so often when they were not occupied with needles or the stale bread she tore into pieces and set outside for the birds. She had always sent River to get it, three loaves for a dollar.

Everyone else had their stories, their tales of women met in bars, of dreams or providential breakdowns while passing through. What had brought her here? A town of lesbians, a sort of gay New Albany, nestled in a pocket of pine trees atop the Continental Divide? She had heard rumors of a communal village, of artists, writers, organizers, where the front line of a new culture was being forged. Flyers came to her home in the city unsolicited, announcing weekend retreats and guide services, a lesbian bed and breakfast club. Though her inquiries went unanswered, she persisted in her vision of a utopia of clean, well-lit homes where the community discussed relevant issues, a printing press staffed with articulate revolutionaries, a loving and loyal group who met each other's needs and cared about the changing of the guard in a new America. All with a splendid view of the mountains, clean air and organic produce. She was sorely disappointed. Here, she found women barely scraping by, touching in their farfetched plans for making money, an untouched press needing parts and someone trained to run it, a close group of friends who gossiped and were alternately affectionate and critical of each other. In short, just like her neighborhood in the city. Only colder.

She had realized soon enough that her ideas didn't fit. They loved her, River knew, because she had helped Hatty die, because she had learned her part to the African rhythm on the saucepan. Because of the meals they shared and the danger. But they didn't love her for her ideas. River was the one they had always feared would come to Emeryville: the tattooed, shaven, muscle-shirted bull dyke who would blow their cover. It didn't matter that bikers came through, grabbing at their braless bosoms, or if a sudden influx of the homeless arrived to compete for their shacks and their jobs. If all the insane from the Home escaped and came to Emeryville, with their diapers and unzipped flies, the lesbians would stand next to the miners and the regulars in the bar and welcome them. But River, sitting on her girl friend's lap in the Mint, was not welcome. They liked her better at the seance than when she marched along the proposed highway with a picket sign. They wished she would grow her hair and find a steady girl friend. "You want the world changed, but by people who act and look like you," she'd accused them. If it wasn't for Hatty and the wards she'd left her with, River would have followed Gina out of town.

Maggie was sleeping when the dogs, vicious with River's gunshots in their ears, rampaged her yard. The blizzard was no camouflage for the goats, spot-lit in the dim corral they were cornered in. There was not much left to save when Maggie found them, although in despair she loaded their mangled bodies into the back seat of Gertrude's car and drove them to the vet in the city. Maggie slept, curled in the fading scent of the goat barn, for a month. "Dear Gina," she wrote, "is the grass really greener somewhere else?"

Work on the new highway continued grudgingly for the few hours of daylight left in the north before solstice. When at four, the bare sun sank behind the canyon wall, the heat of the day evaporated. The tomato leaves were slick and black with frost and the horses slept, lying next to each other on the ground until noon. The overnight end of summer had left no time for squash seasoning on the vine. June, in her sheepskin slippers, plucked frozen peas, beans and sweet corn from her garden and put them into a laundry hamper. "Oh, you poor things," she sputtered, "I worked my ass off all summer and for what?" she asked Myrna, lifting her robe to moon the sky. "See?"

Some liked winter. They sharpened their skates, checked the number of tins of colored ski wax, didn't drive, had gas heat. They went on holiday in February and had satellite dishes in their backyards. "Isn't it lovely?" Deeva said, meeting June outside. Deeva's satellite dish was painted with a forest scene, a doe and a pond. After this first commission, Maggie had spent days designing dishes with pastoral or historical scenes. Lewis and Clark. Buffalo Jumps. Rodeos. Jeanette Rankin placing her solitary vote against the war. Rosetta, dancing her famous spider dance for the miners, the spiders made of cork, rubber and whalebone, imported and shaken from her skirt in the finale, her feet showered with sacks of gold. Maggie stole the idea from Lola Montez. She wasn't sure if Rosetta danced, since she wasn't an actress, like Lola, but a whore. Unfortunately, few in Emeryville could afford satellite dishes, let alone designs painted on them, except for Deeva and Eddie, who commissioned a young stag. And Maggie was not given to walking door to door.

The wet stars, sparkling and shaking drops like the head of Maggie's dog, had finally broken through, and word passed that Maggie was hosting the last campfire of the season. When June and Deeva trudged up the path and into the light of the bonfire, the frozen ground was cracking, turning to mud near the pit. Even BJ was there, after putting her children to bed, dragging her lawn chair along and sitting so close to the flames that she was beginning to smoke like a foundry.

Cold from searching the newly-covered ground for firewood, Myrna crouched low to the fire, brushing snow from her swollen hands. She shivered. It wasn't the breath-less cold of midwinter, but the new chill on her still sun-burnt body. And it was Gina leaving. Before she was ever really here, Myrna thought. Myrna had wanted to tell Gina so many things and they came back to her now, especially among women or near a fire. Stories about herself. Her life. How once, when she was a girl, she had begged her grand-mother for a pair of moccasins. She was not too young to make them, she had pleaded, although the old lady thought she was. Finally, her grandmother gave her two soles to patch on the worn bottoms of her brother's. Swallowing her disappointment, Myrna had sewn all day, finishing the ragged pair just before supper. To the delight of the entire family, her grandmother slipped them on over her own tiny feet and paraded them up and down before the table in a mockery of a round dance: Myrna had sewn the soles on the wrong feet. Shamed, Myrna took the moccasins to her bed where she spent the night pulling the threads and starting over. The next morning she showed her grand-mother the completed pair and, without saying a word, her grandmother traced Myrna's feet onto a thick piece of buckskin for a pair of her own.

Gertrude sat with her back to the fire. With the swept light of the last few weeks, the foliage gone, she could see further and better, could make out hidden tributaries and game trails, the glacial and volcanic breasts and kneecaps of her home. More and more, she found herself studying them, bent on escape. "I need to talk about Ellen," she sighed, not turning around.

No one acted as if they'd heard. BJ glanced at Jake and Maggie continued to roll her cigarette.

"She's been getting hate mail. Hate mail. Christian ladies across the state, trapped in ranch-style houses with only the TV and their children, hate her. Whole societies of churchwomen write letters. Lutheran study groups, Baptist auxiliaries call her a monster. But they want her. They make her promises of salvation. They invite her to visit."

The women stared at the flames.

"You know what else she gets? Fan mail. Stacks of it. At least a letter a day, mostly from adolescent girls and boys, rodeo stars, 4-H Club winners, thanking her for her courage, for her example. I've seen the letters. They're pitiful."

Gertrude had expected Ellen to return to work shamed and more than a little defeated. In the end, as they had thought, there had been no charge and hence, no challenge to the law. But Ellen returned smiling, incorrigible in her attempts to talk about it all: jail, television, anything, in the plodding, unrestrained speech Gertrude had forgotten. Ellen didn't seem to notice when people walked away, averted their eyes, shunned her. Or that Gertrude shunned her, as she did, or that they ate separately, as before.

And why should she sit with Ellen? Despite everything, they were different. Very different. To Gertrude, lesbianism was intelligent, a heretical, stylish, guarded intelligence, a self-imposed exile to Parisian gardens, Colette flashing her pale skin through a toga, a code, a club of writers, the red lips and nails of Bauhaus painters, Carmen McRae and Afro-Cuban rhythms, a just dessert, Adrienne Rich after dinner. Ellen had asked her once, "Do you only sleep with beautiful women?"

"No," she had answered, "of course not," but yes, yes, of course she did, why otherwise? Lesbianism was a pleasure, a choice, a distinct advantage, not a campaign, not loneliness, rejection, degradation. It was she who rejected. She rejected heterosexuality.

But, as she sat, watching Ellen as the others did, from the other side of the cafeteria, no one came to sit with her either. Or talked to her during breaks. And Gertrude's eyes? Almond shaped, the color of dark honey? They avoided them, too.

"Listen," Gertrude remembered Ellen saying during one of their first conversations, "Do you think if I lost weight or didn't have my yard they would accept me? Do you honestly think they accept you?"

Gertrude turned around to face the women at the campfire. "Whether we accept Ellen or not, she still gets rape threats, although no men were apparently interested until she said she was a lesbian. Spit on, called names. People in her yard at night, setting fires, stealing the animals. And what else does she get? She gets shunned by women who profess to support each other. Champions of the underdog. And after she took the rap for us."

"Nobody asked her to," Myrna said.

"Who asked Rosa Luxemburg? Martin Luther King? Crazy Horse?"

"Now, Gertrude..." Myrna began wearily.

"What did she do that was so bad? Besides claim the right to be one of us?"

"On television," BJ reminded.

"She's not one of us," River said.

"Why not? Because she's fat? A witch?"

"Gertrude, half of us are fat, too. You know the difference. What right does she have to speak for us?"

"You have something against single women, then? Is that it? What if I told you she was my lover?"

"Why are you defending her? Why doesn't she defend herself?"

"Not to change the subject," Deeva began, "but I wonder what the Reverend has in store for us. Elections are in two weeks."

"Us?" River said, raising her eyebrows.

"What is this getting to be, a closed club?"

"It's almost as if he were running for election," Gertrude agreed. "You see him more on TV than the candidates."

After the appearance on *Good Evening, Montana* the Reverend Boyd had become an instant celebrity. The Christian Citizens now had branches throughout the Northwest. Their slogan, "Morality Before Equality," was hard to argue against and their endorsement was all some fledgling politician from Two Dot or Sheep Creek needed to win his seat in the state legislature. The legislature, which met every two years, whether it needed to or not, swelled the population of the dusty town on the flats which was the capital. Part city, part ranch town, the suited government workers walked its main street alongside cowboys and spitting mountain men whose attire hadn't changed since the gold rush. The legislature was a highlight for landlords and parking meter maids. Otherwise, no one paid it any mind because nothing ever happened there. The most anyone could hope for was legalized blackjack. But this year was different.

The headlines were a testament to the Reverend's success as both a spiritual and political leader: "Homosexuality a Crime." "Confessed Witch in Emeryville Set Free." "Crackdown on Lesbian Sex Rings." The articles were as sensational as the reporters had promised the women they wouldn't be. The stories were mostly about the fact that lesbians existed at all in Emeryville, akin to the discovery of timber wolves in the yard of a couple in Minnesota. How they got there, why they came, their sexual and feeding habits were of the same interest.

The Reverend now had clout. His sermons were broadcast live over a local radio station. His presence was requested at countless parishes and he was asked to sit on school boards, youth boards and to lecture to colleges. He persuaded the governor's office to issue warnings to the public that the state stood ready to prosecute any cases brought to the courts. He urged police departments to hold workshops, teaching patrolmen how to spot criminal activity. Since there was not one gay bar in the state, he directed them to women's resource centers, gourmet restaurants and to community theaters. Some people had always known about the lesbians in Emeryville. Now, they were a legend, to the extent that anyone coming out of the closet said, "I'm moving to Emeryville."

"What I didn't understand at first," BJ said, pouring a cup from her thermos of mulled wine and leaning closer to the fire, "is why he moved here. It just didn't make sense."

"What do you mean?"

"Why a home in the country? Going back to the land presumes you have land to get back to," BJ answered.

"There she goes," Deeva said, preparing herself for the inevitable lecture on the expenses of single parenthood and how difficult it was to keep the rent paid. "You forget, I always go out of my way to help people. It isn't so easy to have property either. Look at the other side. I get blamed for everything."

"I'm not talking about you, Deeva. I'm talking about the distribution of property."

"I don't charge half what I could for the rooms I rent in Emeryville," Deeva continued, as if she hadn't heard, "including yours."

"Nobody knew that lot was for sale until the Reverend moved onto it. Did the church own it?"

"The church owns the church," Gertrude said, "so it doesn't have to pay a dime in taxes. It probably owns his home, too."

The women had grown quiet, thinking. Maggie owned the dump and June held the deed to the hotel. That left the land around the school, the church, Deeva's houses and the Mint. Twenty or so private homes. Forest Service land. A banker from California had arrived a year before to claim a hundred acres up the west-running creek, building a log cabin from a kit and surprising them all. Because land up the creek was not property. It was the creek, where they hunted elk and cooled off by pools caught in the arms of granite. No one lived there. They had watched as the man, who apparently made enough money to buy and build in the same season, laid fences of barbed wire to keep their cattle out and closed the hole to swimmers.

"I've been studying power and where one gets it," BJ continued. "Money. Property. Religion. All this trouble, from the names they call my children, who, by the way, have lost a playmate a week since the Reverend came, to that awful paint on my house. What else would you call this but a police state? All due to one man's crusade. He had religion, true, but Billy Graham never had much influence five minutes after he left this state. Money? We know better. But, property? Just how much property does this man have? And where did he get it? It was then that I got the idea to look in the county records."

The women moved closer as BJ lowered her voice. "I must have looked ridiculous in the wig and house dress I borrowed from Sara Corrigan, but the secretaries only smiled and pointed to the courthouse drawers. They must have assumed I was there to check a mining claim. And you know what I found out? The Reverend is worth a fortune, but only if sagebrush was gold."

"The trailer lot?" Maggie said.

"He owns most of the private land skirting Emeryville. Whatever isn't in the name of the state or the railroads. And all registered in the church's name."

"Where did he get the money to buy that?" Deeva was nearing the end of her inheritance and had been con-

templating selling off a few pieces of property herself. She
wondered if the Reverend would be interested in a prime
tract of timber next to the creek.

"He didn't buy it. He inherited it," BJ said smugly.

"From who?" June giggled and tucked her arm underneath BJ's.

"From no one other than his great-grandfather,
Jimmy 'No Man's Gonna Ever Stick It To Me Again' Boyd."
BJ smiled triumphantly. "The First."

"From Rosetta?" The women fell into a huddle of
laughter, slapping hands and throwing their arms around
each other's waists and shoulders. Surely, they had something valuable here, they repeated, until a branch snapped
and they turned to see a deputy, his gun drawn and pointed
toward them. Their arms dropped stiffly to their sides.

"Hold it right there." Another man stepped quickly
from the shadows.

"What's the charge?" Myrna yelled, the first to regain
composure.

The policemen continued to aim their guns toward
them. "Shut up, squaw," the deputy yelled.

The stars barely flickered behind another bank of
clouds. The women flocked nervously. "Call another car,"
said the deputy. "We got too many here for just one." He
leveled the gun at the group, then turned to shine the
flashlight toward the disappearing figure of his friend.
"Hey, Larry, you might want to have them notify the
press." The sheriff will be proud, he thought. In months of
patrolling Emeryville uselessly, they had found nothing
but a few gay newspapers. They had followed a lead regard-
ing the poor waitress who was molested in the cafe, but
they found her living with her female tennis coach, attend-
ing college in Mountain View. She had refused to testify.
"OK, easy does it. I want everybody moving down the hill
in single file."

"Why'd you go that way?" his partner asked when
they arrived at the road. He was aiming his flashlight past
the women and into the stand of lodgepole pine so thick
even the deer avoided them.

"She said it would be easier," the deputy said, staring
at a cluster of red willow. "Now, where in the hell did she
go?"

"Let's get out of here before any more of them escape," the man said. They separated the women into the two patrol cars.

Gertrude watched Myrna step into the back seat of the car with Deeva. She knew Myrna could have slipped off easier than any of them. "I hope Maggie sends someone to watch BJ's girls," she whispered as the car pulled away.

In the dark of the patrol car, Deeva was frantically applying lipstick and checking her watch. "Do you think it's too late to call my lawyer?"

Myrna noticed how the car pulled out onto the highway heading south. They were going to the county jail, not the station in the city. They were lucky. The jail had no separate facilities for women and only two large lockups. They wouldn't be searched and they would remain together. She could see Deeva's face in the green light from the dashboard. Deeva looked terrified. Myrna reached across the seat and placed her hand over Deeva's cold fingers. "Don't worry. It'll be fine."

"Don't touch me," Deeva hissed under her breath, throwing Myrna's hand from her lap.

When they arrived at the jail house, a sleepy-eyed circle of journalists greeted them, shivering and yawning in the glare of the lamps. As each woman stepped out, psychedelic spheres of flashbulbs snapped before their eyes, but Deeva was prepared. The photograph on the front pages of the newspapers the next morning revealed only a cap smashed over her face, with her figureless in the oversized coat she had borrowed at the last minute from June. She groped her way out and up the steps, guided by the arm of a patrolman.

Myrna's eyes were like the coals of a jumped deer and in the pictures, hers was clearly no surrender. Gertrude, whose legs and arms had become too complex to arrange harmoniously, waved in exasperation. BJ wore sunglasses, but she needn't have bothered. Their names were printed plainly in order of appearance.

"Obviously, there has been some mistake," Deeva whined as they herded her in the front door. She held tight to the hat with one hand and rummaged in her pocket for phone change with the other. "I want to call my lawyer."

"Lady, get that hat out of your face."

Deeva opened her eyes to the fluorescent office. She had been sure her aunts would be there to explain and take her quietly home. "I want to call my lawyer," she repeated with lessening assurance.

"No phone calls until morning."

"You can't do that," Deeva shouted, aware suddenly that they were meant to spend the night.

"They can do," Myrna said, "anything they want." She scowled at Gertrude. As if in one sentence she could explain to Deeva the role of the police in her life. Police were the men with bullhorns who stopped her on the streets. They had a right to know why she wasn't in school when she was a child and why she wasn't at work when she grew up. They took babies away from whomever they felt shouldn't have them and they locked fathers up for months. Police were the last people she would call for help, who appeared when she least wanted them. The number of Indians who hung themselves with their belts in Montana's jails was suspiciously high.

"No, they can't!" Deeva beat at the arms of the men who were trying to lead her to the cell. She was weeping long after the door clanked shut behind them. "Wait until my lawyer hears of this."

"Don't bother," Myrna said, lighting a cigarette and blowing the smoke toward the small window. "We'll be out by morning."

"She's right," Gertrude said, retrieving her thermos from her waistband. "You won't have to spend too much on legal fees to get out of throwing your arms around a group of women at a campfire."

"They got what they wanted," BJ sighed, dejected. "The Reverend got his headline. And just in time for the elections. And we, guilty or not, are going to be famous right along with him."

Deeva made a pillow of June's coat. "I wish I had learned gospel singing. This makes me think of the South."

"You don't learn gospel," BJ snapped, "you live it."

Myrna groaned. They still had to spend the night together in a very tiny cell. "Gospel," she said, "would be awfully difficult to find in this area, don't you think?"

On the night of the dead, Gertrude tapped into BJ's party in a top hat and tails, twirling a baton and running through a fast time step in an express performance for a short Ku Klux Klan member and a small cowboy with a large, silver badge. As the children burst into applause, Gertrude hugged them. "I see your mother has strictly avoided any reference to witches with your costumes this year."

"She said what could be scarier than this," the cowboy said. "But she says she won't take us out for Halloween. Will you?"

"We'll have much more fun here than knocking on any of those doors out there. Besides, they're haunted."

"Really?"

"Come see Jake," the Klan member said, grabbing Gertrude's arm and leading her to the muscled and hairy legs of a giant ballerina, her calves a mine field of purple bruises. But Jake only motioned for silence, her hands returning to BJ's shoulders.

"Girls, go to the kitchen now and pick out some music for everyone to dance to."

"But nobody's here yet."

"Go."

BJ hung up the phone wearily. "Every agency I've called, from one coast to the other, says the same thing: take your children and run."

"But we already have custody. It was decided by the courts when you got the divorce."

BJ shook her head, ignoring her. "Where would I run to? And with what? I don't have any savings. I've been living on child support and welfare."

"Not to mention my salary," Jake grumbled.

As Myrna had predicted, they had been released the next morning. But the damage was done. When BJ walked in her front door, Maggie, who was cooking breakfast for the girls, informed her that the calls had started with the first edition of the papers. The most frequent caller was BJ's ex-husband and his lawyer, with the news that he was suing for custody.

"Now, he wants them," Gertrude said. "Before, you couldn't get him to take them for a weekend. What's up?"

"The situation has changed. I'm a lesbian. His ex-wife is a lesbian. He is, naturally, embarrassed."

"I don't see how he has a chance."

"He just got married. Next thing you know, he'll join a church. I wonder if he'll go so far as to get a full-time job."

"Now, now," Jake said.

"His mother called," BJ said, shooting Jake a mean look. "She pleaded with me to give them up. My sister called, saying my brother will never speak to me again. My mother called, saying I could have it all if I ever outgrew my stubbornness. 'You're nice looking. You're smart. Lesbianism, Barbara,' she said, 'is an oppression you choose.'"

Deeva arrived and was strolling through BJ's rooms, acting the landlady she was, reading the backs of postcards, examining photographs and paintings. She stopped in front of a piece of Japanese pottery. "BJ, did you happen to borrow..."

"For god's sake, Deeva," River said, following her in. Her usual attire was transformed into that of a gangster by the mere addition of a gun sling, a cigar and the thin mustache she had created from her own pubic hairs. She lowered her voice. "BJ is talking about losing her kids."

"If there's anything I can do to help, just let me know." Deeva lifted the pot to search for its signature.

Jake elbowed BJ. BJ shook her head. Jake said, "She needs money."

"Who doesn't?" Deeva laughed and continued her rounds.

To her surprise, River lifted her by the lapels and slammed her against the wall. "I don't think you heard what she said."

Deeva was choking. Her eyes searched the room, panic-stricken, for allies. The door opened and her eyes came to rest on Myrna. She begged, "Myrna, please help me."

Jake nodded to Myrna, who began to slowly read Jake's lips from across the room. "BJ needs money to hire a lawyer."

"OK, OK," Deeva gasped and River let her grip go. "Why didn't you say so. Send the bills to me."

"I think I speak for everyone when I offer the money we raised for an emergency bail fund in case anyone was arrested," River said.

Myrna was dressed as usual, only with a cowgirl hat on. "Maybe after the elections everything will return to normal. Maybe those senators will get him a television show or something and he'll move out of here."

"He got his headline," BJ said blankly. She was staring out the window at the soft dark which came so early now. Drifting home, led by the tall ones with flashlights, were the dim forms of goblins, clowns and Disney characters. Only the year before, she had designed their costumes, spent weeks sewing sequins on dozens of sheets, cut holes for their heads in pillowcases. None of those children had turned queer from the chocolate chip cookies she passed out nor their parents from the brandied coffee she served them. But this year not one of them had shown up at her door.

"How are the kids taking it?" Gertrude asked, her voice lowered and glancing to the two girls dancing to Motown with Deeva in the kitchen.

"They're smart kids. They knew what to expect," BJ said. "I've tucked them in since they were babies with stories of the underground railroad. Instead of ghost stories, they got the Holocaust and South Africa. They understand intolerance. They understand oppression. But it's different when you're in grade school and suddenly have no one to play with."

A few women slipped out of the room uncomfortably and into the kitchen to dance. Those left behind bowed their heads and stole looks at one another. BJ sighed. She hated conviviality, between men, among children and now, with these women. Here she was again, the mother scolding, the whispered about, the encroaching, the unincluded. Here she was, reminding everyone to brush their teeth, pay the bills, remember the children. And now, this preacher to take care of, as if she needed another headache. As if she needed a god. When all her life she had been directed, bullied and battered by them.

"It's moments like this that make me wonder if they're not fighting my fight," BJ said. "If it's fair to keep them in a town where I have to lock them inside for fear of people poisoning them."

"Maggie?" Myrna said, as someone entered the room, the skull of an elk fitting perfectly over her head.

"How'd you know it was me?"

"What do you call that costume?" Underneath the stag head, which had bits of gristle and drying meat clinging to the bone, was an exact replica of the miner's body, the flannel shirt, wool pants, red suspenders.

"I call it a half-breed."

Myrna wrestled Maggie to the floor. When Maggie got back on her feet, she touched the band of Gertrude's top hat. "Where'd you get those fancy duds?"

Gertrude tipped her hat. "I took advantage of my recent notoriety by suggesting to the owners of the new Italian restaurant in the city that I serve as their maitre d'."

"Sorry to hear you got laid off, Gertrude."

"Polite way to fire you, wasn't it?"

"Ah, who cares? I needed a break from that house of horrors." Gertrude dropped her eyes. "Besides, I can't take it like Ellen can. People whispering behind my back, pretending I don't care."

"The drop in pay, though? From a nurse's salary to a waitress?" Deeva said.

"I am not a waitress. I am the host." Gertrude bent her elbow as if she were offering her arm. "I take particular pleasure in showing the ladies to their seats. Slipping their wraps oh, so slowly off their shoulders."

BJ laughed for the first time that night. Because she had spent years as one of them, shopping and sharing babysitters, lunches, carpools and trips to the laundromat, she knew what Gertrude meant. She, too, could pick out the woman drawn to her hairdresser while the capable fingers shaped each curl. The wives who would like black stockings or those who dreamt of a woman in work pants with rough hands. "I have yet to meet a woman who hasn't fantasized at least once about making love with a woman."

"And who could resist a woman in a tux?" Gertrude said.

"How easy it was!" BJ exclaimed, forgetting her troubles for a moment. "How we'd meet during the after-

noons, in our offices, our homes, in cars with no regrets and
no need of explanations. We all knew why we had to leave.
We would breeze in late to pick up children, fix the dinner,
apologize as if we'd stayed too long at the mall. The scent
of a woman on our sheets was not the betrayal it would
have been if it were from a man." It was a pleasure
unwatched over by the judges, the husbands, the bosses
and the gods. A place she wasn't sneaking from their sight
nor insulting them like River did. Forgetting them completely. That, BJ mused, was freedom.

"Let's go in the kitchen with the girls. I promised
them we'd bob for apples," BJ remembered.

"It's way past their bedtime," Jake said.

"Mom, quick!" One of the girls came running into the
room.

"No, it's time to wind down, like Jake said."

"No, look! June's outside trick or treating!"

The women hurried to the window. There, in the
middle of the old road through Emeryville, robed in a nun's
black wool habit, stood June. Alone. The spanish moss she
had saved from a trip to the rain forests of Oregon was tied
plentifully and eerily through her hair and, on closer
inspection, they could spot the wreath of dead cottonwood
leaves, richly colored and molded by the frost, and June's
face, darkened with something which had smeared like
blood. "Ohhhhh," the two little girls shuddered. "What's
she doing?"

The faces of everyone in Emeryville could be seen at
their windows and no one missed the small skull of beaver
or marmot which June carried in one palm, out like an
offering. A wisp of smoke, trained like a snake, wafted from
the center of it. "Must be sage," Myrna whispered, "because
anything else would have to be relit."

"What's sage?" one child asked, white as a ghost.

"It's good. Don't be afraid. It's for cleansing the home
of evil spirits."

The women watched in hushed silence as June
carried the dried and burning leaves to the four boundaries
of the town. East and the night sky broke over her head
into mists. South and she moved toward the watching
women. West and a dust she was kicking up, frothy at her
ankles, now swirled to her knees. North and the peaks,

blinded by a storm. June stopped and, in a weighted, dreamy dance, held the smoking skull to the stars. Animal skins hung from the sleeves of her gown. "We're sick of you, Old Man! Bringing your jerks to town! We're sick of your stupid laws!" June raised both hands into the air. "Destroying this land! Stealing our children! Who do you think you are?" She threw back her head. "You! Abraham! Apollo! Adam! Listen! We're sick of it! Sick, sick, sick! And we're fighting back!"

Even River, who had so long ago disavowed the gods, held her breath.

The polls were wild in the days before women's suffrage. Every election at least one man was killed, usually the incumbent. They voted in the Mint or the Gold Nugget or the Silver Dollar or the Copper King or the Jackpot or the Smith and Wesson. Most could barely write and signed their ballots with an X. The ability to read wasn't enforced as a requirement. Rosetta, who never lived to cast her vote in Emeryville, used to suggest, "Put stalls out, throw 'em some grain and they'll behave." And indeed, when suffrage triumphed, first in Wyoming where women were tough as nails, having no trees to hold onto in those awful winds, that was the first thing the women did, served coffee and donuts and made them form lines.

Election Day was no longer a cause of vigorous celebration, falling, as it did, in the prime of hunting season. No one crowded into the Mint to watch the local returns. A slice of moon moved in and out of wood smoke and shadows, and the sky was black before supper. Hearing that the coast was clear, the women met in the bar, their felt-lined boots dripping from the foot rails like laundry as they thawed.

"Nothing easier than hunting by headlights," Myrna said as the illegal shots boomed from the ridges above Emeryville.

Gertrude nodded. "Just pray they don't come by here. Isn't it time one of us got a good television?"

"You're welcome to watch mine. I have to get these girls to bed soon." BJ was watching River teach them how to play eight ball. BJ wore the expression her face had grown into since the suit was filed against her. The bars seemed to be already formed between them, the sentence passed. All she could do was stand and run her fingers over the steel.

"What's wrong with this television?" Myrna asked. "Eddie's already upset that no one appreciates his improvements." Eddie was convinced the new highway would put Emeryville, if not on the map, at least located on the way to the places which were. He installed a giant-screen TV. He had plans for a game room, a keno caller, a battalion of poker machines, blackjack, if the state would only change its mind about that sport. Since the Reverend Boyd was becoming such a big shot, Eddie had had second thoughts about the Reverend. Eddie thought he might be able to put a gambling bug in his ear.

"Eddie's a traitor," Gertrude said. "He can hardly wait until the highway's done."

The only part to be completed stretched two miles from either end of Emeryville. Construction was stalled due to weather and an unforeseen circumstance. Where the east-flowing creek emptied into the green river, twisting between cliffs and heading for the Columbia, was a bluff, stained orange with lichen and crowned with an enormous bald eagle's nest. Renovated and added onto each year, the nest teetered over the edge of the outcropping just enough for a carload of environmentalists to notice.

The old timers could have told them. They had watched the great-grandparents of the eagle learn to fly. The women could have told them when the eagle left and where it flew to. Those who had chickens knew it well and cursed the laws protecting it. But no one asked them. The highway's progress slowed while countless men in offices drew up alternate routes and lawyers planned ways to circumvent the laws. The women could have told them not to waste their time. Two weeks before the storms, before the eagle left for the salmon spawning on the northern river called Two Medicine, the bird was found, dead, tied to a survey stake at the foot of the steep and troublesome cliff. Construction, it was announced, would resume in the spring.

A few cars sped by and June jumped from the bar-stool. "Slow down!" she shouted, sticking her head out the door.

"Please," Gertrude said, "don't call attention to us." She hated this season, the hills spattered with blood, trailing from the wounds of the poorly shot deer, the tufts of fur caught by their frantic leaps over fences. "I can't stand it when they come in here. Waiting for us to ask what they've killed."

"You won't have to yell at those cars much longer, June. The new highway runs half a mile from town instead of through it."

"You think that will make a difference? This canyon will resound with the traffic as if we were living next to a racetrack."

"Can we please talk about something else besides fighting progress? Sometimes you women sound as if you'd rather be back scrubbing furs on rocks at the river," BJ said.

"Who was washing whose furs where?" Myrna said.

Deeva patted BJ's hand. "When's the first hearing?"

"Why? Are you going to write it on your engagement calendar?"

"Come on, BJ," Gertrude said, risking an arm around her friend. "What do you want us to do?"

"Kill him."

Deeva tried again. "Why does he want them so badly?"

BJ rolled her eyes. "He doesn't want them. Don't you see? They have nothing to do with it. This is his way of getting even."

"For what?"

BJ sighed. "For everything, Deeva. For everything."

Jake called from the far end of the bar. "All the candidates backed by the Christian Citizens have won. Even Nelson Bates of Bates' Post and Poles. They've asked the Reverend Boyd to say a few words."

Reverend Jimmy Raymond Boyd rolled three times past the screen before the camera of the local network centered him. Another moment passed while the wrong soundtrack spun off an interview with former teenage rodeo queens. "I am happy to be serving the people of this great state," the queen said, out of sync with the Reverend's lips. The Reverend Boyd was pacing the steps of the capital impatiently as if he, too, were waiting for his words to catch up with him. "Together, we can make this a home you all will be proud of," he said finally, "and not the laughingstock of the country. We have big plans for this legislature. Big plans." He bowed his head. "With the blessings of Our Lord, of course."

"Well, now that he's got his cronies in, maybe we can relax," June said.

"Maybe you can relax," BJ said, putting on her coat.

"BJ, don't worry. We're all behind you."

River was shaking the little girls' hands. "We've got to stick together, right?"

"Just remember," Gertrude called, "you're not alone."

BJ turned to grab her purse off the bar. "How do you figure?" she asked on her way out the door.

8

As Rosetta lay dying, the doctor cut the many rings off her swollen fingers and wrapped them in a cloth in his pocket. If she had known, she would have aimed the shotgun she kept, loaded and propped at the foot of her bed, and picked off his pecker. Once the pain began, however, Rosetta stepped out of this world in style, high heeled and furred, clutching a bottle of homemade gin.

High heeled was right. She had asked her girls to dress her in her finest gowns and every bauble she owned weighing down her neck and wrists. She had always worn too much makeup, a stage makeup that came with the trade, designed to take the place of sincerity, but when they brought the bowl of cosmetics to her, her hands fumbled. She could not for the life of her remember what pot of rouge or cream was for what. Her last days, dying from the complications of childbirth, Rosetta was dressed like a queen, but her faces were garish. And as Rosetta lay dying, the doctor, who had ridden horseback from Dry Gulch, stole her rings.

As was his nature to do. Life, liberty and the pursuit of happiness. Cross out happiness. Fill in wealth. What the history of this country is based on. Hunger for land? Shit, they couldn't fool Rosetta. You don't eat land. And a sorry meal it'd be in the West, dry and cracked as beef tongue, so many rocks you'd split your teeth. They didn't come out West 'cause they were starving. They came out to get rich. Progress, she used to tell her girls, is the straight line from one bank to another. It ain't got nothing to do with time.

Time was the straight line you meant to walk from point A to point B when, out of nowhere, point F stops you flat outside your door. That's what happened to her when she'd gotten pregnant. She had been too old to think about childbearing. And yet, her girls had begged her. It won't trouble you at all, they'd said. They would take care of the baby. All she had to do was provide a name and, sooner than she'd thought, an inheritance. Like the old fool she was, she had agreed. True to their word, they'd brought him up rightly. How could she have known that when he was old enough to leave, he wouldn't waste a minute, selling the hotel for a song, and right out from under those who had so pampered and adored him?

She'd only watched long enough to see her girls scattered. And at their age! Poor, hired out to less kindly homes, or worse: married, tied to a cabin and garden patch beside it while some man charted his destiny. Saloon gals, actresses, prostitutes; they were the ones with the pianos, the featherbeds. They never ran out of cocoa or bath salts. Act a little bad Shakespeare, or sing those sappy romantic songs they loved: With ten men to every woman in those days, Rosetta's girls were objects of reverence.

Since then, the town had interested her less and less. She'd been ready to forfeit her ties to it completely when she felt a tug at her waist and before she knew it, found herself plummeting into the unconscious body of an overweight virgin on a dirt road in back of her old hotel in the still, and probably forever, smoky town of Emeryville. Emeryville? Ha! The Indian trails, the mule trails, the towns, the rivers, the birds, even the stars were stamped with the names of the white men who had the audacity to believe themselves the first to see them. What if she rose in the morning and greeted the sun, calling out, "Good Morning, Rosetta!" And who was Emery, but another hard drinker like the rest? And a lot less observant at that.

History was obscure. Legends? They only dragged them out for special occasions, like their grandmother's china. And, if memory was the territory of the dead, the dead were losing ground. Few knew their names, even fewer knew to call them. Time was when people spoke regularly to their dead. It was nothing to go to the shed and have a tête-a-tête with the ghost of grandpa. Not anymore. People were afraid of the dead. Even their own relatives.

But Ellen. Ellen had a reputation with the dead. Nothing scared her, they said. Rosetta had been about to decide that Ellen's reputation was unwarranted that night when she arrived and Ellen, instead of recognizing her, had acted like Rosetta was a message in a bottle. Unasked for. Unanticipated. Unmiraculous, too. Rosetta was about to decide that Ellen really did have hypothermia (after all, the dead sometimes got sucked into the fevers of total strangers) when Ellen mentioned the church.

Churches were trouble if you ever heard of trouble. Rosetta had more than her share of run-ins with them, what with them bringing their ideas to whet the appetites of the unimaginative, stoning the whores, killing their own brothers. When women like Rosetta came out West, nobody cared about their pasts, who their parents were, how they got their money. She didn't have a heart of gold, but it wasn't exactly empty either. But there, every time she turned around, was some preacher, calling her sinner while his congregation raped the Indian women, dragging in the Indian women to confess their sins. Rosetta always made sure they left, those preachers. She could because she was richer and had more of a following.

But here they were again, stirring it up. Leaving Ellen, who had followed her like a puppy to the door, Rosetta was intent on a quick trip through town. It hadn't changed much since she was alive. Fewer houses, fewer bars. The same rutted roads. No horses tied to the posts outside the Mint, although their scent hung heavy in the air. The stars still held the village close and the song of the

creek...Oh! It could tell your future if you listened hard
enough. And there, in front of her, was the hotel, in no
worse shape than when she left it. The garden a bit more
unkempt. Lanterns in the windows as if she had just lit
them. Her knees bothered her now and there were more
steps than she remembered. She gripped the handrail, her
shoes in one hand. Soon, she heard laughter and—her eyes
filling with tears—music. There was nothing in heaven or
hell like the music made by an untuned piano and washtub
bass.

Rosetta wasn't surprised to find half the town piled
into the sturdy four-poster bed in her old room, or even one
of the men who stood, dressed and put on his preacher's
collar. Her hotel had been the focus of the dreams of many
in her day and she had seen more than one holy man in
that bedroom before. But when he spoke his preacher's
speech, admonishing someone, as they always did, for
luring him there, the legend circled around and around like
a tired dog and came to a rest at her feet. What a pack of
stray pups she'd unleashed on the world!

Since that night, Rosetta had tried to return, but
getting anyone's attention in Emeryville was like waving
outside the attic window to someone who lived on the first
floor. Even Ellen seemed preoccupied. There was only so
much the dead could do. She had been about to give up
when, smoothing the hips of the low cut dress she had been
buried in, she caught sight of herself in the mirror of the
world, the streaks of red on her wrinkling eyelids, the
powder piling up in the creases of her nose. "What are you
thinking, Rosetta, you old whore," she laughed. "You don't
call them. They come to you."

The windows inside the cafe were papered with a foil
of frost, glinting like aluminum whenever the electric beer
sign flashed. The women sat at an oilcloth-covered table in
the back, the piles of boots, scarves, mittens and hats
strewn in a circle around them like petals off a flowering
bush. For weeks, the temperature hadn't risen above zero
and many nights, it had fallen to fifteen below. During the
day, the blue sky glistened as if through a sheet of ice.

"Ah, I'm finally getting warm." June, tucked into an expedition parka, lifted her face from the steam rising from a stack of pancakes.

"I hope so," Gertrude said. "That coat's rated to forty below."

Like deer who watch a cabin for months, waiting for the door to open, the car to start, and seeing no one, gradually make their way onto the lawn at dusk, so the women began testing the waters of Emeryville. Encountering only taunts while walking past the school yard or into the hills, only insults as they sat outside on their stoops, mugs smoking in their gloved hands, they became braver. The last bastion was the cafe and they had been meeting there since February. To reclaim the cafe was as close to reclaiming the town as they could muster their spirits to want to.

June grabbed the honey and drizzled it over her lunch. Since she'd returned to the cafe, new items had been added to the menu on which, previously, coffee was the only thing not grilled, mashed or french fried. June ordered, as if it were inconceivable to serve salad without sprouts, tea which was not herbal or lettuce that was not iceberg. Her wish was the cafe employee's command, not because she tipped generously or whined insufferably, but because no one in Emeryville could forget her Halloween performance. They were, frankly, afraid of her.

"Could I have a tiny glass of real milk for my coffee?" June pointed to the nondairy creamer on the counter.

River bobbed a tea ball of wintergreen in her cup, her earlobes bruised from the cold. "Coffee contributes to the dependence of Third World countries on our demands for drugs."

Myrna pushed her chair back from the table, blowing smoke in a direction to minimize conflict. "Speaking of imperialist demands, I'm afraid that the Reverend has got us this time."

"Surprise, surprise," BJ said, sharing Myrna's cigarette.

"I don't see how he can get away with it," Deeva said. "Aren't church and state to be kept separate?"

River rolled her eyes, but ignored Deeva. "What bothers me is that we have no choice. It's going to be a state monument in our town and we, as citizens, have no choice."

"And we are the ones who will have to look at it day in and day out."

June stirred maple syrup into her coffee. "It's not going to be that bad. It could be worse. It could be that mutilation."

"You mean the Crucifixion?" Deeva gasped.

"At least, it's a woman. At least, it's the Virgin Mary," Gertrude said.

"A woman with no choice of childbirth, no access to abortion and then, of course, no power to save the child she has," BJ remarked. "Story of our times. Story of my life. If it's not already written over these hills, it might as well be. It's written on every mother's face."

"How's the trial going?" Gertrude asked delicately. It was rare to see BJ in town. Even rarer to spend time with her.

BJ shrugged. When she wasn't traveling miles on buses with no heat, she was driving in borrowed cars to meetings with lawyers, psychologists and teachers. She had also tried the feminist lecture circuit. Her plight as a mother and a lesbian were the concession every women's group needed to make to social issues. After the first few treks, bundled in a space blanket and scraping the frost from the bus window into shavings in her lap, to sleep on floors and eat mass chili with twenty ex-college girls for little money, BJ realized that they went home from these meetings feeling better than she. They founded no support groups, lobbied no legislatures, raised no money to hire lawyers or babysitters. Not one letter found its way to an editor. She could almost hear them saying, as they filed out the door, "It's sad, but she should have known."

"We really want to know," June probed.

"Look, I'm tired of it," BJ sighed.

They bowed their heads to their cups, all but Deeva, who felt a need to insist. "I don't understand why you think it's our fault."

"I said I was tired. Tired and, I might add, broke."

"And I don't see how you can expect me to pay all those bills. Goodness knows, I paid a lot of them."

"They do pile up, don't they?" BJ said flatly.

"It's only fair that I send the rest her way," Deeva said, turning to the group defensively. "I wasn't the one who had the kids in the first place."

"I realize it's my problem and not yours," BJ said. The judge had almost dismissed the case, as her lawyer had assured her he would do. After all, she had full custody already. There was no proof of neglect or incompetence. The children's grades were good, although lately, when they didn't want to go to school, she could think of no reason to make them. There was no change in economic status, no change of residence. But as she stood to leave the pre-trial hearing, in her nylons and pumps, resenting her ex--husband in his jeans, the prosecution shouted, in a desperate, but obviously planned move, "But your Honor, she is a lesbian."

The courtroom had grown hushed. "Objection," her lawyer called, but before any argument was made, the judge leaned forward and asked, "Is this true?"

"Pardon me, your Honor," BJ said, "but could you tell me if my answer is legally any of your business?"

In subsequent trials, the judge allowed the prosecution to enter as evidence the newspaper articles of her arrest, a videotape of Ellen's guest appearance on *Good Evening, Montana* and a taped testimony from the children on which they admitted that, yes, their mother's sexual preference was known to them. She had not wept. But, when she heard their small voices, trapped inside the cheap machine, colorless, defenseless, used against her, she knew she was going to lose.

Her family became thick and sour as a soup too long untouched. Inside their heavily draped home, they lied for one another, letting in no one. "No, Mom's at the lawyers." "No, they've gone out to play." "No, Jake, I'd rather you didn't come with me to the courtroom." The girls alternated between clinging to BJ and pushing her away, threatening to live with their father. They had few friends left and no one was to be trusted. They fought with each other and with BJ. BJ accused everyone. As if every feature of the husband—a daughter's nose, Jake's quick temper, the way one child sliced an orange before peeling it—was another betrayal, was evidence of him gaining, slipping in through the loose casings of her windows like the cold and undermining her. Jake accused: only love for him would elicit such defense.

The other women had tried. Gertrude brought presents, imported coffee or catalogs, slices of cake, books from the library in the city, but she was thanked politely at the door. Maggie's offers to baby-sit were refused or, when accepted, paid for with more than BJ could afford, a bottle of Italian wine, roses. Their gifts were too late. She would not be favored. BJ glanced around the cafe table at these women who, punished by her silence, formed an invisible web outside her. Virile, athletic, with no responsibilities, they played with revolution, taunting the state and church. What did they have to lose? Their presence was a daily reminder of the blame she leveled at each of their heads, for their failure to prevent this was somehow a greater betrayal than the enemy's.

Deeva was more than ever determined to change the subject. "Why doesn't he put it in his own yard?"

"It is in his own yard. Or was his own yard."

"I can't believe the state went for it. Not only did they buy the land from him, but they're going to pay for the statue, too."

"If this doesn't get him a television show, what will?"

"Tourism is down in Yellowstone," BJ said. It didn't take much to figure out why the Reverend would want to erect a ninety foot statue of the Madonna and Child above the town of Emeryville or why the legislature agreed to his plan, even to providing the publicity and a National Guard helicopter to lift it into place. The highway was under heavy criticism. The schools were poor, the university system crumbling and, despite all the promises from the contractors, there were still few jobs. People were beginning to comprehend that the new roads through the belly of the state, which they would be paying for whenever they filled up their tanks, led nowhere. There was no place to commute to. No attraction for those driving through on their way to vacations in other states, none but the Bitterroot Pit, the largest strip mine in the world. "But Christ is popular again," BJ said.

"That's true. Fundamentalists are clogging the airwaves and selling out the auditoriums. Survivalist groups have founded entire towns in Idaho, luring people from across the Bible Belts, people who have never heard of Idaho except for Idaho potatoes, and they probably thought it was a brand name," River said. "The government probably feels there's no reason a few of those tourist dollars couldn't swing up this way."

"Besides," BJ said, "the Reverend's calling in his favors. If it wasn't for his endorsement, half of them wouldn't have been elected."

"But why Mary? The Virgin isn't very high on the Protestant agenda."

"And Protestantism never went over big here in Emeryville either, right?" BJ continued. "What better way to court the Irish Catholics?"

"He doesn't call it the Virgin Mary," June said. "He calls it 'Our Lady of the Canyons,' and says it is dedicated to all mothers."

"And since it's state funded, it has to be a work of art, not religious. They ran a competition for an artist from the state to do it."

"Mary will look like Annie Oakley," June said.

"There'll be Brahma bulls in the manger and Jesus will be wrapped in a bandanna," Myrna said.

"Do you really think it'll be a western artist?" Deeva asked.

"What other kind are there? Our only museum is devoted to the cows and cowboys of Charlie Russell and what painters survive, spend their lives trying to improve on him," said Gertrude. Scanning the oils of tipis and buffalo, of wranglers and mountain men which were in the contemporary galleries, she often wondered if the West had changed in the last one hundred and fifty years. The challenges met by modern artists—how to react to the skyscraper, to television, to, at least, the camera— remained in the future for these artists. "These guys are still trying to draw a good horse."

"The Madonna will look like the rest. Even Sacajawea looks like she just stepped off the Mayflower." Myrna had been accosted with it since childhood. The bronze roper in the town square in Cumberland, his face lined and mean, a lariat suspended above his head in a deadly caduceus. Lewis and Clark, more familiar than saints or politicians, their stories more at home here than the Greeks'. Lewis and Clark smoking pipes on the hilltops. Lewis and Clark in the airport. Lewis and Clark, carved like Mount Rushmore, above the entrance to her school. Lewis and Clark on a multitude of highway signs, always pointing ahead. As a girl, she had thought one day she would catch up with them.

"Our Lady of the Canyons," Gertrude spat in disgust. "And who of us would have guessed that the Reverend owned the crystal rock?" Ever since she had read the announcement, a small blurb under congressional news, when she closed her eyes, the bluff of borite shattered like a sun, its tiny teeth clattering like an avalanche. She had tried to imagine a statue, spoiling the view of the peaks, or how it would be to pass it on a solitary walk. Perhaps she could erase it, her mind airbrushing it out of the canyon the way it did the telephone lines through the valleys, the outcast blue and unnatural greens in the clay banks near mine tailings.

Maggie sat silently. Her silence was nothing new. Emerging from days alone in her cabin, Maggie usually glared at them as if they were there to steal her meat. She calmed down with time, took her hands from her pockets, her hat off her head. River had long ago relinquished her obligation to include Maggie in conversations. "And what are you feeling about this?" she would ask in the round robin approach which was her trademark. After countless attempts, to which Maggie, burrowing further under her stetson, would grumble, "nuthin," River left her to her oppressions. Maggie was a grump when she was sober.

But this time, as Maggie stood, tipping her stetson, she looked steadied, as if with a secret, and when she smiled, the tracks around her eyes broke into the marks of skaters on the river. "If man was made in God's image, where do you get the image for God's mother?" She bowed. "They picked me to carve the Madonna."

Several minutes passed. She thought them simply too stunned to applaud. "What's wrong?" Maggie finally asked, anticlimactically.

"How did this happen?" BJ frowned.

"I applied. It was an open competition. I guess I was the only zealot who qualified." Maggie chuckled.

"But why didn't you tell us?"

"I'm telling you now. I just found out myself."

"Why didn't you tell us you wanted to do it? That you were going to apply?"

Maggie sighed. "You know how long it takes to get agreement around here. And I didn't think I needed your approval. What if I didn't get it? I've applied to lots of things before."

River was shaking her head, baffled at how this could have slipped past her. "It's the perfect strategy. It's ingenious. Get one of our own to betray us."

"Betray? It's better I do it than some asshole with a palette knife in one hand and a skinning knife in the other. Or don't you agree?"

"How much are they paying you?" River demanded.

"I thought," Maggie shouted, throwing her hat to the floor, "you'd be proud of me."

"We already were proud of you," June said, smiling indulgently.

And it was true. Maggie's art was precious to them. The summer she painted only clouds and the winter she was seldom seen, drawing charcoal comets and round, black stones, belonged to them. The making of her art was as inseparable from their lives as the white bark of aspen stretched tautly over its trunk, was as specific and healing as the inner sleeve of willow June used to cure headaches. This art was not for everyone. These sculptures, these drawings, oils, pastels were artifacts, shards of a culture they were forming, but which seemed lately to be vanishing before their eyes. A time they felt free. They were sure no one else could be trusted with them.

"You say the Reverend doesn't know you're the artist?" Gertrude said.

"No one's to know until the unveiling. But I've asked to remain anonymous, regardless. No sense causing a stir. I'll get my reward."

"Are you going to tell us what you plan to do or do we get to be as surprised as the Reverend will be?"

"Since when has any of you been concerned about what I'm working on until it's finished?"

"But Maggie," River said, "this is public art."

"It's the crystal rock," Deeva said.

Gertrude interpreted. "It's important what kind of image comes across. It's not just you this time. You're one of us."

"I'm an artist," Maggie said, leaving her hat on the floor and kicking open the door, "and I don't belong to anybody."

Gertrude found Maggie the next day, burrowing deep in her shack. The sun, as the door opened, gazed into the dark like a flashlight.

"Maggie, come out of there!" Gertrude was determined to flush her out like the blue grouse hiding in the brush. "Those miners must be your kin because you're hibernating just like they do."

Maggie grumbled from the shadows. "So, what's the verdict? Your friends decide what they want me to sculpt?" If she had a shotgun, she would have aimed it. She was sick of company, in particular, these women. She'd been thinking more and more of when she was young, of how she rode horseback for hours and never saw another human being. Lately, it seemed like all she heard was snowmobiles and this constant babble of conversation. It was supposed to be a quiet country, the North.

"Maggie, you'll never change. If you're not a hermit, you're a whore."

Maggie stomped into the light in her long underwear, her hair matted, her boots unlaced. "Just leave me alone. I already decided I'm not gonna do it."

"Do what?"

"I see what you meant. You're right. I'm turning it down."

"But I wanted to tell you something."

Maggie interrupted. "They leveled the sight yesterday."

When Maggie stormed out of the cafe the afternoon before, she had thought herself on the way home. She had walked fast, head down, up the south slopes dotted with snow, the cottonwood unraveling into pale bark below her. The cold air flew into her chest and lodged there, beating painfully close to her skin. When she stopped to look ahead, she was not heading home, but to the low, round hill, distinguishable from the sweep of ridges which circled it only in that it rose out of the prairie of sagebrush self contained.

She could just make out the ledge which hid the borite on its other side. It was a rock. Not a temple, not a church. It was no shrine, no mecca she was heading toward. It hadn't the magnificence of Canyon de Chelly, nor the view from the nearby peaks. How to explain what it meant to the many who walked to it, who seldom spoke of it, who hadn't even a common name for it, only their own, private ones. There was a time when people would spend a whole day watching a rock like that, the softer stones tumbling to the surface, the lichen sprayed across its flanks, marveling at how time could turn a rock clear and golden, capable of shattering light. She had learned so much when she paid that kind of attention to life, not the cut down, parceled out, bite size reality presented to her as life, not the events, plot, time line of a life, but the rich articulations, visits with ancestors, animals, the body itself loud with chemistry and the faintest imaginings.

Maggie stopped and the hawk in her chest escaped through her lips with small, high-pitched shrieks. Smoke rose from the top of the hill she was moving toward. She stood watching as the sound of thunder rolled toward her through the thick particles of cold air. An hour after the explosion, the small stones still rattled and Maggie was safely warm and at home, the nuggets tumbling inside her, her bones less solid, more frail.

"They're pouring concrete for the slab as soon as the weather warms," Maggie told Gertrude. "Thirty feet of the ninety will be the tower she stands on."

Gertrude wiped the hair out of Maggie's eyes. "We heard, but Maggie, you're not the one who caused the explosion. You're just the one left with the rubble."

Maggie turned back into the dark of the cabin.

Gertrude grabbed her arm. "You can't blame us. We were prepared to hate the statue, no matter who did it. It's like the cross held toward the witches during the Inquisition, the burning cross marched through the towns of the South."

Maggie motioned to a chair and shut the door behind Gertrude. "What miserable, human piece of junk could heal that wound? What could I make that would replace it? I'd be just another white person, making my mark, carving into the trunk of the tree."

"Maggie, remember when Myrna brought her brother up here and he asked you who gave you the right to use sage?"

"Yeah, I told him the sage did," Maggie chuckled, but instantly recovered her frown. "Gertrude, I'm telling you. I don't know what I'm doing."

Gertrude sank into the offered chair. "That's what I came to tell you. Everyone was so mad when you left. I went to talk to Ellen. What she said makes sense. She thinks the Madonna will speak for herself."

The stone was delivered on the back of a logging truck, three pieces of granite so large they must have dynamited a mountain for them. She'd been a fool to think the government would spring for marble. After the cranes had lifted them, positioning them upright in the clearing behind her studio, after the crew set up the scaffolding, the rocks looked captured as Gulliver, trapped in the webs of line. It was then that Maggie recognized them as those which fell during the last explosion for the highway. They had lain on the side of the graded path all winter like a fresh kill or three fallen gods. "So," Maggie said, circling the pink stone, flecked with gray, "you're from here."

Maggie sat under a yellow pine, a safe distance from the rocks which loomed, unpredictable, until the moon brushed past the needles and caught in the uppermost branches. She leaned back on her heels, her spine against the trunk, thinking. What did she know? She knew the North was built on granite, hard, older than their paltry histories. It grew beneath the feet of everyone who lived here, under the valleys, the mountains and now, as it rose, unburied, skeletal, above her, the granite seemed to float, as she had been told the land floated—the continent afloat in granite. The Father of Us All, as the Reverend liked to refer to his police chief of a god, was a pup compared to the life cycle of this granite.

She had been told that it took skilled masons, trained in the ways of stone, to see inside granite, to how the grains, never apparent on the surface, were lined with crystal. Only they could imagine how each shock wave from the chisel would fan out. The angle of the tool, which way the rock would cleave, how the sound could guide them by its hollowness or brilliancy, these were matters of developed feeling. To carve it, Maggie thought, shaking her head, she knew too little and too much.

Waves of moonlight washed over the surface, which was as pebbled and ridged as the shell of abalone. The stone trembled with shadows as the winds carried clouds, owls, bats and leaves between it and the light overhead. When Maggie thought of the word, "mother," it was the curved slope of the view outside her window which came to mind, not human, surely not biblical. She had traced and retraced that slope with her fingers and, later, with pens. Mother was a stone dropped into a pool of water, was a word, animal, whispered inside her when she met other animals on the trail. It was like the ticking clock she held next to abandoned kittens to calm them. It caused those wild and guarded to reveal themselves, unafraid.

But Madonna? The Madonna was a mother who lost her son to a crazed mob. Marah, the root, meaning bitter. A bitter Madonna was BJ. Losing, too. What could she say about this rock that wouldn't be burying it again?

Maggie picked herself up to go to bed. As she walked past on her way toward the cabin, she let her palm brush across the rock's surface, night-cool and damp, without commitment. To her surprise, she felt an eyelid open under her touch. She stopped, studying the stone as the flat colors changed to liquid and back, the moon traveling in and out of the clouds. Again, and her fingers were following strong, carved cheekbones. She felt certain of the angle of the chisel. The moon seemed far, too far for a human hand to touch, but here was this rock, near, reachable. As if she could call it sister, could ask it what it thinks of her life.

In the weeks which followed, Maggie's hands landed and left the granite like a flock of birds. She had wanted to carve a powerful Mary, with muscles like Jake's and a thin beard like her own, dribbling from the chin like moss. A Madonna with a crew cut, maybe an Afro, a cross tattooed on her arm, definitely a beer belly like Myrna's. She pictured her in jeans, in western style. Our Lady of the Canyons would be a cowgirl and capable, like the women she knew. She looked forward most to the child, a large infant, wiggling from its mother's arms, one leg dangling in the pose of the paintings she studied in the books. Only the swaddling, draped across its waist would expose, not a tiny penis, but a girl's vulva. Maggie had spent many evenings close to her stove, cackling at the dyke Madonna and her daughter, Maggie's laugh like a family of crows picking over a carcass. She even imagined herself as one of them, pulling strands of the Reverend Jimmy Raymond Boyd's hair in her beak, digging her talons into his chest. She should have known that revenge was never as easy as it seems.

When she tried to carve anything that she didn't already feel under the surface, anything which didn't align with the veins of quartz tunneling, meeting and colliding like the paths of an ant farm—a beard, perhaps, or something as innocent as an ear—the images would stop and it was impossible to score one line in. The granite would harden like diamond, as she had been told it would if it was exposed to air for years. The statue emerging was unlike anything she had planned.

It was at one of those times, when the rocks sat mute and ignoring her, when she had bloodied her fists uselessly with the hammer and the rock chipped into small, awkward arrowheads, when she left the clearing, deserted and doubtful, that the women began to visit. Not all at once. Only a few, at first. June bringing a pot of rosemary to freshen the cabin. "Rosemary is for memory," she told Maggie, continuing a conversation Maggie didn't know they had started. "Rosemary had white blossoms until the Virgin threw her cape over it on the way to Egypt. It was an azure cape and turned the flowers blue."

No one mentioned the statue directly, nor did a single person duck behind the studio for a closer look. They sat with her awhile, or walked with her, uncannily arriving just as she had helplessly lain the chisel down.

"River, I can't stand it," Maggie said as she approached her shack. "This way of working takes forever." River was waiting with a salve, made from the last year's comfrey, and a sock, and she started to bind Maggie's swollen hands with them.

"What's your hurry? You act like it's still the gold rush."

"But, this isn't anything like the gold rush. Who ever heard of a miner waiting for the gold to surface?"

When the rhythmic beating of the chisel stopped, they came, as if someone knew and sent them. And no one asked to see it. And no one asked when it would be done.

"It's weird, Myrna. Sometimes, I think it's talking to me."

"Of course, it is."

"That," Maggie said, taking a long drag from her cigarette, "makes me feel crazy. How could a rock talk."

"Maggie, don't go stupid on me."

Myrna remembered with what exasperation her grandmother had answered her questions as a child. "Because they do," she would repeat, when Myrna asked, year after year, why the brains worked for tanned hides. "But, isn't there a story? How we came to know?" she would ask. "Myrna," her grandmother would say, studying her, puzzled, "we have always known these things."

Maggie was grinning. "OK, Myrna, if by chance, granite could speak, how could I understand it?"

Myrna felt like her grandmother when she said, "Isn't it enough to know you do?"

Maggie wished, when the rocks hardened and the images stopped for good, when the day she approached the stones to find them finished, the pieces would rise, one after the other, like angels over the stand of quaking aspen, become weightless, and she would watch the granite halo, the breasts, the robes pass across the sky toward the site and become whole. But the trucks and cranes came as before, leaving her alone by the yellowing grass, watching the grubs scatter. Two weeks shy of her deadline, and Maggie was through.

The day of the unveiling, in April when snow should be weighing the lower boughs to the ground, the Reverend Jimmy Raymond Boyd stopped to marvel at the tulips. Tulips were not the only surprise. Azaleas were blooming the color of old lace, flourishing in the month where snow usually alternated with rain. Though the meteorologists had been predicting, besides the falling of California into the sea, besides the surfacing of islands and the gradual sinking of others, the formation of a tropical belt in

Montana, no one who had ever lived in that country of approaching glaciers would believe it. It was odd, though. The weather in Emeryville had become almost balmy.

Hours before the public would arrive, the Reverend was picking his way through the prairie. It was good the statue was so far off the main road. No hoodlums would climb so far to vandalize it, especially with the barbed wire the state had stretched across the boundaries of what was once his land. It had been years, perhaps since he was a boy, since he had walked in the woods on purpose. He noticed the bright patches of moss campion. "Like pincushions," he thought, as sagebrush grazed his sleeves.

He had spent a lot of time figuring it out: the souvenir stand right off the proposed exit, a franchise of postcards, small replicas and memorabilia. The state had agreed to let him lead tours, even to accept donations when the pious wanted to make pilgrimages. He still had pull in the legislature, had insisted on the steps, made of concrete, the brass handrails, planters and a poured sidewalk through the sage. Out of his own pocket came the snowmobile for those who wished to make the trip in winter. After all, if tourists endured the extreme cold and snow to visit a geyser in Yellowstone, they would surely pay their respects here. He envisioned strings of colored lights on the pines at Christmas and a sold-out weekend at Easter.

"Nature doesn't thrill them like it used to," the Reverend had said to the legislature. "We need more, something the tourists can't get anywhere else." If only the Lady would talk, like the oil slicks on the sides of tractor-trailers in Carolina, which transformed into images of Christ, or like the wooden shrines of the Madonna, who spoke to the Mexicans, he would never have to set foot in these mountains again. He could almost taste it. Our Lady of the Canyons would be more popular than the Virgin of Guadalupe.

Atop the hill, disguised in tarps and line, the statue stood on its enormous concrete slab. Sisal twisted back and forth across the canvas, wrapping the artwork like a hostage. For the dedication and the unveiling, he had the promise of live, network coverage. It was up to the artist now, whoever he was. He only hoped the man was equal to the task. "Thank you, Father," the Reverend mumbled as he knelt under the statue, the fat, cumulus clouds passing east over the prairie as shadows.

Who would have thought the nightmares, surreal and illuminated as his vision of Calvary, would turn out to be the answer to his prayers? They were enough to wake anyone. They were one reason, in fact, why he'd joined the ministry early, when he was barely an adolescent—to escape them. They frightened him. They attracted him. Definitely, they confused him, unsure as he was of their origin, whether racial, familial or biblical. Because of their claim on him, he suspected them of evil. Of course, he had never told his father.

Since he was a child, over and over, it was the same dream. In it, he found himself naked in a room, the dark walls slit with eyes. It did no good to hide, either, because under the flounced spread of the huge four-poster would be more eyes, skin, hair and teeth. Since he'd moved to Emeryville, the frequency of the dream had increased and the bed had grown large enough to accommodate an entire community, the miner and Loretta, a vortex of naked bodies, sucked into and under the sheets; the two singing sisters, divested of their Sunday best; a strange woman, tickling him with ostrich feathers; all the women he had made it his personal vendetta to condemn. The nightmare always seemed to last forever and more than once did he think he had drowned in its folds, before he was spit out, trembling, his pajamas soaked with sweat, on his own twin bed in the trailer.

Perhaps it was his newfound prestige, his authority, his prayers, but one night, slipping through the smoke of Emeryville's houses toward his biggest nightmare, the Reverend Jimmy Raymond Boyd felt something had changed. The waiting rooms were empty. Peeking into the parlor, the Reverend saw the woman who lived there, her bare breasts filling out the bibs of a pair of overalls, one nipple slipping around the strap. "Jesus, help me," he whispered to himself, but he was glad she was preoccupied. She was plucking the strings of a country bass and crooning an old blues about money.

The bed, as he feared, was large, but he was grateful that this time, when he climbed in, he found it empty. He had not, however, anticipated the stench of sweat and previous sex. He became immediately asthmatic and would have wakened had it not been for the woman who entered, humming softly and holding a book. She was wearing a worn flannel gown, her graying hair was pulled back from her face and she was smiling. She had almost the same features as he, the long nose, the sunken owl-eyes. She seemed harmless enough. Best of all, when she crawled in, no skin of hers touched his. Even her legs were stockinged. As she began to read aloud, in the slow, enunciated prose women use for the old or very young, he felt his head fall onto her shoulder. Cradled, he let himself relax and she stroked his thin hair, tilting his lips to where he nuzzled and sucked, moving them from one slick nipple to the other until her stomach rose toward his, her spine undulating along the sheets, and she called his name. Loud. "Jimmy!" she gasped, fumbling with the fly to his pajamas.

"Shhh," he hissed, but it was too late. Rosetta, rank with rose water and rye, shot into his life.

"I should have never named you, you little bastard," she whispered, her lips grazing his earlobes.

Jimmy rolled to his side and pulled the blanket tightly around him. "I don't know who you are, old woman." He spat. "Whore!"

Rosetta sat on the edge of June's bed, her ostrich feather robe cloudy in the dim light, and began to calmly trim her toenails. Jimmy listened with horror as they clattered onto the linoleum like calcified, crescent moons. "I could almost feel sorry for you."

"If you'd only believe," the Reverend recited, coming back to himself, despite a faint trembling, "your sins could be forgiven."

"Belief?" Rosetta laughed. "Like I used to tell my girls, belief is like the rouges and powders they sort through each morning, hunting out this or that, what'll make you look good and what'll keep you out of trouble."

"You don't understand. I am offering you salvation."

"Have some respect," Rosetta said, reapplying her lip paint in the dark. "If it weren't for me, you wouldn't have a pot to piss in. You wouldn't, I might add, be here."

"And just what do I have?" Jimmy said, sitting up. "Hundreds of acres I can't pay someone to take, surrounding a town a person'd be a fool to content himself with. Oh, thank you, if you're the one responsible. Thanks a lot. A threadbare church with ten pews and a barrel stove for heat."

"Never satisfied," Rosetta said, fingering the gold nugget she wore, strung on a chain around her neck. "Must be in the blood."

"What do you want from me, old woman? You have been disturbing my sleep all my life."

"Me? Disturbing your sleep?" She stared at the scrawny knees the Reverend was pulling to his chest. She could feel sorry for him, after four generations, still trying to find a way out of this broken-down town. "Listen, little bastard," Rosetta said, bending annoyingly close to his ear, "I might have an idea that'll help you and me both."

The Reverend rose and dusted off his knees. He checked his watch. The reporters were already stepping through the prickly pear and thistle toward him. He smiled, imagining the impression he must have made, kneeling so long in front of the statue, lost in the thought of how it had come to him. A few reporters stumbled, their high heels sinking into the loosened ground of the prairie dog town. The displaced rodents were screaming their protests, baring their teeth and scurrying futilely between the pillaging legs. He knew he should have insisted on paving the whole thing.

"Welcome," he said, climbing down the concrete steps to meet them. "Welcome."

The Reverend joined the reporters under the canopy which the state had erected for its officials, the press and members of the Arts Council, the Tourist Bureau, the Governor and his aides. While he waited for the speeches to begin, he surveyed the crowd, disappointed. Anyone who wasn't squeezed under the awning, who didn't wear a name tag or carry a camera, who wasn't part of the conspiracy between church and state for economic renewal, was from Emeryville, a ragged caste who stood to the back, shuffling and pushing their children closer than they dared go themselves toward the company of suited gentlemen under the tent. The Reverend recognized his flock painfully. They stood apart, even from each other, the retired and those too young yet to leave, the curiosity seekers from the mines and those from the bar, unsure whether to take their hats in their hands.

The Reverend was especially disturbed by the number of those women, whose presence he had not anticipated. He could see how they drew the attention of the reporters, the wind buffeting their brilliant silks, dressed more for carnival in Rio than a church affair. They had their nerve, although they seemed sufficiently penitent, approaching the foot of the statue, one by one, placing green wreaths and garlands, arrangements of wild flowers. Harmless enough, he told himself, until he noticed the fat girl off to the side. What was she doing there, a mockery of a church goer in her tight dress and heels? He hoped the reporters wouldn't recognize her. If she started leaving sacrifices, he would call the police.

The speeches began and he was proud to hear his name acknowledged again and again as first, the Governor and next, the many Council Members applauded his efforts. Soon, it was his turn and not a moment too soon, for the whole flock of women had settled down, cross-legged, even Ellen, on the earth, just like geese. He did not mince words.

"Brethren, when I presented this dream to my fellow statesmen, I was sure of one thing. A monument, dedicated to the mother of Jesus and, therefore, to all women of the world. A testament of the faith of this state's good Christians and a gift to strengthen the faith of those who travel through it. Many of you know the trials and tribulations I have endured in my ministry to this forsaken place, where evil holds sway, a present-day Gomorrah. Many of you may ask, 'Why place an image of Jesus in such a town? Why not reward our communities that are in service to the Lord and not the Devil?'"

A chickadee tossed its black-capped greeting from the crown of the draped figure and flew. A marmot scrambled down the shale behind the shrine. "I have felt no greater calling than the one which led me to this profession. And I know now that there was no better place for me to be than Emeryville. And no better place for this statue. Where, but Emeryville, is the presence of such an ideal of womanhood so needed, what better place for the Mother and Child?"

A signal was given and the National Guard tangled the lines so badly that it was a quarter hour before they were untangled. The audience groaned in suspense. When the heavy tarps finally fell, everyone's hopes and dreams were crushed like the bouquets underneath the fabric. Instead of the Mary they expected, a placid mother with child, a Renaissance Mary, a Venetian mother, a peeling, fresco, Mexican virgin, even a modern, shorn, leather-jacketed goddess, was a rock. A rock which looked exactly as it had when it was loaded onto the back of the logging truck and delivered to Maggie's yard. They could not identify one mark made by the human hand.

The women glared, first at each other, then at Maggie, who stood proudly, her red cowgirl boots shining, while the black Spanish cape and fedora were littered with wood chips and the goat hair which never left the air around her.

"What is this, a joke?" the Reverend cried for them all and was about to say more when the words stopped as if a gigantic slab of granite had rolled into place before the open cavern of his mouth.

9

The logs collapsed into coals and Myrna, gathering her sleeping bag around her and walking with it, the whole of her bedding following her out of bed, rose to put on more wood. Out the window, the night was hard edged with silver and, as she reached for a piece of the split pine, the halved moon set behind the ridge.

For weeks, she had been sleeping the sleep of those who camp in grizzly country, a ridiculous sleep in the face of violence, that humpbacked carnivore, snapping twigs outside a tent. Lately, she had accepted, as those campers eventually did, that the night was not for sleeping, but for sitting straight up in bed, weapon in hand. Myrna knelt by the stove, laying kindling in the sparkling nest of cinders. When the wood caught, she watched the smoke rise to the blackened ceiling above her. Soon, it would be morning.

Her fear was unfounded. For in the years following the Reverend Jimmy Raymond Boyd's crusade, Ellen's confession, the siege of harassment and threats, Emeryville had returned to its poverty-stricken normality. The cows were led from their hiding places, hands were removed from over the mouths of babes, those who had played dead came back to life, but just barely. The lesson of the soldiers had been learned: toleration was one thing, but there were limits to what would be celebrated. They'd been crazy to think themselves exceptions. Even the bikers, their beer money welcome at the Mint, had been told to leave their "colors" at the door.

Those who could finance their exits had done so. The more recent arrivals had only paused and gone on quickly to the bigger cities. The hippies, who had gradually come to resemble the rest of the wool and flannel-clothed population, traded their crosscuts for chain saws after the first heavy and unidealistic snow. When the next few summers of no work beat them down as only the promise of another approaching winter could do, they wired home for money, packed their babies in their pickups and left, too.

The highway was completed just in time for the next administration to freeze federal funding for jobs, education and health care. The Home laid off all but a staff trained in emergencies and Jake followed the construction crew down the road to their next bridge in Idaho. She wrote BJ and sent money, which quickly went to lawyers, and complained nights in trailers and cafes with the boys, dog-tired and veteran, about how their women let the coins just slip through their hands. After the exodus of workers, the new passing lanes were an anachronism before they were used.

An hour after her husband, his new wife and two police officers came for her children, BJ locked the door of her home in Emeryville behind her, carried two suitcases to the bar and asked Sam to hail the afternoon bus. When Gertrude came to visit, she found only a note, asking her to haul what things BJ had left to the bar to give away to Emeryville's poor. In the one festivity of that meager season, River and Gertrude distributed pots and dishes, coffee grinders and sheet music, toys and boxfuls of carefully folded clothing. Eddie, who had purchased her piano, supplied the refreshments, and the locals, rail thin and tipsy, danced to the old tunes while Sam played the keyboard and sang:

> "Shine on, shine on harvest moon,
> Up in the sky..."

while the women sent their young off to tell others, the men dancing with each other,

> "I ain't had no lovin'
> since January, February..."

the dancing men trading purple berets, red straw hats, as the women tossed them from the boxes,

> "June or July."

"Why didn't you tell us she was leaving?" River asked Eddie, scowling.

"She must have figured you wouldn't understand or she would have told you herself. I don't know. But she didn't have much to fight for anymore. The court decided. She lost them. Why should she stay here and hold her head up?"

"Do you think she went to stay with Jake?"

"Jake called the bar the other night. All her letters have been returned to the sender, unforwarded. I guess I was the first one to let her know," Eddie said, swaggering in spite of himself.

"Would you go live in a trailer with a bunch of construction workers?" Gertrude asked wearily.

Deeva sat on a barstool near Myrna, ecstatically watching the revelers. "Wouldn't BJ be thrilled to see how happy she's made them?"

Some of the locals Myrna didn't know, young girls with black eyes and babies on their hips, the pale, almost albino boys. Everyone absorbed in the stacks of glossy magazines and catalogs, in their gifts. "Deeva, I doubt she gives a shit," Myrna said.

They were getting old. The winners of the unspoken contests they used to wage—who could split more wood, dig postholes faster, fell the biggest tree, which had reached an epiphany the day that Jake, an ax in each hand, demonstrated to the rapidly diminishing audience her skill in splitting two logs at once—were now nursing ruptured discs, bad knees and arthritis. No more the days of borrowing a flatbed and filling it with firewood in one long, communal afternoon. They bought their wood now, and probably from the same thugs who had spray painted BJ's home with "Lesbian Cunts," who had once stolen, not sold their wood.

Among the damned, they had, at least, felt distinct from the brutal, slow history which sent teenagers like Tony Gibbs staggering into the bar, blood spattering from a suicide attempt, the skin on his wrists shaved and glistening like ice hanging from the snouts of horses in winter. Only to be admonished, not with hope—there was no hope, no money to leave, no education or luck in his future—that Death, too, was to be tolerated. "You'll die soon enough," Eddie had told him, throwing Tony a bar rag, "why not wait?" The women were reduced, just as the motorcycle gang was reduced, guarding their right to wear their colors, their club jackets, in the bar, by brandishing an arsenal of hand guns and knives. "Boys, please," Eddie had scolded, "Leave your toys outside."

People had always flocked in and out of Emeryville like sparrows on the telephone lines, a continual gathering and draining. But, recently, they seemed trapped as if in a desperate and deathly stalemate. The women bought washing machines, repaired the roofs on their bargain homes and shuffled, like the rest of Emeryville, from one low paying job and long commute to another. Friends who had once been close hadn't spoken for years. Those who had paired up stayed in their houses like married couples. Emeryville had been reduced, too. To a place their homes, not their dreams, were unfortunately situated in.

June took the brunt of this questionable peace, wandering the streets alone like Cassandra. No one listened. She disappeared from Emeryville for months at a time, her car filled with a poetic assortment of junk and treasures, an archetypal ensemble of porcelain dolls, modern art, Native American beadwork and sepia photographs of the booming age of the nearby mines. Only to return with more than when she left, staging flea markets from her rooms, which were attended by an ever increasing number of traders, some speaking in foreign tongues, some finely dressed and repeatedly kissing June's offered hand. They were obviously enamored of her. Many, in turn, seemed to have brought things with them, adding to the barrage of mechanical parts and war memorabilia, which were stacked against her walls. June's home became a swarm of vestal objects, departing and arriving with the busyness of a hive.

"I am just trying to pay for my washing machine like the rest of you!" June would scream out her window at anyone who stared. No matter how desperately she tried, June, at her sanest, appeared the most insane. She rallied against the young men who opened doors for her. "As if I am old enough to be your grandmother," she would scold. She upbraided those whose parents sent them to shovel her walks. "I am not dead yet," she cried. "Who sent you here to insult me?"

Even Gina, who was one of their youngest, spoke in past tense. Lately, her letters were delirious with metaphor, as she told and retold the stories of her time in Emeryville, over and over as if she were stuck there, spinning in her tire tracks the way pickups did in snow, digging herself in. How the town had been like a womb. How much Myrna had meant to her, how much the women taught her, all as if these winds, which were this night circling Myrna's cabin with liquid speed, ringing the small town as if it were Saturn and waking her to the fire gone out, were already scouring their bones. Myrna listened as a hundred windows knocked against their casings. "Damn that girl," she mumbled, lighting a cigarette in the coals, "as if she hadn't chickened out before she'd learned anything."

A garbage can hit a parked car and continued down the alley, gaining momentum. Anything can be lost in these winds, Myrna thought, anything. Just that easy, picked up and set down to blow away. She listened as something caught the handle of the door, as if a sleeve, flapping wildly, then moved on. She was disgusted with herself. She had never been one of those people who saw the blackened stumps of a clear-cut and imagined them to be bear. Myrna would never manufacture danger.

Nor was the night something she hadn't walked through. Leaving for the pitch-black hills after her shift at the Mint was a habit she had carried with her since childhood, like the ragged trunk she dragged from shacks like this to apartments above bars. Her mother's wedding dress was stored in that trunk, along with her grandfather's Bible and the velvet gauntlets and leggings her great-grandmother had made him. The velvet was beaded with constellations of flowers that Myrna had never seen on earth, but which, sometimes at night, she searched for. The night was safe for her. It was there that she was left alone with feeding animals, hunting birds and the winds which carried sounds that, in daylight, were called silence. She had tried to teach Gina this. At night, you could hear yourself breathe, the creek no longer faded into the background, and silence became a bulging package, myriad with overtones.

Nothing like this small, overheated cabin she felt trapped in, a racket of fears and bugaboo voices, all piled one on top of another like Maggie's houses were. And what was worse, she didn't recognize any of them. Not *her* fears, these voices. Voices inarticulate as the banging of doors outside her own, although there were no doors near, and the almost inaudible beat of footsteps pacing and then stopping in front of her home. Not her dream, somebody else's. Not her nightmare.

The feet had stopped again. She could almost see them, right beyond her door. Slowly, she found her boots beneath the bed and slipped the knife from the sheath of rawhide. A strong gust reared on its hind legs and broke over the tar paper roof of the shack like a wave. She stood. The door shuddered and blew open. To no one. Nothing was there. "Oh, for god's sake," Myrna grumbled. "Whatever's calling, I'm coming."

She pulled the earflaps of her sheepskin cap down low and shoved her hands under the arms of her jacket. Outdoors, she felt instantly better. The stars gleamed and the mountains surrounding her were an ambush, rich, lying-in-wait green. She paused as her eyes adjusted to the dark. No lights yet in Emeryville. Even Sam would be in bed after swamping the bar. Not a sound. The dogs were curled like wolves, their backs to the wind. The air was bright and, as she started to move, the ice of the furrows crunched under her boots.

Hard to imagine such a town once supported two hotels. The only new addition to the photographs taken in 1919, which Eddie kept behind the counter of the Mint, was the new fire hall. The post office, which had celebrated its one hundredth birthday the year before, was housed in the same one-room office the telegraph had once occupied. The stone jail was built in 1880. Two cells and room for the jailer. And the church. Then or now, trouble if you ever heard of trouble.

Despite his plans, the Reverend Boyd had returned to his congregation. Our Lady of the Canyons was unconvincing to clergy and laymen alike, although he made a thin living selling postcards and tours. It had become a cult thing, attracting artistic types and the kind of low-class trash who frequented the fortune tellers in the cities, those who advertised with neon, outlined hands or tarot cards painted badly on boards and placed on sidewalks. Nothing he could count on. He had even thought to have it removed discreetly after the hubbub and had actually entertained bids for the cost of someone doing a plaster cast of a more recognizable Mary, one with veils and, at least, a face, but the state had put an end to that. Soon after the unveiling, a letter from the Governor had arrived, thanking him for his support of the Fine Arts. A polite way, the Reverend Boyd thought, of dismissing him.

Ironically, the citizens of Emeryville were kinder to him. They bought their postcards from him and chips of the rock he collected after storms. They sent their women to him for tours. Since he had resumed his services on Sunday mornings, the chapel was noticeably fuller and, where before, there were only coins, bills sometimes found their way into the offering plate. When he was invited to dinner after church, they sent him home with cakes and pies. As if he had joined their club of failure. This did not make him happy. He was paid enough to stay and not enough to leave.

Myrna was climbing well above the cloud of wood smoke which marked the town of Emeryville. The tips of the willow were encased in ice where they hung over the stream. Bundled for the worst, she was surprised to find the temperature mild and the winds, although still strong in number, diving through the pines just above her head, but no lower, as if she were untouchable. She unwound her scarf. Near solstice and the ground was still open. What snow had fallen was only a crust under the bushes of juniper. Not a good year for the hunters, unable to track their prey in the firm soil. The miners had already begun their complaining about the future droughts. She looked above her to where, beyond the thick curtain of douglas fir, Maggie's cabin would be.

Maggie made candles this time of year, stubbornly melting the wax on her wood stove and dipping the wicks, cooling them in a pail of water. No one could tell her it would be cheaper to buy them, that she could be doing something more valuable with her time than spending the three days it took to make enough to get through the winter. Maggie lived the way she had been living for fifteen years, with no running water, no indoor plumbing, no electricity and no telephone. "People are always talkin' about living their ideals," Maggie said. "Well, I live 'em." Her neighbors up the creek, a retired couple from Arizona who spent their summers in the mountains, had asked Maggie to share in the costs of installing an electric pole. "I almost did it," Maggie had told Myrna. "I almost got caught up in all that nonsense, and just because I like 'em."

The only concession Maggie had made to turning forty was the gnarled assortment of cottonwood branches which she nailed upright to her stairs. She felt her way down this forest in the night, their limbs weathered like her short hair had begun to, the color of driftwood.

The stars tossed back and forth between the trees and Myrna heard, as if in waves, the winds crescendo. Remarkably, not one hair on her head stirred. It was as if she were in a room, enclosed, watching a storm. She could hear how it ploughed through the stiffened grasses. It startled her when it landed like a fist on the panes. How she wanted to open those windows, let the night she had come out to meet fly in, precise and ruthless as an owl, for the cold to land with sharp talons on her skin. But she walked the dirt road, higher and further from town, unbuffeted. Where the creek took a sharp turn and left the path of the road for higher ground, she paused. She lit a cigarette with no problem, with only the cup of her hand guarding the match.

She leaned out over the rail of the logging bridge, out over the water. The moon, which had set hours before, was still lodged in the creek, a cloudy, celestial movement under ice. If she followed this creek, it would disappear under an avalanche of boulders, each the size of a house. It would thin to a low whistling below them. If she climbed further, she would come to a place where she had watched, laughing, as Gina sank in boggy patches of fern and mud. Later, they had seen a moose, intent behind the alpine fir. It was Gina's first summer and she had thought the moose a horse. Gina. What kind of vision would you give up out of fear?

Myrna turned from the creek and headed off the road to an unmarked trail that anyone but she would lose, which climbed through a dense stand of lodgepole, crested a high mountain park and descended a dry creek bed to the other side of town. Its tunnels, its detours, circling acres of knee-deep windfall, were engraved on her soul. Not even Gina knew of the creek bed to keep to between the obstacle pine or would guess the wide path beyond the thickets of chokecherry and willow where the trail began. Myrna hoarded its secrets, the hidden clearing where she was sure to see moose, the nests for eagle and red-tailed hawk, just as the hunters hoarded their secret places. She knew it would comfort her. She might catch dawn from the top if she hurried.

By certain signs—a root breaking ground and twisting just so—she knew she was approaching the high, flat clearing where she would rest before her return. Only from above, from the distant peaks surrounding it, was it apparent, hidden as it was from all sides by thick slopes of conifer and an inner rim of aspen. In summer, it was awash with lupine and shooting star. In winter, it was a canvas against which, binoculars in hand, she had watched herds of elk move together, dark against the snow. She thought of those elk now, of how they would sniff the air, lifting their heads from their feeding, how they would falter and stare toward the granite peaks she was viewing them from, although their sight and smell were useless. The trails were there, to the creek-side, for watering, but there were no animals in sight. No tracks in the thin snow. Scanning the edges as she entered the gray light of the clearing, Myrna suddenly realized that she felt exactly like those elk with her above them, ever since she had left the stuffiness of the cabin. Caught by the same current of attention. Precise and from a distance, she was being followed.

A twig snapped. Not an animal. She heard nothing. Again. Not animal what she feared. Something else. A snap or shuffle. Something caught her eye in the tamped grasses near her and she went to it cautiously. With her boot, she poked a bright orange from under the ash. It was a hurried job. Whoever had built that fire was near, had probably heard her coming. She stood, motionless. She stood as the winds, pacing back and forth in the shadows, gathered strength for when they would approach in earnest.

It was the hour of ambush, the hour of lead. It was the hour when soldiers waited, stiff-kneed for the legal hour of slaughter. A dangerous time for the hidden, the hunted. The hour of Sand Creek. Of sleeping villages. Of women and old folks, the sleeping camp. Her heart was beating like sharply pointed stars inside her body. Its beating echoed off the steep cliffs, which were copper, awesome and silver in the growing light. It was the hour of locked doors slowly being opened. She heard a rifle cock. The held breath. Something whispered inside her, "A man with a gun."

Myrna felt her knife rise like a fish to her hand. She felt the heat of a memory inside her. Gina pleading, "Please, there's no time." Gina warning, "Something terrible. I've seen it." And Myrna, always impatient, replying, "We've all seen it, Gina. But going away won't stop it. There's nowhere to go." Myrna knelt to the warm stones at her feet and began stirring the ash. She pushed the charred twigs into a pyre. "What makes you so goddamned brave?" she remembered Gina asking.

No sooner had she knelt than a droning above in the pines descended and the winds came, yellow-eyed and agile, hanging on by their tails. From every direction they came, trampling the dead and dry thistle, cutting wide paths through the grasses. From deep in the forest, she heard limbs cracking. The fledgling fire sputtered and went out. Myrna, crouched over the smoking embers, shielded her eyes from the snow which came, pelting into her face, and searched the meadow. Animals were entering from the violet edges, an elk, running heavy and blind through the flying branches, a moose, shaking blood from a wound in its ear, the blood turning black in the drifts, and above the din, she heard them advance, the rifles being loaded, the traps set. What shots she heard seemed small in the clamor.

Myrna bent over herself, her hands over her ears and still they came, a stampede of the wounded. She heard them stumble and fall, all the easily shot deer, flushed out from their sleep or feeding, a blizzard of the dead, burning her skin, her eyes, the deer dead, the elk fallen, the moose, all the dead animals. "Stop, stop!" she cried, but still, they came, fast and blustering. A cow elk fell an arm's length away, the pale inner coat which she grew in the winter spilling out like batting. She heard the screams of the calf's, like a child's, exactly like a human child's, following her mother's reckless trail of fur, caught in trees and barbed wire fences.

The meadow cleared, but far to the edge, in the sleepy light, was the movement of figures. The figures were people moving, she could see that now, only a handful. They were staggering, half dressed, rubbing their eyes as if from a fire they were fleeing. There were women and they were clutching children and belongings. An old one was hobbling, hurrying to keep up. Hobbling, too, the old men and one, holding a folded blanket in front of him. Was it like her own, the pattern woven to map this very line of mountains, following one after another and the red, green and blue stars which fit between them? "Who are you?" she called. The old man seemed to hear her. He raised his head as if searching the meadow. In his face, she recognized her own set mouth, her shadowed eyes. And he fell, too, just like the animals. Myrna ran across the meadow toward him.

"What the hell are you doing?" someone shouted and she stopped cold between the fallen man and that voice, familiar but dim, as if reaching from across the world. She heard the rifles cock. The held breath.

"Come back!" the voice said, straining across more than time and distance. Myrna stood, caught between recognitions. She could almost feel the shoulders tense, the guns raise.

"Save yourself!" the voice cried against the grain of the wind.

And suddenly, Myrna knew. "Whose dream is this anyway?" she shouted back, just as Gina saw Myrna fall to her knees, the front of her mackinaw blooming a brilliant red.

There was nowhere to go. She sat and sat. She did not know how long she sat there. Months or years could have broken over her head, color entering the way the day is born, generous, missing nothing, the selfish nights collecting, calling it all back in. She sat there so long, she couldn't say when the sounds began, just out of earshot, like a quick movement to the side. They were, to tell the truth, a little aggravating. She had cleared a place for herself in her grief. She was lodged in it.

The sound continued. She would call it a tapping. "I'll ignore it," she decided.

It was irritating. Like the tick of an irregular clock an hour before the alarm. Tick. Tick, ick, tick, ick. Then, tick. A moment. Tick, ick, tick. Soft as a stick pushed into the summer soil. Nothing she could put a finger on. Nothing she could fall back asleep to.

"Leave me alone," she said. "I have died of grief."

Tap. Tap. Tap, tap. It was like the sound of footsteps, too. Many footsteps, and these were not high heels they were stepping in. Not the heavy boots of soldiers. Certainly not the skis of a search and rescue team. When she found herself listening more closely, in spite of herself, she heard them more as skins, like bare feet padding the ground. Stopping here. Closer. There. And digging, too. Like the sound of a stick pushed into the soil. She remembered hearing of how the Indian women used to dig roots with sticks. Camas roots. All kinds of roots, wild onion, turnip, the bitterroot's pink and leafless flower. There was a tale about the bitterroot. Something about the root's two legs. No, about them being red. She couldn't remember. Myrna would know. She wondered if it had helped Myrna to know.

Just when she had accepted the digging, when the fitfulness of its rhythm no longer bothered her, when over time, it had stretched into a pattern and she had made a peace with it, the humming began. Low, almost gospel, like the minor chord she woke to on Sunday mornings in the black neighborhood she lived in in Seattle. "It couldn't be," she said to herself and her voice startled her. She thought of those women, up early and dressed in their Sunday best, picking their way through the previous night's parties, dragging their children along the littered sidewalks. Their choirs, a sorrowful, magic, churchgoing hat of a music, yellow topped with feathers and a dazzling silk rose.

Tap. Tap, tap, tap. The footsteps were zigzagging across the meadow like the prairie dogs did. How they would scurry in one direction, then rise on their hind legs, taking one look back. Then, down. Then, swiftly running ahead. Then, back. She listened as the footsteps approached. Then, grew distant. Like a band of grouse, hurrying from the safety of one bush to the next while a red-tailed hawk shrieked and circled overhead. And all the while, above the pattering, the song, an off-key thread, like an old woman playing cards alone, humming. The way Hatty used to hum over her crocheting when she thought none of them was around.

Without missing a beat, the melody was exchanged for the precipice of hysteria June's voice sometimes teetered on, a tawdry wail she tried out in laundromats and public showers, growling the blued notes. Sultry, then shy, the song moved from one voice to another, rising and falling as if it were a drum, passed from hand to hand. It seemed an old drum, this song, burnished and veined, as if from having years of music pass through it. The song grew as they picked their way through the bodies, the dead, piled and embracing. She thought of those bodies, the animal bodies washed out from where she was sitting, in concentric circles like waves. She thought of how they would be lying, entangled, the long hairs, the winter grasses, the stiff and rolling hides.

Her legs were cramped and her jeans soaked from the snow. "I'll stand," she said, "but they can't make me look."

The singers were gathering in close. She could hear their breath hit the air like the round, rawhide drums Myrna had taught her to beat without pause. Layer upon layer, the sounds joining hands and climbing. The song was not sweet. She could no longer tell that it was women who were singing it. Parts she could recognize. Notes she had heard as a child. A melody caught under the creek beds of watercress, willow and mint. The green overtones of running water. A ribbon of something she'd heard once, lying between Maggie's thighs, but that she had seen more frequently circle Myrna when she was absorbed in something she loved, building a fire, blowing on it.

"Listen," Myrna would say, as the smoke rose through the skinned poles of the tipi with deafening noise, and it was as if she had reached over and turned the volume up. The creek in the wind, the wind in the trees, the wood in the fire, all came rushing at her ears.

The song was not sweet, but it was she whom they were singing to. The voices passed above the dead as a cloud would, erratically, as if they were pausing, touching one bone, singing into it, then the next. And now it was near, near as the first steps she had taken alone on this land, the hills cloudy and muted as if spring were just below the surface, the flowers, the yellowed, barely green tips of trees. She recognized it as what she had followed to Emeryville, what she heard past her fears and vague intuitions, past what she wanted, past even Myrna. Immediate, breaking inside her body as if it were hers.

The song was not sweet. It was a murky pool of a song, layered with the brilliant dead, the peppered and frosted leaves of aspen, threads of golden grasses, spinning, thin as smoke, and smoke-colored stones, bone, bark, all swirling into her as the grains of tea swirl and collect in the bottom of a Japanese cup. Gina looked in the cup. Her eyes opened, just as the flowers of jasmine, dried and fragile, floated to the top.

It was raining in Seattle when Gina woke. It slowed, quickened, slowed. There was no traffic. From the quiet and not the light, she guessed that it was well before dawn. She didn't move, listening. The rain fell with differing speeds. She lay, wrapped in the dim, small room which was stained the color of June's winter teas, those brewed of chicory, licorice, the warming roots, warmed by this blanket, the memory of sage and wood smoke, which they had given her. She hadn't heard the rain like this for how long?

She lay, waiting. She thought of Emeryville, of that small, inconvenient town. She wondered who would be left, who would be angry at her leaving. So few had stayed once the trouble began. "We're from different worlds," Myrna had said, "different worlds." What if she were remembering everything wrong?

Gina lay as the rain hit the pavement below softly, as if someone were stepping through a forest of dry and fallen leaves. There were casualties there, she knew. There were still no jobs. And against all hope, BJ had lost her children. "So," Gina said to herself, "I won't have to stay forever." And still, she lay there, waiting.

She thought of Hatty, of how she would sit in the Mint, garrulous with drink, her voice coarse from too many cigarettes. How she would greet each new customer, her voice indistinguishable from the gulls which were outside Gina's window now. "Did ya ever do anything right?" she would yell, laughing, her words, to friend and foe alike, appropriate, as Glenn's "boomboom" was appropriate.

"Gina," she remembered Hatty saying, "What else you got talking to you this strong?"

10

It was midnight and Gina stood in a cloud of exhaust, while the driver searched below the bus for her bags. Smoke rose from the houses, smaller than she had remembered them. The entire town, smaller than it had seemed while she lived there. She looked down the dirt road. Fifteen, maybe twenty telephone poles, lining the road like crosses. The sand dunes of mine tailings, the spire of the church. Had she told herself the right tale? Over and over, for twelve hours since Seattle, her stories, their stories wrapped into hers, filling in the parts when she was gone with their letters. She thought of the postcard Gertrude had sent just last year, the kind sold in the bar, photographed before the blasting and bulldozers had taken away the swimming holes and eagle nest. "Few take the exit now," it had read on the back. "Oddly enough, the highway has created a sanctuary."

The air was dry, still, almost metallic in its lack of moisture, the temperature brisk. She had left during the first harvest of Seattle's gardens and boarded a bus to where it was barely spring. Gina shivered. The streets were empty as she had expected, but standing alone, this unnerved her. Emeryville. She was sure the driver had called it. What if everyone was gone? It wasn't impossible. The population here was subject to the same threats their ancestors battled, their number withering with each new outbreak of influenza, the gold running out. Gina had visited the nearby ghost towns, their cemeteries crowded with the small stones of children. It was a fragile existence. Why couldn't it happen now?

She slung her pack over her shoulder and thought of her friends, so compelled to live this harsh life, compelled as if they were animals gone to some ancestral feeding grounds. And yet, the gold was gone. The buffalo, the grizzly long gone. Over the years, she had asked them to tell of how they had ended up here. Gleaned from the divergent and elaborate tales of accident and fate, of last-ditch job offers, of totemic callings, of the simple fact that some were born there, was a common thread: They had all followed women to this place. Gina adjusted her pack and walked toward Myrna's. She hoped Myrna was sleeping alone.

The door was, as always, unlocked. "Myrna?" she whispered, entering. In the dim light from the Mint's street light, Gina surveyed the once familiar room. There was Myrna's tin stove, the fire glinting like stars from its sides. Gina was stunned by the simplicity. In all this time, Myrna had collected nothing. There seemed even less, if this was possible, than before. She'd forgotten how Myrna dared the extremes of this poverty. She immediately thought of all she could have brought with her: glasses, curtains, a teapot. A new ax. Gina exhaled deeply, relieved. Only one figure lay there in the dark.

She sat on the edge of the bed. She knew Myrna was awake. No one could sneak up on Myrna in her own home. "Mind if I sleep here?"

Myrna lay flat on her back, her arms cupping her head from behind.

"Still no pillow?" Gina said. "Can I light a lamp?"

"Out of kerosene."

Gina reached to her pack for a flashlight, then decided against it. Myrna knew who she was.

"With all this talk of the Madonna, I expected to see an angel floating like a planet above the town. Spotlighted. What happened?"

"Gina..."

"I'm a tourist, I'll admit it. I came to see the tribute to feminine virtue. I came to pay my respects."

"Gina, go to sleep."

"And nothing. No neon, no travel guides. I must tell you, I am disappointed."

"Do you want to sleep here or what?"

Gina knew better than to throw her arms around Myrna. "Look, I agree that we have a lot to talk over."

Myrna was studying her like she studied animals which came too close, determining whether they were wounded or infected. She watched Gina like a mixed blessing and said, "Did you bring wood in with you?"

"No, sorry. I forgot. I'll get it right now."

When Gina returned, Myrna was snoring, but she had unzipped her sleeping bag and spread it as a blanket over the bed. Gina grabbed the gloves, which were drying on the hearth and opened the small door of the stove. She threw in a log and damped the chimney. In a raku bowl on the floor, Gina recognized Myrna's stash of sweet-pine. She pinched the dried needles and watched them spark as they hit the hot surface of the stove-top. The scent rose, clear and sweet, more evocative of her life here, of the trails, than sage or willow or wood smoke. And yet, she had never found it in these mountains and Myrna swore it was from far away.

"Sub-alpine fir?" Gina would drill Myrna. "Cedar?" When they walked, she would point to this tree and that, sure Myrna knew since she kept the needles wrapped in newsprint under her mattress.

"It doesn't grow here, Gina," Myrna would repeat. "I get it from a friend."

"Then why do these mountains smell like sweet-pine?"

"I don't know. Maybe it used to grow here."

"Come on, Myrna, is this another thing you won't share with white people?"

"You give me too much credit."

"No matter what I do, how much we've gone through together, there are certain things you don't trust me with, right?"

"Damn it, Gina," Myrna had said, stamping her foot, "you always think I'm some kind of medicine man. That I'm trying to trick you. You trick yourself. I'm only going to say this once. I wish I did know. But I don't. And I would tell you if I knew."

Myrna was asleep when Gina crawled in next to her. The burning sweet-pine had entered Myrna's hair like the smoke of a fire entered you, followed you, left you smelling of the burning trees.

Gina slept long, into late afternoon, and when she woke, Myrna was gone. She heard the crack of splitting wood and leaned her head out the door. The sky was close, promising rain. "Morning," Gina called, as Myrna set a wedge in the center of a gnarled round.

"There's coffee on. Hurry and drink it. You wanted to see the statue before the sun sets, didn't you?"

"Let's wait awhile, maybe after I've been back a few days."

"Gina?"

"I know, I know. I'm sure that whatever Maggie made is beautiful, but I was just kidding last night. I can see the statue anytime."

Myrna continued to look at her, eyebrows raised.

"How can you forget the crystal rock so easily? Remember the first time I discovered it, at dawn, and on my own? That time the deer came so close I thought she would walk into me?" Gina said. "I don't see how you can forget. You went there as much as I did."

"Maggie didn't destroy it." Myrna paused. "So, you're still ignoring whatever you don't want to look at?" she teased.

"I came back, didn't I? Besides, I heard it was a joke."

"All the more reason to see it."

"Anything else you have planned?"

"Dinner at Maggie's. Six-thirty. We can time it to arrive around then."

"A potluck?"

"No, I think Maggie's cooking."

Gina groaned. "No easing back in, I see."

"It's not that things have changed that much, I can tell ya," Myrna said, as they climbed past the slash-and-burn piles the Forest Service had left five years before and where the poor still got their firewood. Gina had watched them returning home from a day there with their chain saws, blackened as if they were chimney sweeps.

"I don't expect much."

Myrna's steps rocked expertly but slowly as she waited for Gina, panting behind her. "Take it easy. They say it takes three weeks for your blood to thicken for this air."

They walked, letting their bodies adjust to each other as to the change in elevation. They had already made their way up to the spring, past the burrows dug into the side of a slope by miners a hundred years before. Gina stopped to inspect the walls, barely holding with rotting lumber and mud. The scars from the placer mines were slowly closing in.

Myrna was hiking ahead, talking loudly, as if she were a docent in a museum. She wore the same plaid mackinaw she had worn when Gina met her. "You should hear the locals talk about it. In a couple years, they'll call it Pompey's Pillar, like they did that other poor rock. They'll say a massacre happened there, or that it's where Sacajawea changed her baby's diapers."

"Can we please rest a minute?" Gina called. "I can't hear a word you're saying."

The gray sky was low, nestling in the limbs above them. Myrna waited for Gina to catch up. "So, tell me about the unveiling," Gina said. "What a trick Maggie played. Just like the emperor's new clothes."

"It's not what you're thinking," Myrna said, remembering how they had waited with the rest of Emeryville for the tarps to fall. When they did, others besides the Reverend Jimmy Raymond Boyd were visibly upset. For instead of the work of art they had so painstakingly nursed

Maggie through, the work of revolution or revenge, of
heretical tribute or Native vision, was a rock. Cracked and
torn from the inside of the mountain, with hunks of quartz
and agate still feeding on its sides. When the Reverend
yelled, "I'll sue," forgetting the statue had been paid for by
the state, the women had been about to agree, seeing at
once how Ellen had made fools of them again by talking
them into supporting Maggie.

"Maggie, how could you..." River had begun, when
her words stopped on the dime that the Reverend's had.
Because the public was crowding the steps. Reporters were
snapping photographs and scribbling wildly. They over-
heard members of the Tourist Bureau who adored it. The
Governor, his chest swelling with pride, posed at the
statue's feet. The journalists plied the Art Council director
for details. Who was the artist? Why had he wished to
remain anonymous?

The locals, silent and inconspicuous during the
ceremony, waited until the suited had left to approach the
Madonna. A thin, teenage boy in blue jeans held down the
lower wire with one boot and lifted the upper with his
hands, helping a line of children to slip through the barbed
wire from behind the statue. Canes and walking sticks,
wheelchairs appeared out of nowhere. The women of
Emeryville watched as their neighbors knelt with their
pains and their prayers, clumsy in their salutations, calling it Jesus or God or Mary or the names of dead husbands
and sisters. Some held lengthy conversations, some
hurriedly placed crosses or clippings from fragile newspapers, coins and, in one case, a covered dish of food on the
steps, just as Myrna or Gertrude had left tobacco or sweet-
grass near the cliff of crystal rock. Picnic baskets and
coolers were fetched from under the sagebrush. Cans of
beer, fried chicken pulled from the overgrown sluice lines.
There was laughter.

The sun circled above the stone face, then behind it.
The women had stared, trying to remember the rock the
statue had replaced, its deceptive dull side, the crags and
crevices which would catch each wave of light. They could
not remember it. Behind the statue, birds were flying with
sticks and mud for nests. The sage hills surrounding it
were broadcast with deer. And suddenly, they could not

imagine the landscape without the Madonna. It was as if
it had existed in the same spot for an eternity, as much a
part of their lives as the peaks or the flat-topped buttes to
the north. It was a landmark. They remembered it and
they remembered hearing stories of it. Their ancestors
could never have found this place without it.

"Remember when the highway crew had to remove
the stone fence around the Old Cemetery?" Myrna asked
Gina.

"Beautiful fence," Gina said. "BJ got some of those
stones, didn't she?"

"Some? She salvaged most of them. She marked each
one so they would fit tight as they had before. You saw the
fence she made around her yard."

"That's a lot of work for somebody to go off and leave."

Myrna frowned pointedly at Gina. "Look who's talking."

"Anyway?"

"Anyway, Hatty came by one day, telling BJ how
she'd passed that fence every day on her way to school as
a kid. She remembered how she would balance on it."

"Must have been one of Hatty's drunk days. She
wouldn't have passed that cemetery."

"No, no, don't you see? In BJ's yard. That's where she
thought she balanced on the fence. If that fence wasn't
there before, it should have been." Myrna paused. "The
statue is like that."

Gina grinned. "I believe you."

Myrna smiled for the first time that day and the lines,
which flocked from her eyes, were exquisite. She hadn't
changed much. Her hair, still black, her lips dulled in the
cold to the color of willow bark. But Myrna's belly, grown
through years of serious bar conversation, was gone. Gina
risked a pat on Myrna's stomach.

"Quit drinking?"

"No one to drink with." The creek puttered next to
them, too early for runoff. There was snow in the pockets
between stones.

"Give me a break. You never needed someone to drink
with before."

And then, Myrna laughed. How good to hear that
laugh, hearty and deep and hoarse. No one laughed like

that in the city. No women dared. No men, Gina doubted, could. "I had to keep my eye on things while you were gone. Did a pretty good job, don't you think?"

"Very funny," Gina said, boxing at Myrna, who backed away, abandoning the road for the roadside. Gina chased her to a stand of aspen, feigning blows until she came close enough for Myrna to trip her. As she tumbled into a large bush of sage, its bitter scent protesting as she crushed it, she had just enough time to grab Myrna on the way down. They wrestled, laughing and awkward in their winter clothes. Gina helped Myrna up, still panting, and they stood, their arms on each other's sleeves.

The crows were calling from the other side of the ridge. They stood close, their bodies not touching, but almost touching, as if their bodies were the hands they used to hold, palm to palm in the tipi late at night, measuring the differences in breath and heartbeat, in temperature, in the ability to measure. They stood, two women in the forest of aspen, as if in asylum, the bark split and tight across the cold trunks, the creek windswept below them and above them, a wind from the north. Until those differences joined forces, shuddered and became currents.

Gina slipped her hands under Myrna's coat and her mouth opened toward her, moist and hot and red. Red and alive under the web of winter aspen.

"The Madonna can wait," Gina said.

The snow was falling, drifting steadily, was a whisper. The wind was not whispering, was rich and well-mastered, was almost a cornet through the canyon, was ballad and wet in the blue tips of pine.

"I could drink this air," Gina said as the flakes melted cleanly on her face.

"Here, wear my gloves. You're delirious," Myrna said. "We're almost at Maggie's." Below them, eclipsed by gray and green and the shadow of the mountain, a lantern flickered.

"I'm nervous. Who do you think will be there?"

"June. Maggie. Probably River. Deeva will be curious. Why are you nervous?"

"Because I left. Because I've been gone so long."

"You know what I always say. Once you're part of a circle, you never really leave it."

"You don't always say that. June always said that."

"What matters who said what? Or what happened to whom?"

They were nearing the first of Maggie's hand-me-down houses. The candles shed their blue through the windows, the light turning the forest even blacker. Another storm in the trees, the sky opaque as petals. Maggie was smoking outside her door, an odd-smelling and clumsy cigarette, the stems of whatever was rolled in it breaking through the paper.

"What is that, marijuana?" Gina asked.

"Mullein. I'm trying to quit tobacco." Maggie smiled at Myrna. "I'm trying to quit everything. But what the heck? This calls for a celebration. You got one that'll stay lit?"

Myrna shook a cigarette from her store-bought pack and Maggie, despite her small frame, lifted Gina in a hug that took her breath away. "You've missed some good times, Gina."

"I'm sure I have."

"So, what did you think of the statue?"

Gina looked at Myrna and blushed. "The statue?"

"Our Lady of the Canyons. Myrna said it was the first thing you asked about."

"You must have had some inspiration, Maggie."

"Are you going to invite us in or not," Myrna interrupted.

"Oh, my. Of course, I'm sorry. Everybody's waiting."

Entering the warmth of Maggie's cabin, Gina was surprised to find, instead of the remnant band she had expected, that the number of women, if anything, had grown. By the ease and friendliness with which they shared the crowded room, Gina guessed this occasion to be but one of many. They sat on pillows and logs and on the floor, drinking wine or chamomile, just as they used to, but those who smoked now went outside to do so. One by one, they rose to greet her, making room.

"Maggie must anticipate a lengthy withdrawal," Gina whispered to Myrna, motioning to the harvest of mullein, the dozens of bundles drying from the rafters, the soft leaves losing shape, the tiny yellow flowers falling to the floor. The floor was dusted with them.

In the flickering light of Maggie's candles, Gina spotted a sad shape, crouched like a struck dog near the back door. "Hey, Ellen," Gina said, "did you ever get rid of that freak of a yard?"

Ellen turned red and said nothing. But Maggie, who had come up behind her, her arms barely reaching around Ellen's waist, frowned. "Why give her a hard time, Gina?"

"I can see there've been a lot of changes while I was gone," Gina scowled.

Maggie's expression softened. After the granite had left her yard, as abruptly as it had arrived, when, after months of working on the Madonna, of their daily conversation, it was gone, Maggie sat, the words hardening like pebbles in her eyes, becoming as impenetrable as she was before. It was then that Ellen showed up, puffing from the climb and carrying a bottle of Wild Turkey from the Mint.

"I've heard you've been to bed with just about every woman in Emeryville," Ellen said, catching her breath. "Why not me?"

Maggie didn't budge from under the tree she was propped against. She sat, studying this woman, this mythologized, wrong-turn, edge-of-the-cliff taboo they had gauged their lives by. Close up, Ellen seemed thinner. And she had as many dead floating around her as the rest of them did. "Good question," Maggie stammered.

Ellen pulled the whiskey out of the brown paper bag. "You have glasses or are you going to make me drink from the bottle?"

Maggie, who slipped up on women, who opened and closed like the granite did to her chisel, had laughed. "Sure, Ellen, come on in."

That night, they talked long into the dark, first by the stove on braided rugs, then in the lamplight of the bed, trading back and forth their answers. Ellen was not at all what Maggie had imagined. Undefeated, unremorseful, there she was, sassier than them all and criminal to boot: not pretty, not dieting, demanding as hell and not happy in the least with what was asked of her. Maggie's hands began to move toward Ellen in the manner they had become accustomed to, muscled, unhesitant. And Ellen?

Sometime during the night, no, even before that, when Gertrude first listened to her, as far back, maybe as Rosetta, Ellen had felt something growing, stony and sharp-edged under the rolls of flesh, the acquiescent years of self-banishment to the care of the dead, ancestresses or animals. Something like flint which sparked when she took a step in any direction. It was not Maggie who undressed her.

Ellen had her own question for Gina. "Why'd you come back?"

Gina hesitated. The commotion of her entrance had settled and the sound of the creek shimmered through the walls like the sound of two cymbals in the moment after they are struck, spilling over, showering. The women were all watching her. She listened. Hiding behind an over-grown fence of willow, the creek, thin, holy, flashing when-ever the moon hit. It seemed to grow louder the more attention she paid to it. She could hear the currents form and re-form over and under each rock. Overtones. Under-tones. So loud and occupying that the city had seemed to Gina quiet and empty after it. "I guess I needed to know if this was all true." She glanced around, embarrassed. "Deeva, what happened to your boyfriend?"

Deeva scowled. "He left me."

Gina laughed, throwing her arm around Deeva's shoulder. "Now that you're free, are you going to try women again?" she teased.

"I am not free," Deeva snapped. "I am well over the age of disco-dancing. Where do you suggest I find a woman my age in Montana? The rodeo? At the bridge clubs?"

"Seattle's not so bleak for older women."

"You may not understand this," Deeva said, "but I have responsibilities here. Unless someone wants to buy my property from me at even the same price I paid for it ten years ago, which is highly unlikely, given the present market."

The fire snapped in Maggie's stove. Myrna kicked the door open and stomped in, knocking the snow off her boots, with a load of limbs in her arms.

"Any word from BJ?" Gina asked.

"She hasn't forgiven a one of us."

"What about the kids?"

"Husband's still got them. Word has it they're enrolled in Catholic school."

Gina sighed. "At least, the boys of Emeryville don't bother you as much."

"The boys are now men," River said.

"Really, no one's bothered us too much since the Art Show at the library. Somebody threw a pair of copulating Barbie dolls, fastened together with rubber bands, at Maggie."

"What else?"

"Gertrude, tell her about the paper boys."

"You knew the Grady kid. He's in high school now. I always invite him in. His folks are real poor."

"For butter cookies and expresso, can you imagine?" June said.

"He likes them," Gertrude continued, smiling at her friends. "So, one day as I was paying him, I heard his friends below, waiting in the stairwell. They're yelling something, but I can't quite hear what it is."

"They're yelling, 'Dyke! Dyke! Dyke!'" River added.

"It wasn't until after he left, when River called me, that I realized what they had been saying. She knew because they had done the same thing to her earlier."

"By then," River said, "we were so hopping mad, we agreed to meet at Gertrude's car and hunt them down. We went speeding all over town, up one back road and down the next, until we saw them, cowering at the end of a logging lane."

Gertrude finished the story. "We skidded to a halt, jumped out, ready to beat some respect into those kids, when we discovered that what we thought was a gang, huddled under the tree at twilight, was a Forest Service sign. Dead End, of course."

"Old goats," Maggie cackled. "Blind old bats."

"At least, all they did was call you names," Gina said. "It could be worse."

They all stopped laughing. "It was worse," Gertrude said. "In my haste to meet River, I thought they had thrown soda against my walls. Only when I came home later did I smell that they had pissed up and down my stairwell."

Gina lowered her head. Gertrude, who remembered ceremony as if their lives were something she had arrived to put the finishing touches to. Myrna, unshakeable. June, with her sideshow announcing itself in their ears like a carnival barker. Maggie, never lonely. They were faultless, strong. She had depended on them to remain so. But, now, as they met her around Maggie's fire, she found Myrna thinner, Gertrude laughing less and June a good twelve feet closer to the ground.

"Did you call their parents?"

"River called every parent in town."

"And then, I worried that their parents would beat them."

"Well, they do," Gertrude said, "you know they do."

Gina looked in Gertrude's eyes. She knew the way stories grew tangled or low, when they grew too sad for the telling. But they were telling her the truth so she resisted her impulse to say something to make them feel better. "I'm sorry."

"Parker on the tape deck cheers me," Gertrude said, recovering her smile.

"What about you, June? How are you doing?"

June was cleaning the last of the brownies out of the pan with her fingers. A rhinestone brooch the size of a hand, shaped in the Star of David, was pinned to the yoke of her Guatemalan tunic. "It's been very cold since you moved out of my house."

"June! That was so long ago. That was way before I left Emeryville."

"So what? You think it was easy getting used to sleeping alone again?"

Gina was speechless. "I thought you understood," she said finally.

"Understood what? That Myrna was younger, darker, that you had a crush on her? What did you tell me that I could understand?"

Gina bit her lip. She was tempted to argue, to say it didn't happen that way, that this sorrow was untrue, not at all how she had imagined it, when she thought of something Hatty had said, late one winter night in the Mint. Hatty, downing whiskey and beer in celebration of Christmas. "Just remember," she said, "your story is only a small part of the story, a very small part. But the big story, that will always be a part of you."

Gina walked over to June and put her arms around her waist. June burst into tears. Gina ran her fingers through that hair, matted with twigs and webs and the crumbled leaves of herbs which June had given up straining out of her hair rinses. "So, tell me," Gina whispered, "it was pretty bad?"

"While you were gone," someone began, while Myrna slipped outside for more wood.

Melissa Kwasny was born in LaPorte, Indiana and educated at the University of Montana, where she studied with Madeline Defrees and the late Richard Hugo. She spent the next ten years in Montana, writing, teaching and performing with the Jane Finnigan Quintet. She is currently living in San Francisco, where she teaches in the California Poets in the Schools Program. She was recently an artist-in-residence at the Headlands Center for the Arts.

Photo: Amy Jeanne Appleby

▓ spinsters book company

Spinsters Book Company was founded in 1978 to produce vital books for diverse women's communities. In 1986 we merged with Aunt Lute Books to become Spinsters/Aunt Lute. In 1990, the Aunt Lute Foundation became an independant non-profit publishing program.

Spinsters is committed to publishing works outside the scope of mainstream commercial publishers: books that not only name crucial issues in women's lives, but more importantly encourage change and growth; books that help to make the best in our lives more possible. We sponsor an annual Lesbian Fiction Contest for the best lesbian novel each year. And we are particularly interested in creative works by lesbians.

If you would like to know about other books we produce, or our Fiction Contest, write or phone us for a free catalogue. You can buy books directly from us. We can also supply you with the name of a bookstore closest to you that stocks our books. We accept phone orders with Visa or Mastercard.

spinsters book company
P.O. Box 410687
San Francisco, CA 94141
415-558-9655